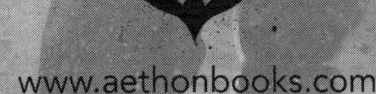

# RICK PARTLOW
## DROP TROOPER BOOK TWELVE
# BLUE FORCE

www.aethonbooks.com

**BLUE FORCE**
**©2023 RICK PARTLOW**

This book is protected under the copyright laws of the United States of America. No part of this publication may be reproduced, stored in a retrieval system, or transmitted, in any form or by any means, without the prior permission in writing of the publisher, nor be otherwise circulated in any form of binding or cover other than that in which it is published and without a similar condition including this condition being imposed on the subsequent purchaser. Any reproduction or unauthorized use of the material or artwork contained herein is prohibited without the express written permission of the authors.

Aethon Books supports the right to free expression and the value of copyright. The purpose of copyright is to encourage writers and artists to produce the creative works that enrich our culture.

The scanning, uploading, and distribution of this book without permission is a theft of the author's intellectual property. If you would like to use material from the book (other than for review purposes), please contact editor@aethonbooks.com. Thank you for your support of the author's rights.

Aethon Books
www.aethonbooks.com

Print and eBook formatting by Steve Beaulieu.

Published by Aethon Books LLC.

Aethon Books is not responsible for websites (or their content) that are not owned by the publisher.

*This book is a work of fiction. Names, characters, places, and incidents are the product of the author's imagination or are used fictitiously. Any resemblance to actual events, locales, or persons, living or dead is coincidental.*

All rights reserved.

ALSO IN THE SERIES


*CONTACT FRONT*
*KINETIC STRIKE*
*DANGER CLOSE*
*DIRECT FIRE*
*HOME FRONT*
*FIRE BASE*
*SHOCK ACTION*
*RELEASE POINT*
*KILL BOX*
*DROP ZONE*
*TANGO DOWN*
*BLUE FORCE*
*WEAPONS FREE*

# [ 1 ]

My opponent's eyes locked on mine, daring me to keep my gaze there. It was a trick. The late Sgt.-Major Ellen Campbell had told me that the temptation to watch the enemy's eyes was a trap. The eyes could deceive, could feint, could lead you astray. You didn't watch their feet either, because if they were good, their footwork could be just as deceptive.

No, you watched their hips, their center of gravity. When their weight shifted, you knew they were going to strike, and when you saw which way they were distributing their balance, you knew which side the hit would come from. Of course, *these* particular hips were pretty distracting all on their own, and it was all I could do to keep my attention on the fight instead of on Victoria Sandoval's legs. She grinned under those dark, intense eyes.

"You're not thinking with your big head, Cam," she warned me.

I laughed, though I didn't lose my concentration. She was *trying* to distract me. That's why she'd worn the tight gym shorts and cut-off t-shirt instead of her usual sweats.

"You really want to win that bet, don't you?" I replied softly, the padded mats on the gym deck squeaking beneath my bare feet as I shifted my weight, circling around her.

"All or nothing," she confirmed. "We're tied at three matches apiece, and we arrive back at Yfingam in three hours."

It was a tribute both to our boredom and my own need to relieve the nearly constant tension of the last few weeks when we'd made the bet in the first place. We'd been sparring with each other for years, of course, just to keep in shape, and we were probably more serious about it than most Drop Troopers. That was mostly due to Top's influence, her conviction that a Marine was always a Marine, whether in or out of their battle-suit, and they should always be ready to fight even if they were naked. But the bet... that was taking things to a new level.

Vicky moved. She was damned fast, and if I outweighed her by eighteen kilos, well, the speed made up for some of that. The kick was the snap of a bullwhip, and if I'd tried to block it, it would have likely made my whole arm go numb for a second. Luckily, I didn't try. Bruce Lee once said the best way to block a strike is not to be there when it lands. He probably meant something philosophical by that, something about avoiding fights when possible, but I was a Marine and fighting was what I did, so I chose to interpret the advice in my own way.

I'd sidestepped the second I saw her weight shift and her foot snapped through empty space, the wind of its passage cool against the sweat beading on my face. A push to the back of her leg, just enough of a brush to send her off-balance, make her take an extra second to regain her footing. Enough for me to duck into a leg sweep on her plant foot.

She cursed loudly, slapping an arm on the mat to spread out the impact. I lunged toward her, grabbing her in a rear naked choke before she could get her feet back under her. She patted my arm immediately, sighing in disgust.

"Why the hell did I do that?" she asked, slapping the plastic again as she sat up. "That was stupid, just showing off."

"Top always said don't kick someone above the waist," I agreed, clambering to my feet and offering her a hand up. "Of course, I kind of broke that rule myself when I was fighting Colonel Hachette in his office."

It seemed like years ago, not weeks, when I'd had to resort to smacking Hachette upside the head to snap him out of his funk after Top's death. It had worked, barely, and Hachette had redeemed himself, sacrificing his life to ensure the destruction of the Womb, the gigantic brown dwarf that had been turned into a nanotech factory putting out the engineered Skrela warriors and their hive ships. It was gone now and so was he, leaving *me* in charge of the mission.

*Whatever the hell the mission* is *anymore.*

We'd made peace of a sort with our original target, the rogue Tahni General Zan-Thint, though how long that would last was anyone's guess. We'd destroyed the Skrela, which made Yfingam and the other colony worlds out here in this stretch of the galaxy safe from their predations, but that left extant the ones behind the creation of the inhuman threat in the first place.

And *that* was the secret that had caused all the tension we were trying to work off here in the gym of the starship *Orion*. Because while everyone else had bought into the lie that a faction of the Resscharr, what we knew from legend and from the artifacts they'd left behind as the Predecessors, had created the Skrela as a punishment for their own people for wiping out the only other intelligent life they'd found off Earth, we knew the truth. Well, I *suspected* the truth.

The Resscharr had left behind something else besides their artifacts. They'd left behind their sentient artificial intelligences, including the one in the gateway we and Zan-Thint's Tahni had used to travel out here from the Cluster, the section of the galaxy otherwise closed off from this one by an artificial twisting of the laws of hyperdimensional physics that cut off all the Transition lines out to the rest of the universe.

That AI, which called itself Dwight, had copied a piece of itself into the computers of the Tahni destroyer and yet another into the systems of the *Orion* and had proven invaluable in the information it had provided us as we'd hunted down the remnants of the Resscharr and the last of the gateways they'd brought with them. Dwight had made it clear to us that he didn't trust the Resscharr, and after a while, neither had I.

There were a lot of reasons not to. They'd admitted they'd tried to kill off homo sapiens 70,000 years ago because they considered us a threat to their plans for the galaxy and the Tahni they'd engineered, so it hadn't been too hard to believe the AI we'd discovered in one of the Skrela genetic repositories along the way to the Womb when it had told us that the Resscharr had wiped out the original Skrela and that a faction of their people who called themselves the Condemnation had reengineered the vaguely insectoid species into a weapon to punish their own.

Until Dwight had made a mistake. Just a small slip, enough to make me suspect that there'd been no Condemnation, that the Skrela had been created by the AI as revenge for the Resscharr using them as virtual slaves.

Meeting Vicky's eyes there in the gym, a chill passed down my spine that wasn't just the sweat on my back drying under the vents of the air conditioning. She was thinking the same thing I was and probably wishing we could talk about the problem, or better, share it with *anyone* else. But we couldn't, because Dwight was in our systems, listening through every microphone, every personal datalink, reading every message. I'd managed to get Vicky alone on one of our shore leaves and whisper the truth to her while we'd left our 'links behind, but the opportunity hadn't come since. I was in charge and could, theoretically, have ordered another shore leave and tried to get Captain Nance off the ship, but Dwight wasn't stupid.

It wasn't just that the AI had lied to us, just that Dwight and his kind might have been responsible for billions of deaths, but that we had recovered the last gateway. It was anchored to the hull of the *Orion*, and we were hauling it back to Yfingam to take the ship and all our people back to the Cluster. Our ship with *Dwight* in the computer systems.

How the hell could I bring a genocidal computer that could take control of a military warship all the way back to Earth? What if the thing decided that humans were no better than the Resscharr and needed to be wiped out?

"All right," Vicky sighed, wiping sweat from her face and falling into a fighting stance. "You're up one fall to zero. Let's try it again."

I nodded and took up my position, though I suddenly didn't feel as enthusiastic as I had a few seconds ago, either about the bet or Vicky's shorts. Well, about the bet anyway. Too many things trying to pry my attention away from the fight. Not just the thoughts of our predicament, but the other crewmembers in the ship's gym.

The clank of exercise equipment, the grunt of people working out, the whoosh of breath from runners on their treadmills, all that was a usual background noise and I could shut it out with no trouble. It was the gawkers who were getting to me. The bet was not, apparently, as secret as I would have liked it to be, and those who knew about it also knew this was the last chance either of us would have to win it.

Most of them were Marines and I *could* have just ordered them to leave, but that would have made it even more of a temptation for them to record the thing and post it on the ship's internal nets. At least none of them were platoon leaders or senior NCOs. *Those* I might have chewed out for wasting their time. Bad enough a couple of the handful clustered at the edge of the mats were squad leaders.

"You guys want to use the pads?" I asked, cocking an eyebrow at them.

"Oh, uh, no, sir," one of the squad leaders, Staff-Sergeant Craig stuttered. "We were just, um... here in the gym and were hoping you'd show us some unarmed combat tips." She finished up strong, smiling as she realized she'd come up with a reasonable excuse.

I snorted but turned back to Vicky. Just in time to get a heel in the solar plexus.

"Fuck!" I tried to say, but it came out as a wheeze along with all the other air in my lungs, the concussion of the same explosion of pain that sent flashes of light starring in my vision.

Stumbling backward, I didn't gasp for air because I knew another attack would be coming, and if I didn't want to get my ass kicked I'd have to be ready for it. She went for my thigh, for the common peroneal, and I think it was because she knew how much I hated getting hit there and she was embarrassed that I'd caught her high kick.

This one I had to block because I lacked the breath and the presence of mind to dodge, and yes, my left arm went numb from taking the hit there, but I'd take that every time over limping for the rest of the day. She didn't give up, pressing in, but I had my wits back and my footwork too, and I circled around to her right, springing into a push kick. She turned away from it and took the blow on her arm, but it still put her off-balance and gave me space.

Sweet air rushed into my lungs and I shook myself, shoving down the pain in my chest. Vicky smirked and danced from one foot to another, much more confident than she had been when I'd swept her leg.

"Captain Alvarez?"

The voice in my earbud was all too familiar, and where once I would have merely found the interruption annoying, now it was utterly bone-chilling. I raised a hand to Vicky and put the other to my ear in an automatic gesture.

"What is it, Dwight?"

I was surprised he didn't use the gym's holographic entertainment projector to manifest the avatar he'd adapted for us, a human male in a Commonwealth Fleet duty uniform. He seemed to take some perverse glee in pretending to be human, or maybe it was just to get us to let our guard down and think of him as one of us. This time, he was just a disembodied voice.

"I'm sorry to interrupt your exercise, but I'd like the chance to address you and Captain Nance before we Transition to Yfingam, if you wouldn't mind."

Vicky rolled her eyes, arms crossing in her usual irritated reaction to Dwight. I knew she was feeling the same thing I was, but it was important the AI not suspect we knew the truth. I tried to imitate her, sighing.

"You know, Dwight," I told him, hands on my hips as I fought to catch my breath, "for a fucking sentient computer, you are so damned analog. We're on ship's coms and so is Captain Nance. Couldn't we just do this remotely? Hell, I think we could even keep sparring and still be able to pay attention."

"That is entirely possible," he replied patiently, "but this is something I feel would better be discussed in private."

I shook my head and grabbed a towel, wiping sweat off my neck.

"All right, give us half an hour to get cleaned up. We'll meet the captain in the Operations Center."

The gathered Marines moaned, some of them throwing up their hands, and I couldn't help grin at their disappointment. I nodded to Vicky.

"Wanna call it a draw then? Nobody wins the bet."

"Shit," she said, making a face. "I was really looking forward to you singing the Commonwealth Marine hymn on the bridge in a speedo."

"Later," I promised her, leering. "In private."

"Aw, that's no fun," Vicky insisted, winking. "You do that all the time."

# [ 2 ]

"All right," Captain Nance said, scowling as he fell into one of the padded chairs around the table at the center of the compartment. "You've dragged me in here right in the middle of lunch for what exactly?"

Nance looked a bit worse for wear after our voyage. His doughy, jowly face was paler and more drawn than I remembered, stress lines around his eyes and mouth. I supposed I understood because I saw them in the mirror every night. Too many people had died, and it weighed on his conscience as heavily as mine. Theoretically, the interior lighting on the ship was supposed to provide all the vitamin D of sunlight, but I still swore there was a difference. There's no way I would have mistaken sunlight on my face for the overhead lamps on a ship.

"Dwight?" I prompted, motioning above us at the holographic projector.

The avatar appeared above us and I squinted at him. Did he look more haggard as well? It was possible he was mirroring us again, making his own countenance match ours to make sure we humanized him... or maybe my memory was just going. That was possible too. I hadn't been sleeping very well the last few weeks.

"I'm here," he announced, redundantly. He was *always* there, as omnipresent as God, if lacking the omnipotence and perhaps the omniscience. I wasn't so sure about that one. "My apologies, Captain Nance, but there are things I felt we should discuss before we return to Yfingam."

"Shouldn't Dunstan be here?" Vicky asked. "And maybe Lan-Min-Gen?"

"Or Lilandreth," I put in. I knew the Resscharr matriarch and the AI hated and mistrusted each other, but Dwight hadn't expressly excluded her before.

"Commander Dunstan is a good man," Dwight acceded, and I wanted to ask him how he would know since he'd never been human, but I kept my mouth shut. "But not, perhaps, as serious as necessary for such decisions. And no, I don't believe either Lilandreth or Commander Lan-Min-Gen should be included in this conversation."

Nance made an impatient "get on with it" gesture. I frowned, wondering again if we were clear on the command structure. The captain had agreed that I was in command of the mission after Hachette's death, but I wasn't sure if that knowledge had penetrated into his subconscious. He still acted as if he were in charge, which I wouldn't have minded if he hadn't specifically rejected the idea before acknowledging my leadership.

"My concern," Dwight went on, seemingly unperturbed by Nance's churlish mood, "is for our cargo."

He motioned above him, and as if he'd conjured it out of thin air, an exterior image of the *Orion* taken by a shuttle or an Intercept before our last foray into Transition Space. The ship was a different animal from the cruisers I'd seen during the war. The *Orion* had been constructed for a long-term mission, a jack of all trades and master of none. She wasn't streamlined for combat, more a bulbous collection of utilitarian parts, including fuel storage bays and a habitation drum that could be spun for centripetal gravity when we weren't under boost. She looked like a cross between a commercial transport and a warship... though right now, she more resembled a cargo ship with the gateway artifact anchored to her hull.

The artifact itself was a flattened cylinder, glowing silvery in the light of an alien sun in the image, jutting out from the front of the *Orion* by a few dozen meters and probably outmassing the ship by thousands of tons. Well, it *would* have outmassed the ship if Dwight hadn't powered up the device's gravitational distortion field, the same one it used to construct the gateway, and used it to negate the thing's mass.

"What about the thing?" Nance asked. He shrugged. "I mean, it's a huge pain in the pass structurally. We can't even use the habitation drum with that giant dildo glued to the hull, but other than that, what's the worry?"

"We haven't gone into the details of how the gateway will have to be used once we arrive back at Yfingam," Dwight explained, "but as I mentioned before, the gateway is just the core of the system. You'll have to construct a large framework around it in order to guide the gravimetic energies and pinpoint the exit wormhole." His virtual fingers plucked the silver cylinder off the image of the *Orion*, then sketched lines around it until it looked much like the gateway we'd encountered back in the Cluster, the one that had taken us here.

"Do we even have the materials to build something like that?" I asked, a frown tugging at my face as I leaned forward, trying to get a better look at the facilities he'd drawn around the artifact. They seemed pretty extensive.

"The raw materials should be available in the system's asteroid belt," the AI assured me, "and I can guide you through how to use the energy weapons the Resscharr equipped the *Orion* with to smelt them down. I've examined the construction drones this ship has available for repairs and you should be able to utilize them to accomplish most of what needs to be done, though some of it will have to be supervised on site by humans. You should be able to get by with a few of your engineering crew. That is not the issue."

"Then what *is*?" Vicky demanded, and I had the sense she'd forgotten their underlying concerns in a surge of impatience with the melodramatic games Dwight liked to play.

"The time." Dwight's avatar shook its head. "This is not going to be a quick process. I know you and your people are eager to get home and they may be somewhat impatient, as you humans tend to be. But this construction will take *months*."

"Shit," Nance murmured, running a hand over his face. "That sucks." He sighed as if blowing all the negativity out of him. "But on the other hand, with the Skrela gone, at least we won't have *that* Sword of Damocles hanging over our heads constantly." Nance shrugged. "I'll try to set up more shore leave for the crew so no one gets too mental about the delay."

"That's not what worries you," I declared, spearing the holographic avatar with a glare. I knew on an intellectual level that the image wasn't him, that I could have looked anywhere and he would have seen it, but old instincts died hard.

"No," Dwight agreed. "You need to remember, once you're gone, the gateway will be left behind. And I worry what the Resscharr and the Tahni may do with it in your absence."

I blinked, the thought striking me like a hammer between the eyes.

"I don't think Zan-Thint wants to return to the Cluster," I ventured slowly, trying to process the possibilities. "What could he do if he went back? It's not like we're giving him the Resscharr weapons. He's got one destroyer and a few patrol boats, a few companies of Shock Troopers, and that's it."

Dwight's expression was the sort of condescending pity I remembered from all the adults I'd encountered in the group homes when I'd tried to explain to them the problems I was having with the other kids.

"You've seen what the gateway device can do," he said, laughing softly, "and yet you lack the understanding of the destructive power it holds. Why do you think the Predecessors left *me* to supervise it? Why do you think they didn't simply leave it floating in the middle of nowhere? Because it is far too dangerous to leave in the hands of those you don't trust."

"Okay, Dwight," I said, not trying to disguise the scorn I felt for him, not because of what I suspected but just in the moment from his attitude. "Tell me how it's dangerous, and tell me why I should *care* if it's dangerous way out here?"

"How worried would you be," he asked, cocking an eyebrow at me, "if Zan-Thint opened a wormhole between the vacuum of deep space and the heart of the Sun? Do you *know* what would happen if he did that?"

"He could *do* that?" Nance asked, eyes going wide. "Wouldn't that destroy the gateway?"

"No. The gateway device controls the fabric of spacetime on a level that can cross galaxies. There is not much that could destroy it."

"Would Zan-Thint even *think* such a thing is possible?" Vicky asked, staring at the surface of the table as if she could see the solar system reflected in it. "I mean, he's not you. He doesn't know how the gateway works." Her gaze flickered up to Dwight's image. "*Does* he?"

"Isn't there another copy of you on his destroyer?" I asked Dwight.

"Not a *copy*," he corrected me, sniffing derision at my lack of understanding. "It is a separate piece of the whole that still exists, guarding the gateway you came through. It is *similar* to me, but we are at best brothers, not identical twins. His experience separated from mine the moment we separated from each other." Dwight spread his hands in a shrug. "If you are asking me if he would reveal to the Tahni the destructive potential of the gateway, I can't answer that question. I could ask him, but I wouldn't know if he would answer me honestly. Is this a chance you're willing to take?"

"As opposed to what?" Vicky demanded. "What's the alternative? Could you leave another version of yourself in charge of the gateway?"

"I could," Dwight admitted. "In fact, I may have to in order to control the wormhole. But that wouldn't stop Zan-Thint—or the Resscharr—from destroying the infrastructure around the device and using their AI to take command of it. I offer no alternative because I have none. I only felt the need to make you aware of the dangers. You will have to decide what to do about them."

"What would *you* do?" I asked him, more interested in probing his version of a conscience than debating our course of action. "If you were making the call? What's the logical decision here?"

Dwight's avatar smiled thinly.

"Just because I'm not biological doesn't mean I'm unemotional, Captain Alvarez. My processes may be, at their heart, ones and zeros, but the patterns they imitate are those of a living being. However, what we don't share is your affection for the Tahni or the Resscharr. If I were in your position, I would, perhaps, be more ruthless than you. This ship is much superior to what the Tahni at Yfingam have. You should destroy their space assets. Without them, they are no danger to anyone else."

Nance looked thoughtful, as if he was actually considering

the notion.

"We do that," I pointed out, hoping to head off him *and* Dwight, "and the Tahni and the Karai will probably slaughter the Vergai. And since we're leaving, we won't be around to stop them."

Nance glanced to the side at the display on the wall.

"Well, we're going to have to decide later. I have to get back to the bridge for Transition." He hopped up from his chair and headed for the hatch, pausing there and looking back over his shoulder at me, grinning lopsidedly. "Let me know if you come up with any brilliant ideas, fearless leader."

---

"Do we need to get the company ready for Transition?" Vicky asked me as we paced through the corridors back to our offices.

A stab of pain in my chest reminded me that we no longer actually *had* a Drop Trooper company. Two and a half platoons, more like it. We'd accomplished the mission but at a very heavy cost, and the impact of it was even greater since most of the casualties had come since I took over the company after Captain Solano died.

Vicky's hand on my arm broke me from the morose reverie, and the sympathetic look in her eyes told me she understood what I was feeling.

"No," I told her. "Just have them ready to head down in the drop ships once we hit orbit. They need a break."

That was something else that had changed, and not for the better. Being in command of the mission meant that I couldn't be just the Drop Trooper company commander anymore. Vicky handled most of the day-to-day operations and I had to concentrate on the big picture.

She was quiet as we walked past Fleet crew hurrying to

their positions, and when she spoke again, it was hesitant, thoughtful.

"You remember the double gates back on Hausos?" she asked me, the question sounding innocent enough.

I frowned at her for a moment before the light went on inside my head. "Double gates" was a military term we'd both studied in the history courses we'd had to take for officer's training way back when. It had to do with speaking in front of the enemy, enemy prisoners of war specifically, though there'd been no human EPWs since the Pirate Wars. Military personnel couldn't refer to each other or to their fellows by their real names in front of human EPWs because there was the possibility that one of them might escape or might get word back to their forces, and all it would take was a bright boy with a link to the nets to find the families of those Marines or Fleet personnel and take revenge on them.

"The ones at the Dubrov place, right?" I asked her, playing along. "He was that guy who we thought was our friend but wound up cooperating with the pirates."

Which was an odd thing to say in any normal conversation, since she'd brought the subject up and would probably remember who the people with the double gate were and whether they'd betrayed us to the bad guys. But we had to establish who was who in this code, and I just had to hope Dwight wouldn't notice.

"Well, that's what we *thought* anyway," she said diffidently. I spared her a questioning look and she went on, eyes down the corridor as if she was afraid to meet my eyes. "Sometimes I wonder if we were jumping to conclusions about Dubrov. I mean, it makes sense and I can see why everyone thought so, but maybe there was some other explanation? Could there have been any other way of looking at things?"

I didn't say anything immediately. I knew what she was

asking. I had no *proof* that the AIs had been the ones who created the Skrela. I was working from logic and deduction, but...

"I can't think of anything else that makes sense," I told her, shaking my head. "I mean, he said things to us that he couldn't have known unless he'd conspired with the pirates."

Which was code for the fact that Dwight had asked Lilandreth to come with him to one of the Skreloid worlds because he claimed that the language in the control center was from a time after he'd been installed at the gateway and he needed her help translating it. But we found out later that the Skreloid worlds had been established in the distant past and there was no reason Dwight wouldn't have been able to interpret the readouts.

"He's only human," she said softly. "Whatever else he is, he was just a man, and we don't know what he went through. Maybe we don't know everything."

I'd known Vicky a long time and I could read between the lines. She was asking me if there was some other explanation, if maybe even if I was right, that Dwight might still not have known what had happened.

"Maybe we don't," I admitted. "But you know how the military is. Especially when you're in command. You have to assume the worst." I blew out a breath. Maybe I *wanted* her to be right. "There's plenty of time to think about it. No reason to make any decisions right now, y'know?"

"You're probably right." But she still looked worried. I slipped an arm around her.

"There was a Bible verse my mom liked to quote," I told her. "It was from the Sermon on the Mount."

I paused, trying to remember.

*"Take therefore no thought for the morrow: for the morrow shall take thought for the things of itself. Sufficient unto the day is the evil thereof."*

# [ 3 ]

"It feels like forever since we've seen this place," Nance murmured, staring down at the greens and blues of Yfingam. "We picking up any threats, Tactical?"

"Nothing out of the ordinary," Wojtera reported, barely looking up from the holographic display at his position. "The Tahni ships are on the opposite side of the planet from us currently, but we're running our transponder, so they should know who we are before they see us."

"I always wondered," Yanayev, the Helm officer, mused, floating against the straps of safety harness, "why the planet and the city have the same name. Isn't that a little lazy?"

"It wasn't named by humans," I said, and the woman twisted in her acceleration couch, raising an eyebrow at the explanation. Well, probably not the reasoning behind it but the fact that it was me giving it. For over a year now, it had been Colonel Hachette who'd answered those kind of questions. Or Dwight. If I hadn't spoken up, it probably would've been Dwight. "Just because we tend to name our major cities different than the planet doesn't mean that the Resscharr have the same aesthetic."

"Maybe if Lilandreth were up here for the approach," Yanayev said snidely, "she could give us the lowdown on Resscharr naming protocols."

"Belay that shit, Yanayev," Nance snapped, not looking around at the woman.

I chewed on my lip, holding back a sharp retort of my own. The crew had heard the story that the Resscharr were the ones who'd created the Skrela and it had, apparently, evaporated any good feelings they might have had toward Lilandreth and her people for giving us the cool new engine and weapons.

"Whatever the Resscharr did," I said quietly but firmly, "Lilandreth had no part in it. She's done nothing but help us."

"Yes, sir," Yanayev said, glancing at the deck, abashed. I blinked, though I tried not to let my surprise show on my face. Technically she was a higher rank than me, though hers was Fleet and mine was Marines, but she must have really bought into the decision to make me mission commander. I'd been wondering if the Fleet types would accept it.

"Sir," Lt. Chase said, "we have an incoming transmission from Lt. Campea."

I waited just a beat for Nance to acknowledge until I realized he'd been talking to me. If Vicky had been on the bridge instead of with the company, she undoubtedly would have given me a helpful nudge.

"Put it on the main screen, Chase," I told him, acting as if I'd known it all along.

I wondered in the brief moment between the order and its execution whether I'd done the right thing. Should I have had the call sent to my personal 'link? If it was bad news, should I try to keep it from the crew until I'd had the chance to deal with it? I had the gut feeling that would have been a mistake, that I should trust the crew if I wanted them to trust me.

Campea's face filled a quarter of the forward view screen,

rounded and a little soft for a Force Recon platoon leader, but I knew that was camouflage as effective as that on his armor. He was as tough as seasoned leather, and we'd trusted him to keep a lid on things back on Yfingam for the months we'd been gone. From the haggard, stress-lined look of him, it hadn't been easy. I recognized the background behind him, the headquarters we'd set up outside the city in some old storage buildings.

"Hey, Captain Alvarez," he said, nodding. "Captain Nance." His eyes traveled across the bridge. "Where's Top? With the company?"

I cleared my throat, weariness settling in on me, dragging me down by the shoulders. I hadn't thought of that. He wouldn't know anything about our mission.

"We took some casualties, John," I told him, each word a tombstone weighing a ton. "A *lot* of them. Top didn't make it."

Campea gasped. I'd rarely seen anyone gasp in my life, and even more rarely from a Recon Marine, but this was well earned. The man's face went white, and whatever he'd been about to say caught in his throat.

"We lost Colonel Hachette as well," I went on, deciding to break all the bad news at once. Campea winced, though there wasn't the gut-punch reaction from the news about Top. Perhaps Hachette had been more at arm's length to a Marine first lieutenant than Top. "I'm in overall command of the mission now. The good news is, we've accomplished that mission."

"What?" Campea blurted, eyes gone wide. "I mean, sir?"

"We discovered and neutralized the source of the Skrela incursions." It was a much longer story than that, of course, but I'd brief him on the rest later. "We're not sure if there are any stray elements left extant, but we don't have to worry about major attacks again. And we found the second gateway. We've brought it back with us." Light came back into his eyes, and I hastened to caution him before he got too optimistic. "It's gonna need some work before it can get us all back home, but we did it. What's the situation here?"

Campea took a second to get his thoughts together, and I couldn't blame him for that, not after the bombs I'd dropped on him. He sucked in a breath and launched into it with the calm precision I expected from the man.

"Tensions are pretty high, sir. I *thought* we had an understanding before you left, but it's been months, and it seems like every other day there's another incident between the Karai and the Vergai. We've had twenty-three dead and forty-one injured since you left, and the only reason there hasn't been open warfare is Zan-Thint telling the Karai that he won't support them if they go to war without his okay." Campea scowled. "I think Carella *wants* them to do it, wants to get it over with. She's counting on us and the Resscharr here to back her up, though I've told her over and over that I'm not going to commit my one tiny platoon of light infantry against the entire Tahni force here." He shrugged. "I'm not sure it's gotten through to her, but I'll tell you right now, sir, since the *Orion* is back along with your Drop Troopers, I know she's gonna get worse. I don't know how much longer I can keep a lid on it."

"You've done a great job, John," I assured him, though I really had no idea if he had. That was part of being a commander, reassuring people when they were about to fall apart. Then, if I found out later that he'd fucked up, I could counsel him in private. I didn't have the luxury of *replacing* him, of course, not when we had a grand total of one platoon of Force Recon on hand, but at least I could make sure he understood what I expected. "We'll be coming down immediately, and I guess we're going to have to bring everyone together."

I rubbed thumb and forefinger on the bridge of my nose. I felt a headache coming on.

"Of course," I went on, "the fact we're going to be leaving for good in a couple months may just make it all that much worse."

---

"So, you've moved your headquarters into the fortress," I told Zan-Thint, admiring the view from the balcony of his new office. "I thought you wanted to maintain a separation in everyone's mind between the Tahni and the Resscharr who used to rule from here."

I could certainly see the attraction. The Marines called this place Yfingam castle, though it didn't resemble a medieval tower at all, more akin to something that might have been familiar in late Byzantium, though on a smaller scale. The entire city was a continuous building from the exterior wall right into the central tower, and while that might have been a huge fire risk back in the bad old days, it wasn't a problem when the construction materials had been exuded out of artificial material by nanite constructors sometime around ten thousand years ago.

The balcony was a privilege of the dweller of the tower, which had until our arrival been a Resscharr. Not the technologically advanced type of Resscharr like Lilandreth and the other refugees from Decision though. These Resscharr had abandoned the path of their ancestors for a more primitive existence, left to the lifestyle of their choice by their ancestors who'd transported them to this world, leaving them to the care of the sentient AI buried under the building. The balcony looked out over the other buildings, over the wall and into the fields beyond, so the old Resscharr ruler could keep a watchful eye on the Vergai tending his crops. It was very much an imperial position.

"That was more important at first," Zan-Thint said, waving

a hand dismissively. "Now, well... I think we all know the situation."

There was something qualitatively different about the Tahni officer since the first time I'd met him. Back then he'd been harder edged, unmistakably a line military officer, a hardened combat veteran. Now... those edges had softened, and he'd traded his military uniform for something more decorative and polychromatic, something that brought to mind pictures I'd seen of the way the dictators of small countries had dressed a couple centuries ago.

"Yeah, I suppose we do." I shrugged, looking away from the sunbaked summer fields and into the soft light of the... well, it was less of an office and more of a throne room. It had once been adorned with furniture better suited to the digitigrade legs and body structure of the Resscharr, but Zan-Thint had replaced that with newly constructed pieces comfortable for the Tahni... and us humans. "I suppose Lan-Min-Gen..." I nodded toward the Shock Trooper officer, who stood near the door, hands clasped in front of him, silent as a statue. "... already briefed you on the mission."

"He did," Zan-Thint confirmed, leaning against the curved table in front of the only couch in the room, which was presumably reserved for him. "I must say, it is quite the relief to no longer have to worry over the threat from the Skrela. You have my gratitude." He'd apparently learned something of human facial expressions along with our language, because he attempted something close to a smile. With his steam-shovel jaws and horrific, blocky teeth, I would rather he'd forgone the attempt. "And I am quite gratified as well to hear that you will all soon be going home."

"Yeah, I thought you might feel that way," I said, my own smile thin and showing fewer teeth. "I'm sorry for the loss of your corvettes and their crews. They fought bravely."

"They were foolhardy and heedless," Zan-Thint countered. "Lan-Min-Gen told me of this as well. I regret the loss of their ships as assets, but if I may be brutally frank with you, they weren't good for anything. They couldn't have matched *your* ships, much less the Skrela, and they were useless against targets on the ground. At least on this mission they had the chance to die with purpose and honor."

I glanced sidelong at Lan-Min-Gen, wondering if Zan-Thint felt the same way about his Shock Troopers. They were useless against our Vigilantes and not needed to fight the Vergai. He'd certainly been willing enough to sacrifice them. Would that bother Lan-Min-Gen, or would he accept it with the same sort of fatalism most Tahni seemed to show?

"We'll need a little while to get the gateway prepared to transport us," I went on. "Maybe several months. I'd like to use the time we have left to help establish some sort of peaceful coexistence with the Vergai."

"And may your gods grant you good fortune in that endeavor," Zan-Thint said with an affected snort of amusement. "Their leader, Carella, is a fanatic to the point where she makes me seem reasonable by comparison." Which showed an amazing degree of self-awareness from the Tahni. I wasn't sure if that was a good thing. A stupid enemy was almost always more desirable than a smart one, but if he was to be a neutral neighbor, perhaps perspective was a desirable trait.

"She is." I didn't bother to deny it. "Maybe if her husband hadn't been killed on Decision, we wouldn't have to worry about her, but that wasn't how it went down." I paced in front of the desk, wishing for a chair. Why the hell did he have to be a dick about providing chairs for other people in in his office? "I'm going to work on getting her cooperation, but before I promise her anything, I wanted to talk to you first. Because you know the first thing she's going to ask me when I go to her is whether I've run any of it by you yet."

"And what would you... *run by me*, Cameron Alvarez?" The turn of phrase clearly amused him.

"We're gonna have to organize some sort of power sharing," I said. "Carella won't settle for anything less than her people having a say in how things are run." I spread my hands demonstratively. "Maybe some kind of council with representatives based on population? You could bring the Resscharr in, along with you and the Karai. Maybe the council could vote on a governor for the colony."

Tahni didn't laugh, per se, and Zan-Thint made no effort at imitating the reaction either, but I knew the species well enough to recognize the equivalent, and I eyed him balefully.

"You suggest this thing," he said, "yet you don't propose why I would accept sharing power with a force so inferior to my own. Between my Tahni and the Karai, we control at least seventy percent of the combat power on this planet... once you're gone. There's no reason we should not also control seventy percent of the political power. Or more."

I sighed, crossing my arms, not attempting to hide my impatience.

"Except the whole part about you having to fight another war if you don't. Didn't you get enough of war? Wasn't that why you came out here in the first place?"

"It would be a *short* war," he pointed out. "We would wipe them out to the last."

"And you think you wouldn't take casualties?" I shot back. "You think you have enough people and equipment here to afford them?" I motioned around us. "Because I got news for you, you aren't getting any more trained soldiers or laser weapons or fusion drives out here. What you got is what you got. You can keep it for any future emergencies, or you can waste it now in a pointless civil war."

"Or," he said, coming off his seat on the table and looming over me by nearly thirty centimeters, "I could take *your* weapons, *your* fusion drives while you're still here."

My lip skinned away from my teeth in a snarl, and I didn't give a step despite the differences in our height.

"You can fucking *try*."

And yeah, I was being pretty reckless with my mouth considering that Zan-Thint was in control of hundreds of Tahni soldiers and tens of thousands of Karai warriors and all I had on me was my sidearm. But I'd faced the sort of death he could only imagine, and there wasn't much here that could scare me anymore.

Zan-Thint met my stare with those black, piggish eyes beneath the bony brow ridges, and neither of us looked back at Lan-Min-Gen. I figured he'd back his commander if it came to that, but if I broke eye contact with Zan-Thint, I'd be showing weakness. Maybe it was my knowledge of the Tahni or maybe it was just a lifetime of experience dealing with bullies, but some instinct told me I shouldn't show weakness in front of him.

"Go," Zan-Thint told me, motioning toward the door. "Talk to Carella. If you can convince her to agree to this, I will consider it."

A sigh of relief would have been just as damning as showing weakness, so I simply nodded and turned to leave. Lan-Min-Gen escorted me out of the room and we remained silent down the spiraling ramp from the top of the tower to the main floor. Armed guards lined the ramp, glaring at me suspiciously, though the muzzles of their weapons never wavered.

Lan-Min-Gen waited until we were well past them before he spoke.

"I know you well enough now," he said, finally, "to understand you are trying to do what you believe is right."

The corner of my mouth turned up, though he couldn't see it.

"There's a 'but' in there somewhere."

"The commander was not wrong. The Vergai leader Carella is a fanatic. You will not convince her."

I sighed, nodded unwillingly.

"I know. But I have to try."

## [ 4 ]

"You tell me," Carella said archly, arms crossed over her chest, "that you are going to abandon us here, defenseless, and then, in the next breath, say we should trust the Tahni, the Karai, and the Resscharr, the very ones who enslaved us before your arrival, to honor an agreement to share rule?"

Carella was young, even for this backward world with no concept of anti-aging treatment and precious little in the way of medical technology in general. But she'd aged just in the time I'd known her, lines at the corners of her eyes and mouth drawing maps of pain. The death of her husband, Matis, who'd been the co-leader of the Vergai, had done what years of privation and servitude to the Resscharr and Karai hadn't been able to. It had aged her.

We weren't in her house. She hadn't invited us there for some time, and I hadn't seen her children since months before we left for this last voyage. Instead, she met us in a brick building that I thought had once been a grain storehouse, though the only thing stored there at the moment were crates of the rifles we'd fabricated for their militia. They weren't as careful about those as they were with the energy weapons that had been gifted by the Resscharr on Decision to the Vergai soldiers who'd come along with us. Those were hidden well, because I never saw one after the Skrela attack.

Not that I cared about being invited to her home, but as a storehouse this place had no windows, and it was high summer on this hemisphere of the planet. Even with the door left open, it was damned hot, and sweat was trickling down my back despite at least having a bit of shade from the afternoon glare.

"We're not staying here forever just to make you feel more secure," Vicky told her, unable to restrain her irritation at the woman. "We're going home, and you have to be prepared for what happens after we're gone."

Again, we were all standing. I *knew* that the Vergai invited their guests to sit, so this was just being rude, and I didn't blame Vicky for being annoyed. At least there were no armed guards watching over us, just Carella, the two of us, and Oster and Leesha. Oster had gone along with us to Decision and had taken command of the Vergai militia after Matis' death. He and his wife had tried to act as go-betweens for us with Carella, since she had very little use for us Commonwealth types. They looked uncomfortable watching our interplay, like children hearing their parents argue, but I also noted that *they* hadn't been offered a chair either.

"You could leave us your weapons," Carella suggested, and her words were sharp and bitter even through the translator. "They would be much more useful than your *council*." She didn't pace, she stalked, a leopardess ready to strike, and like us, she wore a sidearm. One *we'd* given her. For some reason, I felt more worried about her killing us than I had Zan-Thint. "Do you believe that the Karai or the Tahni will *allow* us to vote against them? You say representation will be based on our population, but there are fewer of us than of the Karai, even without the Tahni strengthening their numbers."

"Then you need to ally yourselves with the Resscharr," I suggested. "There are enough of them that, between the two of you, you could form a majority."

You'd think I'd suggested that she dig up her mother's corpse and desecrate it from the way her face turned red, and she actually yanked at her hair as if she wanted to tear it out.

"The Resscharr are the ones who brought us here! The ones who enslaved us! Why would they ally with us rather than the Karai who were their soldiers?"

"The Karai betrayed them, Carella," Oster told her, daring to talk back to the woman for a change. He'd been unbearably meek in her presence for too long, and I was wondering why the hell we were keeping him around. "And the Tahni were responsible for their downfall."

"Yes, lady," Leesha agreed, face brightening as if she was delighted to have a positive argument to seize onto. "Surely they would blame the Tahni and Karai for their downfall rather than us! They might welcome the chance to stand up against their conquerors."

Carella peered at the two of them through narrowed eyes, as if she was considering what they said through the filter of skepticism she seemed to have for anything we suggested.

"This may be so," she admitted, finally, squatting on a crate of assault rifles. "It may be."

"Don't forget the refugees from Decision," I said. Her gaze flickered sharply toward me, and I guessed that was for merely mentioning the world where her husband had died. I ignored it. "They know they can't trust the Tahni. And they have no reason to resent you and the Vergai. They also have a much higher level of technology than either you *or* the Tahni, so the native Resscharr here have no choice but to listen to them."

Carella chewed at her lip, staring at the sawdust-covered plank flooring like she thought the truth was written on it by the prophets. I *knew* she didn't want to listen to us, knew she was looking for a reason not to, but I was hoping against hope that she'd finally learned her lesson after everything that had happened since Matis' death.

Nothing is *ever* that simple, and I should have known that better than anyone.

"You're asking me to trust the very survival of my people to the whims of others who have no reason to love us. If you're going to abandon us to this fate, then perhaps we have no other choice than to strike at our enemies first."

Again, I should have probably maintained my calm, but I was no diplomat and, honest to God, this woman was taxing me.

"Jesus tapdancing Christ," I snapped, jabbing a finger toward her. "You know what, lady? For the longest time now, I've let you get away with this bullshit because I felt guilty about Matis. He was under my command and that made his death my responsibility. But honest to God, you've gotten on my last nerve!"

"Cam," Vicky said softly, eyeing me sidelong with a mixture of horror and maybe envy that she hadn't had the chance to say it first. I *should* have listened to her, but I was too far along on this rant to stop now.

"Here's your choices," I told her, counting them off on my fingers. "You can fight, but you'll do it without us. We won't be here past the next few months, and we're not going to help you start a war. And you'll bloody their nose, to be sure, but you'll lose, and they'll either slaughter you to the last man, woman, and child or the survivors will have to run, live like savages in caves. And if they remember you at all, they'll curse your name as the one who could have saved them."

Oster and Leesha winced, and I understood. I was

hammering it home pretty hard. But being subtle hadn't worked, and I would likely have tried the direct approach a while ago if it hadn't been for Top and Hachette looking over my shoulder.

"Or," I went on, folding down another finger, "you can try it our way. Rein your people in. Stop the violence, stop the confrontations with the Karai, and make an honest effort at coexistence. Commit to being a part of the planetary government here and make yourselves so invaluable, so integral to the process, that none of the others can imagine trying to make this place run without you." I nodded, raising a palm to forestall the objection she was about to bring up. "Yeah, it won't happen fast, but if you start now, you can be well on the way there before we leave. That's your *best* option, the one that'll give your people a home here that can last, if you'll just swallow your damned ego and listen to someone else for a change."

I dropped my hands and sighed.

"Or you can all leave. Laisvas Miestas is just a short interplanetary flight away for the *Orion*. The Islanders would be happy for more people, more technology, more supplies. It's where you all were brought from in the first place."

Sort of. They were originally brought from Earth, but there was no way to get them all through the gateway and back there, not unless we came back with the entire fleet. But the other habitable in this system was populated mostly by humans with a much smaller contingent of genetic Tahni. Of course, there was much less land on that world and shitloads of water, which meant everyone who went from here to there would likely have to learn a new trade, but it was better than dying.

"It is a strange place," Leesha murmured, eyes clouded over as if the prospect of going there disturbed her. "If the legends are true, there is sea from horizon to horizon and giant storms that last for days."

"We've been there," Vicky reminded her in a tone much gentler than mine had been. She put a hand on the woman's arm and gave it a comforting squeeze. "The island chains are beautiful and the oceans are rich with life. It would mean a change, but things are going to change, one way or another."

"Carella," Oster said, taking a hesitant step toward their leader, "I know none of us want to hear this, but Cam is right. If we try to fight the Tahni without the help of the Earthers, we'll die. For my part, I would feel more comfortable on a world with other humans where I didn't have to worry about the Karai and the Resscharr and whether they'll decide someday that we Vergai are a hindrance to be removed."

"You would leave here, Oster?" Carella asked, smoothing down her woolen skirts as she stood to face him. "You would travel to the Island World and abandon this place and all that we've worked for?"

"We are all the children of the Islanders," Oster corrected her quietly, eyes downcast. "I would simply go home."

Carella sighed out a long breath, and with it, the outrage seemed to drain from her. She made a shooing motion.

"Go. I will think on this." She met my eyes again. "I will speak to my people, and soon you will have your answer."

I left her with a curt nod, not trusting myself to say anything else without pissing her off again. The sun was lower in the sky than when we'd entered the building, and I squinted against the reddening flares of it still hovering above the horizon. Farmers guided horse-drawn carts down the track between the buildings, carrying crops to storage bins, all an ordinary summer day... except for the militia manning guard posts on both sides of the road, the barrels of their crew-served weapons pointed down. For now.

"Well, that went better than I expected," Vicky said, arm

slipping around my shoulder. "Particularly given how you went all caveman on her."

"Did it?" I shook my head but couldn't shake the feeling that Carella's acquiescence wasn't genuine. "Then why do I think that everything just got worse?"

---

The walk back to our own headquarters was a long one, and I probably should have procured a vehicle for it, but after so many months trapped in the confines of the ship, I didn't begrudge some outdoor time. The dirt road was muddy from horse piss and littered with the deposits from them and the oxen the Vergai used to haul their wagons, so the two of us had set off across the fields instead.

"Oh, man," Vicky sighed, tilting her head back to catch the last rays of the day, "I tell you one thing, once we get back, I want to find a beach somewhere and spend a month just lying in the sun on it. Then we can rent a cabin somewhere in the mountains with a stream nearby and hike in the woods every day for another month. I figure we're both due enough back pay to take care of that."

I said nothing for a moment, unwilling to rob Vicky of her fantasy despite a growing conviction in my gut that we weren't as close to home as everyone thought. There was still too much that could go wrong. I suppressed the thought and chuckled instead.

"It'd be just our luck," I told her, "that Hachette forgot to send in the paperwork for our promotions and pay raises before we went through the gateway."

"Oh, that would truly suck!" Vicky said, a stricken expression passing over her face, as if the thought of not getting paid was just as important to her as the possibilities I'd kept to myself. "That would mean we've been working for free this whole time! That would piss me off!"

"No big deal," I insisted, trying to keep my tone light-hearted. "If they try to screw over our pay, we'll just steal one of the Intercepts and sell it on the black market."

The stalks of grain in the field had been cut down and hauled away, giving the place a devastated look, and here and there I noticed the beheaded body of a snake or the crushed form of a rat, victims of the mechanical reapers. A winged shadow passed over us and a red tail hawk—or at least the genetically engineered equivalent left here by the Predecessors—swooped down and grabbed one of the dead snakes, pecking at it a few times before carrying it away back to somewhere more convenient to eat dinner.

"You're meeting with Lilandreth tomorrow, right?" Vicky asked, changing subjects so abruptly I nearly missed a step. I shot her a confused look and she tapped her ear. I got it then. She was guarding her words against being listened in on by Dwight.

"Yeah," I agreed, trying to sound natural. "I'm going to ask her about modifying the fabricators to produce more Vigilantes. I know we can't duplicate the power sources and weapons the Resscharr gave us, but I think we might be able to work up some conventional isotope reactors from material we can get here in the system."

"Should we tell her?"

I knew exactly what she meant. Should we tell Lilandreth about Dwight, about our suspicion that the AIs had created the Skrela? But I couldn't let on.

"Tell her what?" I prompted innocently.

"About Carella." Her glare made it clear that she was bullshitting and also that she was annoyed I was forcing her to bullshit, but she played along. "If we give her the heads-up about the whole council thing, maybe we can get her to reach out to Carella proactively, convince her that this is a good idea."

And now it was my turn to be annoyed, because I had to come up with a way to answer both questions at once and still sound natural. That took a moment, and if Dwight had been able to look at me as well as listen, it would have seemed like I was considering the question carefully... because I was.

"It's not a bad idea," I ventured after a few seconds. "But I kind of worry about her reaction. She's already in a pretty fragile place emotionally after what we found out on the trip. She and the... Tahni aren't exactly getting along as it is without me bringing this up. We'd have to get her alone and then approach the matter gradually."

She was silent, though I couldn't tell whether she was considering my answer or how she'd phrase the next few words. It was maddening, not being able to *talk* openly to each other without worrying about him listening in. I mean, I suppose looking back on it, most of my life had been spent in places where I could have been spied on, where the military or the government or corporations could have overheard what I was saying, but I'd never been in a position where anyone would have *wanted* to before.

"Who else should we tell?" Her tone was helpless, and I wished I could say something comforting.

"Nance." I worried this wouldn't make any sense but hoped Dwight would chalk it up to the shorthand Vicky and I used as a couple. "But we'll have to wait until he's down here and we can tell him face to face. And damned if that's not about it. It's pretty fucked up that we're in a position where there's no one else to make the decisions. I'm too used to having the buck stop with Hachette."

And that much wasn't an act for Dwight's benefit. As much as I'd bitched about Hachette's decision making, at least there'd been someone above me, someone *else* to blame if things went bad. I kicked at a loose rock turned up by one of the reapers and a covey of quail flushed from the scrub, hooting their alarm.

"Whatever else goes wrong now, there's no one left to blame but me."

## [ 5 ]

"Fourteen thousand tons of tungsten," Dwight counted off with all the enthusiasm of a retail clerk, "one hundred thousand tons of nickel-iron, thirty thousand tons of magnesium, eight thousand tons of platinum..."

Leaning back in the folding chair that was still the only furniture they'd bothered to bring down from the *Orion* to the dumpy little office down on the planet, I squeezed my eyes shut. It wouldn't have been so bad if we'd all been sitting across from each other in person, but Dwight *wasn't* a person, Vicky was running the Marines through PMCS on their suits, Lilandreth didn't feel the need to leave the city, in her words because it would be "a poor use of time and resources," and Nance claimed that he didn't have time to come down for shore leave.

I had my doubts on that one. Having known the man as long as I had, and having been there once myself, I was beginning to think Captain Nance was an inveterate agoraphobe who *really* didn't want to leave his ship. The more I thought about it, the stronger my conviction that this was the real reason he didn't want to be in command of the mission. He knew if he was, he'd have to set foot on a planet at some point.

What it all meant was that I was sitting in a hot, stuffy block building in the middle of summer on a late morning, by myself, watching a sentient computer tell us all what would be required to build the gateway corridor complex. And I was having a damned hard time staying awake for it. I never thought I'd get nostalgic about preventative maintenance sessions.

"We get the idea," Nance interrupted the AI, making a gesture that might have signaled *move along* or might have been something even ruder. "You do know you can just input all those numbers into the ship's system, right?"

"Of course," Dwight said, his avatar taking up a corner of the flat-screen monitor on the folding metal table. Not even a holographic display down here. That had been Hachette's call back when. Nothing went down to the planet that couldn't be carried back to the ship on someone's back or abandoned in place. "But I felt it was crucial that all of you understand what a massive undertaking this is. You should be able to find this sort of mineral content in a single asteroid, and the *Orion* is quite capable of transporting it back to orbit, but the key is going to be the smelting of the ores. It's going to require the use of your main gun, and not in a manner that it was designed for. Overheating is going to be the problem, which will mean extended cooldown periods. You're also going to need to fabricate the construction drones. I can control them if you like, since I know the exact specifications. That would save you from needing a large work crew."

Nance grunted noncommittally.

"I don't know about that. I'm more comfortable with my engineering crew overseeing everything."

Dwight's expression was pained, a picture of strained patience.

"Captain Nance, your ship was constructed by automated construction pods controlled by artificial intelligences much less complex than I. Do you really believe I can't handle this project?"

Nance scowled at the AI's avatar, then at me.

"You're the boss, Alvarez."

Yeah, I was the boss all right. And I knew something he didn't, that Dwight might not be trustworthy. But would the possibility that he hated the Resscharr enough to genocide them be reason enough for him to sabotage our attempt to get home? What other choice did we have? We weren't going anywhere without his help.

"You're in charge of the construction project, Dwight," I told him. "Captain Nance, whatever he needs from the ship, your people give it to him. The key is to get this done as quickly as possible. Things are unstable here, and we don't need to be here if and when they blow up. Everyone copy?"

"Aye, aye, sir," Nance said, the corner of his mouth twisting in a sneer. And that was it, just about all I was going to take.

"Captain," I told him, "if you disagree with my determination, now's the time to give me a well-reasoned argument against it." And while the words were civil and professional, I was fairly certain the look in my eye wasn't. "If you have a problem with me making the decisions, this would also be the perfect time for you to take operational command of this mission... and bear the responsibility for every choice made from here on out."

Nance was already pale, but I thought he went a bit *paler* at the statement. The man *really* didn't want to be in command.

"No, sir," he said, finally. "We'll get it done."

I nodded slowly, satisfied.

"All right, then. Get on it ASAP. I've got some more materials I'm going to need from the mining operation once you bring that asteroid in as well. I'll get you a list, but once the smelting starts, I need those down here as a priority." I had the file ready and sent it with a flick of my finger on my 'link screen.

Nance glanced down at it, his eyebrow raising.

"What are we building down there?" he wondered.

"Security," I told him. "Everyone, get to work. Lilandreth, if you'd please stay on the line?"

I waited until Nance was off the line and Dwight's image disappeared before I went on. Not that Dwight was actually *gone*, of course.

"I do not understand," she said before I could speak, "why I have been included in this conference. It's obvious you need nothing from my people to complete this project."

"Lilandreth," I said, ignoring her complaints and getting to the point, "I understand there are some fabricators inside the fortress. Are those still controlled by the Resscharr, or have the Karai taken them over?"

She blinked, and I wondered if the reaction meant the same thing for her species as it did for mine. If she was surprised by the question, there was no hesitation in her answer.

"The Karai have no concept of how to use the fabricators. And if General Zan-Thint is aware of their existence, he hasn't mentioned them."

"Good. Ours are adequate for most of what I have in mind, but I need over a hundred compact isotope reactors constructed and we don't have the capacity for that. If I give you the isotopes, can you handle the production?"

I was hoping like hell she'd say yes, because the only alternative I had was to churn them out up on the *Orion*, which would have to wait until after the construction drones were finished and would probably take months all by itself.

"Of course." She tilted her head to the side in a gesture I had come to understand meant assent. "It will take the better part of a full month to turn out that many." A pause. "Am I to assume these will be used to replace the losses you took of your battlesuits?"

I watched that inhuman face for a moment before I replied, trying to decide if I trusted her any more than Dwight did. True, she'd been key to destroying the Womb and getting rid of the Skrela, but that had been in her own best interest as well. There was something about her features, something that Top had described once as the uncanny valley, jut close enough to human that I could almost forget what she was, but not human, so definitely not human. It was the same with the Tahni, and I wondered if we'd ever really trust each other on a gut level.

"Yeah," I admitted. "Maybe all our troubles are over and we're about to jump through that gateway back to the loving arms of the Commonwealth and everything's gonna be wine and roses, but I've been shot at too many times to believe that. Right now we're at less than half strength, and if we run into any serious enemy, we're toast."

Golden eyes with vertical irises watched me with a perception that had seemed to confirm the Tahni view of the Predecessors as gods.

"You won't have the upgraded power cells and weapons we gave you," she pointed out. "And more importantly, I know you lack the facilities to implant those interface jacks."

"Before the implant jacks became SOP for the Drop Troopers," I explained, "we used neural halos that could read electrical impulses in the brain through the scalp. It's a microsecond slower, but it's better than nothing."

"And who will you get to wear those devices? Who will fight for you, Cameron Alvarez?"

Was she mocking me? It was hard to tell, but I got the sense she was playing with me.

"I'm working on that," I said, careful to keep my voice neutral.

"You're making a mistake, you know." And there it was, the

other shoe I'd been waiting to drop, and the mocking faded into something darker, grimmer. "Trusting that thing."

Ah. That's what all this was about. Dwight. She'd been forced to sit there and listen to the AI dictate terms to us, and it was gnawing at her.

"I don't see that we have any choice."

"That's what we thought." She tossed her head, the mane of stiff, feathery hair snapping like a cat o'nine tails. "Send me the material when you get it. I will produce your reactors. But they will not save you from the real threat."

The transmission cut off and the screen went dark.

"Lovely," I murmured to no one. Not only did Lilandreth resent us for working with Dwight, she refused to come out here physically so I would have the chance to tell her what we suspected.

I didn't want to get out of the chair, despite the stuffy, humid atmosphere in the old storage building, didn't want to open the door because I knew who was waiting outside. I was looking forward to this conversation even less than I had been the one with Lilandreth. But the job was the job.

Oster was standing outside the door, shuffling from one foot to another, hands clasping his broad-brimmed farmer's hat in front of him like one of the old ladies back on my home street worrying a rosary bead.

"Sorry to keep you waiting," I told the man, nodding to the Force Recon Marine standing guard outside the building. At least she had a cooling system inside her armor. "Come on in."

Oster ducked inside, glancing behind him as if to make sure no one had seen him enter, and I restrained a laugh. There weren't too many of the Vergai who didn't know he'd allied himself with us.

"Have a seat." I waved at the plastic chair, forgoing an

apology for how flimsy it was because at least we *had* chairs available for our guests.

Oster squatted on the thing like he was afraid it might collapse beneath him, staring at the floor.

"I gather you've had an answer from Carella," I said, sitting across from him.

"Not in so many words." He shook his head, still unwilling to look up. "She won't see me or Leesha, or even any of our friends who share our views. She's shut herself off and spoken only to people she trusts, those who are as fanatical in their hatred of the Karai as she is. This is not an answer to your proposal in words, but I feel it shows which path she's taking."

"What about those friends of yours?" I spread my hands. "Would any of them be willing to stand up to her, try to sway the rest of the Vergai to your side? I mean, there's tens of thousands of you just here around the city. Surely there's got to be enough who don't want war with the Karai to make a difference."

"Yet she has all the weapons." Now he finally met my eyes, and there was fear in his expression. "She guards the energy rifles the Resscharr gave us on Decision like they were the keys to eternal life. Even *I* don't know where they are, and I was the leader of our militia. The weapons you made for us are all in the hands of her allies now."

"Yeah, I can see where that might be a problem. What do *you* want, Oster? What do the people who you talk to want?"

"We wish to leave this place." The words came out of him like they'd been extracted by a medieval torturer with hot pliers. His breath came short from the exertion of the admission and he looked as if he were about to fall out of his chair. "It's weakness to say, but the feeling has grown among more and more of us. We know you and your ship are leaving here, and to stay without your protection is slow suicide."

"We can arrange passage for you to the Islands if that's what you want. There *is* another choice though. At least for a few of you, those who're willing." He stared at me uncomprehending until I went on. "We lost a lot of Drop Troopers destroying the Skrela. We can build more suits." I shrugged. "They won't be quite as good as the ones we came here with, much less the improved ones the Resscharr built, but they're a hell of a lot better than sharp sticks and harsh language. We need people who we can train, people who are willing to fight if it comes to that."

"To fight for *you*," Oster assumed. The tilt of his head was skeptical, suspicious. "For your people."

"Yeah." There was no use trying to con him about that. "And in return, they get to come with us when we leave." I motioned upward. "Back to the Commonwealth, to a place where humans run the show and the Tahni have been conquered, where there are *no* Resscharr anymore."

"This wouldn't be for Leesha or I," Oster surmised, the words soft and thoughtful.

"No," I agreed. "This would have to be young men and women who don't have children. There's no room on a warship for children, and even if there were, Marines get killed and I'm not going to be responsible for making orphans. Childless couples are okay, but they have to understand they won't be serving in the same units because they can't be constantly worrying about each other and not the mission." I raised a finger and brought his attention up to my eyes and away from the floor. "Make sure they know this. I don't want anyone who comes into this thinking it's going to be easy or fun. What we *will* do is teach them. We'll teach them about our technology, about our worlds, about how to be a Marine. And if they make it back to the Commonwealth, I'll guarantee them a home."

This would be the tough part, not for him but for me. I had

no idea if I could talk the government into granting land on some colony world to a bunch of refugees from the Bronze Age. But hell, if I had to, I'd use Hachette's old contacts to give them fake identities.

"I can ask," Oster said. He didn't sound hopeful, but then he never really did. "There are always young people who are bored of farming and wish for a different life."

I laughed. I couldn't stop myself.

"Oster," I said, still chuckling, "you've just described every single military force in the history of humanity."

## [ 6 ]

"Hey, sir," Sgt. Czarnecki said, a grin splitting his blocky, square-jawed face. "Didn't think we'd see you again here in the land of grunts."

Chuckles went around the table at that, some of them accompanying bits of partially chewed dinner. These guys *were* Marines, no matter what else they'd been through. Not as many as there had been a few months ago though, and the empty seats in the board-and-nail barn that had become our chow hall were all to obvious.

"Yeah, that's 'cause I never have time to sit down and eat dinner anymore, Top," I told him, falling onto a spot on the bench beside Vicky and giving her hand a squeeze. "Between the locals and the orbital construction and the Tahni, I'm bouncing around like a pinball."

"That's what happens when you get a command slot, sir," the gunnery sergeant told me, shaking his head before biting into a biscuit. He didn't seem *actually* pissed off, of course. The Marines had been more than happy to have one of their own in charge of the mission, even though they still gave me shit about it.

"Here you go, Captain," one of the enlisted who'd drawn KP duty set a plate in front of me filled with the same biscuits, potatoes, and ham as the others, plus a set of plasticware. "You picked a good night to eat with the troops. This ham is off the fuckin' hook, sir."

"We never had it so good," Vicky agreed, stuffing another mouthful of the stuff down. "No soy and spirulina special on Yfingam."

"I might even miss this place," Czarnecki admitted.

"At least it's cooler in the evening," I admitted, nodding out the open windows.

The primary star was touching the tops of the trees, setting them afire with an orange and red blaze of colors, and somewhere a night bird warmed up for his evening performance. It was dark enough inside the hall now that someone had switched on the overhead lights and a small cloud of insects was swarming around them. I kept one eye on them as I tried the ham.

It was tender and glazed with brown sugar, and I closed my eyes and made a purring sound.

"Holy shit, you weren't kidding," I told Vicky, savoring the bite. "I wonder if we can convince Captain Nance to subdivide off a section of the cargo bay for a pigpen."

Vicky snorted a laugh, then coughed as she nearly choked.

"I can just imagine the air purification system trying to scrub out that smell," she said once she'd managed to resume breathing.

"Well, I'm never going back to Earth," Top declared firmly, smacking the table for emphasis. "Only the rich corporate types get this kind of food back on Earth. When I get back, I'm taking retirement, finally, and living somewhere they eat cows and pigs and grow their own vegetables in the ground, not in some Goddamned vat."

"How long have you been in the Corps, Top?" Vicky asked him. I would bet she knew the answer to the day and hour, because Vicky would never have taken command of a company without knowing every detail she could find about every man and woman in it.

"Eighteen years, ma'am," Czarnecki told her proudly. "Was holding out for twenty, but God knows I've used up every ounce of luck I ever had."

"You were in before the war then?" I asked him. I think I'd known that, vaguely, since I'd read the personnel files of the whole company when I took over from Solano, but it hadn't registered at the time.

"Full five years before, sir," he confirmed, nodding sharply before taking in a forkful of mashed potatoes. "I joined for about the same reason you did, except I didn't get caught. I was a teenager in the Upper Danube Development Corridor and got involved with the gangs. They told me to kill some guy and I didn't want to do it, but they said if I didn't, they'd do me first and then kill him anyway. I knew two ways out—either go to the cops or join the Marines." He toasted us with a cup of water. "And here I am." He laughed softly. Well, as softly as he *could*. The man couldn't whisper, couldn't chuckle. Every sound he made was loud, and thank God he'd never tried out for Force Recon. "You know, after I spent five years running maintenance on a security outpost near the Neutral Zone, I figured my whole career would be peacetime bullshit. Then the war broke out and, by the end, I was sure I'd get out the second it ended. Until Sgt.-Major Campbell and Captain Solano came to me and asked me to join this task force." He shrugged. "It kinda felt like we were finishing the job, y'know? Couldn't call the war over if we had this Zan-Thint asshole still causing trouble. Not this time though. Getting out, settling down somewhere, and not leaving ground again."

"Yeah, right," a nearby platoon sergeant scoffed. She was an E5, should've been a squad leader if we hadn't been down so many people. She had short, blonde hair and an upturned nose, and it took me a second to recall her name. Bonaventure. That was it. Sheila Bonaventure. "We know you, Top," she went on. "You'll last about a month before you re-up."

"You just watch, Bonaventure," he told her, pointing with his fork. "Never gonna leave the ground again."

I laughed, not saying much because I was busy eating. I'd skipped lunch... again. This time because the *Orion*'s chief engineer wanted to complain about Dwight repurposing his maintenance drones for the new construction project and Chief Moretti swore up and down that he *had* to have them in order to perform his monthly safety checks.

"So," Vicky said quietly beside me while Czarnecki kept up the banter with his NCOs, "it's been two weeks. Any word back from Oster about the recruits?"

I sighed, my mood tumbling back down to earth.

"He says a lot of the kids are excited about it but they're scared of their parents, who are scared of Carella. And she's not budging a centimeter." I flipped my fork over and let it clatter to the empty plate. "In fact, she's not saying a word to anyone outside her inner circle. Oster doesn't know what the hell's going on, but he knows everyone's keyed up and nervous. People aren't talking to each other, and every time they send a load of food for trade into the city, there's armed guards along and they're all Carella's loyalists."

She grunted, not offering comment. It had all been said at this point.

"It was a good idea, anyway," she told me, shrugging. "We can still use the suits as backups. And maybe put the Force Recon platoon in them."

"I feel responsible for the Vergai," I told her. "I mean, we're the ones who gave them the hope of being free from the Resscharr and the Karai. We gave them weapons, trained them, got them used to our protection."

"You can lead a horse to knowledge," Vicky said with a crooked grin, "but you can't make her think. There's nothing we can do about any of it until the *Orion* gets the asteroid back here, and that won't be for another few weeks, even with that Resscharr drive on the ship. She took the shuttles and Intercepts with her too, so until then, we have no orbital or air support and we can't even start on the new suits."

"Stop being so damned reasonable," I grumbled. Letting my gaze travel around the dining hall, I noted that Lt. Springfield wasn't there and neither was one of her squads. "Springfield on patrol?"

"Yeah, she drew the short straw," Vicky said. "I'll make sure the KP crew saves her and her first squad some food though."

"Where's Campea and the Force Recon platoon?" I should have known that, but I'd been so jammed up the last few days, I'd lost track of the duty rosters. "They're not *all* on watch, are they?"

"Campea is fed up dealing with the Karai and the Vergai and the Tahni and the Resscharr," she said, ticking off each of the groups on her fingers, her tone making it clear that she was quoting the man. "He requested permission to take his platoon on a field training exercise out in the boonies, and since you were busy, I told him to go ahead. They'll be back in two days, hopefully with their quotient of brush-breaking and chest-beating filled."

"I fuckin' envy him," I admitted, sagging against the table. "If I have to mediate one more squabble between the pilots, the engineers, Nance, and Dwight, I will tear my hair out." I ran a hand over it. It was getting longer and slightly curly. "Speaking of which, I need a haircut again. You want to give it to me this time? I did it myself last time and it looked like shit."

"It certainly did," she agreed, her grin mischievous. "You'd better watch out though, if I have that razor in hand, I might start on your back hair."

"Hold on now..."

"Captain Alvarez, this is Springfield, you read me?"

The voice was insistent in my ear, the tone urgent enough that I didn't even bother complaining about dinner being interrupted.

"Yeah, I'm here, Springfield," I said, standing up from the bench, moving toward the door, Vicky right behind me. "Go ahead."

"We have a situation at the stockyards, sir. Armed Karai facing down armed Vergai and crowds are gathering. Do you want us to intervene?"

"Shit," I hissed, breaking into a run toward the reinforced barn where we kept the Vigilantes. The suit would be the quickest way there for me. "Make your presence known, Springfield," I said, voice strained at the sprint across the gravel and dirt. "Do *not* fire unless fired upon by a weapon that can breach your armor, but feel free to use yourselves as a shield between them as long as you don't think you're putting your squad at risk. I'll be there in five mikes. Copy?"

"Copy that, sir. Hurry."

Vicky was right beside me, running as fast as I could, which probably meant I needed to get more PT time in, but I was too busy to think about that.

"This shit has been a long time coming," she said, disgustingly not out of breath as we passed by the guards at the storage hangar, ignoring their salutes.

"It's a miracle it hadn't happened already," I agreed, stumbling to a halt outside the doors, slapping a palm against the ID plate we'd installed. "Probably was only because we came back. Bought us a couple weeks."

The security indicator turned green and the doors unlocked with a magnetic click, pushing easily inward at the touch of my hand. The lights came on with the opening of the door, revealing the extensive modifications we'd done to the interior of the old barn, the BiPhase Carbide reinforcements, the buildfoam filling, and the maintenance cradles for the Vigilantes. It wasn't quite up to the standards of an armory on Inferno, but it was a damn sight better than nothing, and the only way the Tahni could break into it was with one of their assault shuttles.

"Do we want more troops backing us up?" Vicky asked me as we both scrambled into the open chest plates of our Vigilantes. I didn't need to search for mine any more than any of the Drop Troopers in our company would have. We drilled this constantly whenever we were onplanet and every suit went in the same cradle every time, no exceptions. A depressing number of those cradles were empty now, but it didn't change the order.

"No," I decided, pulling the chest plastron shut, our conversation transitioning automatically to our 'links. "One squad plus us will be enough to be a deterrent without making it look like we're attacking."

The lights inside the suit flickered on as it sealed, but I didn't need them to find the cords for the interface jacks. My fingers went to them automatically, guided by years and years of practice, sliding the jacks home into my sockets with a familiar click. Readouts snapped into coherence in my HUD, and the suit went from a lifeless lump of metal to something lithe and deadly, a part of me just like the sockets.

I pulled away from the gantry, spiked soles pounding into the cement floor, and squeezed through the partially open doors as the Fleet Security guards scrambled out of the way. Five or ten steps to make sure I didn't fry those guards and I hit the jets.

Once upon a time, I would have been able to ride the jump jets for a few hundred meters before they overheated, then had to rumble along with the straight-legged, troll-like gait of the Vigilante. Not since the Resscharr had upgraded the suits. Now we could fly for kilometers, for several minutes at least, probably up past a half an hour if I was daring enough to try it. I wasn't, because these upgrades, while incredibly useful, were irreplaceable, and I didn't want to push them harder than I had to.

The primary star was below the horizon, but I spotted it once again as I shot a couple hundred meters above the ground, a glinting red at the edge of the western skyline. The layout of the land around the fortress was spread below me, a one-to-one scale sand table. The military compound was a small section at the corner of the Vergai lands, open, untended fields separating us from the farms like they considered us an infection to be isolated.

The farmlands stretched on forever, on every side of the city, dotted by barns and farmhouses, enclosed here and there by split-rail fences penning in pigs and cattle, goats and sheep. The Vergai had been the peasant farmers in the feudal state the Resscharr had run on Yfingam before our arrival, with the Karai as the warrior class. That was still the arrangement to some extent, though now the Vergai got paid for their produce rather than giving it away for the privilege of being allowed to live on their own land.

Trading for *what* had been the key sticking point to getting the new arrangement settled, and it was still the main problem. The theory had been that the Karai and the Resscharr would begin to grow their own food, supply themselves, and put everyone on a more equal footing, but it hadn't been as simple as that. The Karai had never done anything but learn to fight and maybe a little mining on the side, while the Resscharr had, well, never done *anything* except order other people around, and though the Vergai had made efforts to teach them agriculture, those had yet to yield results.

Instead, they'd worked out a crude and halting form of trade. It was temporary, could never last, because it involved the exchange of horded raw materials and metal tools, and once the surplus of those were gone, we'd be right back to where we'd started. It was amazing the ad hoc process had lasted as long as it had, but the center of it all was the market. The market was just inside the city gate, and I knew it made the Vergai uncomfortable just to venture within the city walls, since that had once been the prelude to a quick beheading by the Karai, plus they weren't allowed to go armed inside the city walls.

Which meant that when Vergai traders went into the market, they usually left their vehicles and their armed guards out in the stockyards, the pens just outside the side entrance to the city... the side next to the Karai steadings. I couldn't see the stockyards from this side of the fortress and I wasn't going to try to soar over the top of the main tower, so I curved around its walls and the Tahni anti-aircraft emplacements followed me with their coilgun muzzles, their targeting lasers setting off flashing yellow alerts in my HUD and setting my teeth on edge.

I held my breath and prayed they wouldn't take a potshot at us just out of sheer spite. It wasn't likely, not without Zan-Thint's okay, but these were Tahni we were talking about, and not just your run-of-the-mill Tahni but ones who were bitter and angry enough about the war that they'd joined up with Zan-Thint's insurgency. I was sure they were calling in and asking him for permission, and honest to God, I could imagine him thinking about it carefully before telling them no.

Finally, after what felt like an eternity floating in the firing arc of the turrets, we were around to the stockyard side of the fortress. The outside of the walled city was basically hexagonal in shape, but not perfectly so, as if the Resscharr designers of the thing had felt like playing a cruel joke on obsessive-compulsive humans who might one day catch an overhead glimpse of the place. One of the imperfections was the gate beside the stockyard, jutting out like the docking umbilical on a space station, the tunnel reaching through the gap in the cattle fencing.

Well, *livestock* fencing. In this case, the livestock penned there were sheep, which made sense. Neither the Tahni nor the Karai ate meat, but the Karai, unlike their Tahni cousins, did make clothing from wool and leather. The Resscharr had descended from meat-eating dinosaurs and ate anything that moved, including humans if they got desperate, or at least that was the rumor. I didn't know if the sheep were the responsibility of the dozen or so Vergai gathered at the outer gate to the stockyards, but I did know who they were guarding them from.

There were only six of the Karai. It would have been difficult for me to count them from a hundred meters up, but the suit's targeting computer had analyzed the situation quite extensively and provided me with a threat assessment for each of the thermal signatures it had detected, including the sheep. The sheep, it had decided, were mostly harmless, while the Karai had three Tahni KE rifles between them, the Vergai were all armed with the slugshooters we'd fabricated for them, and the squad of Drop Troopers was exceptionally dangerous but considered friendly.

Springfield was doing what I'd told her, putting her people between the two groups, but it was easier said than done. Vigilantes are built for mobility mixed and firepower, built to destroy hardened targets. What they *aren't* built to do is play tag with a bunch of unarmored humanoids, and it was only a matter of time before one side or both figured out the Vigilantes weren't going to fire on them.

Unfortunately, that time was just before Vicky and I landed.

## [ 7 ]

I couldn't tell who fired first. KE rifles had no thermal signature, and the muzzle flash from the chemical-propellant slugshooters came nearly simultaneously with two of the group of Vergai stumbling backward, dropping their guns. We were seconds from a total slaughter and there was no time to think.

I did something stupid.

I *knew* when I did it that it was stupid, but Springfield was already yelling at the two groups over her external speakers to cease fire and it wasn't accomplishing a Goddamned thing, while I was still thirty meters up with a bird's-eye view... and an energy cannon aimed straight down.

I wish I could say that I had a clear targeting screen and was dead certain sure that I was dead certain sure I wouldn't hit any of our suits or the combatants, but the truth is, I was going by my gut and a scant half-second glance when I pulled the trigger. The actinic bolt of alien energy slammed into the center of the group, sending up a spray of vaporized soil and one poor, luckless sheep. The concussion sent the whole lot of them sprawling, hands covering their eyes, though it had little effect on my squad of Vigilantes.

Smoke was still billowing upward from the explosion when I touched down at the center of it, Vicky descending on a column of fire right beside me. Our jets sent small whirlwinds and eddies of smoke spiraling outward, clearing away the haze and showing the carnage for all to see. Four of the Vergai were down, one rolling side to side, clutching at his leg and moaning while the other three were motionless, splattered with blood. Three of the Karai had been hit but only one was clearly dead, the other two still conscious and moving despite red-stained wounds in their torsos.

"Nice entrance, sir," Springfield said, and her tone attempted to be light and bantering, but she sounded as nervous as I felt.

"We have three autodocs set up in our medical tent," I said, not indulging in any bullshit. "Pick up the wounded and fly them back there immediately."

I didn't wait for her to reply, just switched nets to the general Tahni frequency and sighed, not really wanting to make this call.

"General Zan-Thint, we have injured Karai at the stockyard. They're going to need medical treatment and we don't have the equipment for it. Could you send down some of your medical people?"

"Injured how?" Zan-Thint answered more quickly than I'd thought he would, as if he'd been watching and knew exactly what had happened.

"There was an incident between the Karai and the Vergai," I said, my tone neutral, not showing any of the frustration and anger roiling in my gut. "We can straighten out what happened after we see to the wounded."

"We will discuss this later, Alvarez."

*Oh, I'm sure of that.*

Springfield had been giving orders to the patrol squad while

I was busy, because they were already gently lifting the Vergai wounded in the arms of their battlesuits. Well, as gently as *possible* when one hand of the battlesuit was pretty much welded to an energy cannon and the other was a savage claw meant for ripping metal. It was risky, but the wounded looked pretty bad—tantalum needles traveling at 3,000 meters per second did a shitload of damage, and I'd have been surprised if even two of the four lived.

While the Vigilantes evacuated the Vergai wounded, I busied myself with something even more crucial to saving the lives of the ones left, kicking away their weapons before they recovered from the shock of the energy blast. I didn't have to tell Vicky what to do. She grabbed the KE rifles from where the Karai had dropped them, the lefthand claw of her Vigilante big enough to clutch all three in one grip. Then she clenched her fist and metal screeched in protest, twisting the outer housings of the weapons into unusable scrap. Not even the Vigilante could break the tungsten core of the rifles, but it would take a few weeks in the Tahni armorer's shop to get those things working again. Vicky tossed them to the ground in front of the Karai and the ones who had regained their senses glared at her.

"Who's in charge here?" I demanded over my suit's public address speakers, hoping whoever it was hadn't been one of the wounded, because they were already jetting back to our medical tent.

A short, broad-shouldered man who looked like he was in his twenties pushed himself to his feet, wide, white eyes peeking out from bushy black hair and a full beard. His hands were shaking, though I didn't know whether that was from the post-adrenaline dump from the firefight, the residue of the shock of the energy blast, or pure fear at the three-meter-tall, faceless metal giant yelling at him.

"I am Pontus," he told me, stuttering, hesitant. "I brought

this flock..." he turned and motioned at the terrified sheep huddled against the far rail fence of the stockyard, bleating pitifully, "... here for trade with the Karai and Resscharr. But those thieving bastards tried to steal them from us!" He pointed an accusatory finger at the Karai, who were also coming to their feet. "They lied and said they'd already made payment for these sheep, but the Karai *never* offer payment until they see the merchandise! It's been the same for months!"

"Filthy Vergai scum!" The Karai who yelled the epithet was pretty much a Tahni in a leather harness as far as I was concerned, and except for Lan-Min-Gen and a couple of his Shock Troopers who'd been on the boat with us, all of them looked alike to me. This one had a few flash burns on his face and arms, courtesy of me, which was the only way I could separate him from the others. "Just because *you* deceive yourselves doesn't mean that we Karai share in your dishonor! Our sub-chief has told us that we shipped you a ton of iron ore in exchange for three wagon loads of cattle hide and you shorted us half a wagon. These animals were repayment for this slight, and now you have added murder to your sins!" He waved a hand at one of the fallen Karai, one who was clearly dead, his throat ripped out by one of the slugs from the assault rifles. "You have killed a fine warrior and a direct cousin of our leader, Nam Ker. He will never allow you to live in peace after this."

"Springfield," I snapped. The platoon leader hadn't left with the casualties and was still standing between the two groups. "Who fired first?"

"I'd have to review everyone's camera footage, sir," she admitted. "I heard the chatter of the Vergai rifles and the sound of the KE rifles discharge at the same time. Both sides were yelling pretty loud, and I was facing the wrong direction."

*Shit.* I'd been hoping she could settle it, *really* hoping that the Karai had shot first and I could shame them into retreating. That wasn't going to happen.

"Cam," Vicky said. "Behind you."

I turned back the way we'd come, toward the Vergai farms, and saw what she was talking about. Vehicles. They belonged to the Vergai because we'd fabricated the things for them, simple, alcohol-fueled trucks that made it easier to haul their crops and equipment. Fuel came from stills which had the side-benefit of producing high-quality grain alcohol, though at the moment, I wasn't sure if that was a good thing.

These particular trucks had been turned into what they used to call, back in the day, technicals. The rear covers had been stripped off the cargo beds and each of them mounted a crew-served machine gun on a pintle, which were little more than toys when I was in my suit but could do some real damage to the Karai. Vergai militia were packed in around the guns and I cursed, wondering how the hell they'd rolled out so quickly. I knew Marine reaction teams that *wished* they could get into action only ten minutes after the call went out.

"Aaaaannd here comes the other side," Vicky said.

I didn't have to turn this time. My HUD alerted me to the flyers, the views from the 360-degree video pickups around the outside of my helmet projected over the mapping software and sensor readouts laid out in front of me. Three Tahni flyers with Karai troops along as cannon fodder, plus a platoon of Shock Troopers, pouring out of the city's front gate and heading this way.

One of Pontus' group made a rush for the rifles I'd kicked away, but I grabbed him by the back of his rawhide jacket and tossed him back among the others. He tumbled backward with a woof of escaping breath, then glared at me.

"Don't be stupid," I cautioned him—all of them, pointing a

clawed finger at the group. "Keep your mouths shut and stay away from those weapons."

"This is bad," Vicky opined, though she sounded calmer than I felt.

"Yeah. Spin up the rest of the company and get them ready to hop over here if we call. Not yet though. Don't want to escalate."

The Karai were still bellowing in their own language and I wasn't paying close enough attention to hear the translation and the Vergai were yelling back, but neither approached each other or tried to squeeze past our battlesuits. The plaintive bleating of the sheep drowned them both out, and like them, I didn't want to *be* here, wanted more than anything else to hit the jets and get out before either set of reinforcements arrived, but it was too late for that.

The flyers landed first, touching down outside the fence, thank God, or those poor sheep would have started chewing off their limbs to squeeze out of that fence. Clamshell hatches flew open and Karai warriors poured out, setting up a perimeter for the Tahni medics, their field kits hanging off their shoulders as they ran over to the wounded, clambering over the rails of the pen.

I'd never been impressed with the Tahni level of commitment to their troops, but these guys went to work on the Karai with practiced efficiency, though I didn't watch. There was something about treating a living body like a machine to be fixed that I'd never cared for. The Karai were watching them though, their eyes on the wounded... particularly on the one we'd been told was Nam Ker's cousin.

The Vergai had ceased to glare at us with resentment and were now content to hide behind our bulk, using us as shields from all those KE rifle muzzles pointed their way. The trucks were still on their way but they were a good minute out down the road, and if the Karai wanted to, they could cut the surviving Vergai down in seconds.

They wanted to. I could see it in their eyes, in the spastic bunching of their shoulders, their white-knuckled grasp on the unfamiliar weapons. They were bunched together, way too close, the characteristic of troops who haven't done much fighting against an enemy armed with ranged weapons. But one Karai pushed through them, no weapon in his hand but a harsh, jagged look to his face, a scar running down one side. They may have all looked alike to me, but not this one. I would have recognized him from a kilometer away and walked in a different direction if I had.

"Nam Ker," one of the Karai who'd been among the original belligerents stepped up to greet the huge, hulking warrior, the leader of the Karai on this world. "It's your cousin..."

Nam Ker said nothing, shoving the other male out of the way and kneeling beside the gravely wounded Karai. The casualty wasn't breathing and the Tahni medic tending to him had stepped back, making a gesture of negation to Nam Ker. The Karai commander knelt beside his cousin, palms flat on the dead male's chest, and when he lifted his hands, red dripped from his long fingers. Nam Ker traced lines of blood across his own face in V-shapes, then threw back his head and howled, a wail of agony that transcended culture, religion, or even species. We'd both come from the same genetic line a million years ago or so, and that was close enough.

Nam Ker had a good set of lungs on him and the banshee wail went on for over ten seconds before he collapsed to the dirt, cradling his cousin's head in bloody hands. Even the other Karai looked impressed with the demonstration of grief and fraternal love, their attention wavering from the Vergai to stare at their commander. When he finally pulled himself together, Nam Ker pushed himself to his feet and turned to stare daggers at... well, maybe at the Vergai, and maybe at *us.*

"My cousin," Nam-Ker roared. "The son of my father's brother! A warrior of unbroken bloodline back to the beginning, back to the first Karai who came to this place!" He waved his arms like a blood-and-thunder revival preacher haranguing the colonists on one of the outlaw settlements to repent. "You've robbed me of my family, taken my blood, and I will have blood in return."

"Nam Ker," I said, restraining an instinct to pop open my chest plastron and speak to him face to face, "this wasn't targeted at your cousin. They had a disagreement about payment and someone opened fire, we don't know who."

"You think I *care*, human?" If his voice had carried during the wail, it echoed from the far hills kilometers away now. "You think I give a damn what their excuse is? He was my family. His spirit cries out to me for their lives."

"You listen to your spirit," I warned him, pointing off toward the trucks, now only a couple hundred meters away, "and you'll be starting a war. Hundreds, maybe thousands of your friends and relatives will die, and you're not guaranteed to win. What do the gods say about that? Do they want you to sacrifice hundreds of other lives to avenge your cousin?"

The trucks screeched to a halt, and the muzzles of the Karai weapons shifted from the handful of humans behind our battlesuits to the Vergai scrambling off the backs of the vehicles. The fifteen-millimeter maws of the machineguns swung toward the Karai... and toward us. The Vergai militia swarmed around the other side of the Tahni flyers, and we were seconds from disaster. One wrong move, one inexperienced finger jerking a trigger, and dozens of people would be dead. Just for a start.

I recognized the man who stepped forward from the thirty or forty Vergai militia, though I didn't know him well. I'd seen him in Carella's personal guard, always at her arm with a gun in his hand. He was tall and lanky, not as young as the others, a bit of gray in his beard. His name was Dallan, and if I remembered right he'd once had his own family, a wife and two children, but they'd died in a plague that neither the Resscharr nor the Karai had suffered from or sought to help alleviate.

"We want our people back," Dallan announced, ignoring us, speaking directly to Nam Ker. "Return them to us or we'll open fire."

"Dallan," I interrupted, turning up the gain on my external speakers so that all the Vergai could hear my voice. "This is Captain Alvarez. You need to pull your people back. We can sort this mess out, but not if all of you are standing around and pointing guns at each other."

"What do you care of our differences, Alvarez?" he demanded, lip curling in a sneer. "You and your people will be gone soon, leaving us to our own fate, so why don't you get an early start and keep out of our affairs?"

"Keep out of *your* affairs, asshole?" I barked back at him. "Who the hell do you think gave you that rifle you're waving around like an idiot?" I flipped a metal hand that weighed thirty kilos in a casual motion that smacked the weapon right out of his grip and sent it clattering to the ground. He stepped back, eyes going wide. "Who do you think built those trucks you decided to reconfigure as weapons? Who do you think has kept you alive this long, you ungrateful fuck?"

And yeah, I was getting angry again, but this time I wasn't going to slow down. Maybe if I kept their attention on me, none of them would pop off a round at the Karai by accident. I took a step closer to Dallan, forcing him back.

"You listen to me, and you pass this back on to Carella. You are *not* the big dog in this fight. You are not in charge here. If you want to survive, you'd damn well better start thinking with your big head. Get your people back and wait for the grown-ups to straighten this out."

"Stuck in the middle again, eh, Alvarez?"

It was hard to recognize a Tahni voice, since they all sound like Marine drill sergeants who just inhaled a lungful of helium, but this one I knew, even though the alien's face was concealed behind the helmet of a set of powered Shock Trooper armor. I could even read the rank insignia on the chest of Lan-Min-Gen's armor plating after all the time we'd spent together on the *Orion*.

The Tahni ground force commander led a full platoon of Shock Troopers through the midst of the Karai, not being too gentle about brushing them aside. Technically, the Karai were the peers, the allies of the Tahni, but from what I'd seen, it was more a case of Zan-Thint and his people simply taking the place of the Resscharr as the HMFICs with the Karai relegated right back to their role as muscle, and not very smart muscle. Nam-Ker's eyes were unreadable under those bony brow ridges, but if I had any sense of the body language the Tahni and the Karai shared, I would have been willing to bet he resented the intrusion of the Shock Troopers.

"Oh, you know how it is, Lan-Min-Gen," I told him, sighing with relief. He was, if not a friend, then at least a comrade-in-arms. "Nice seeing you here. You think there's any way we can end this without anyone else getting shot?"

Lan-Min-Gen snorted, a sound that meant much the same thing for the Tahni as it did for us.

"I imagine there'll be a reckoning for this with the general," he said, "but I see nothing to gain by involving us all in a useless fight that would undoubtedly kill many of us, the Karai and the Vergai... and none of you."

I was hoping that last had been in jest. I was sure the Tahni had a sense of humor, but I'd yet to meet the human who understood it. Either way, he lumbered up to Nam Ker in the waddling gait of the powered exoskeleton, the armor hanging off it scarred and battered from hard use.

"Nam Ker," he said, "I grieve for the loss of your cousin. I will remember him in my nightly devotions for all his service to the Karai. Perhaps we should take his body somewhere more appropriate for the days of observation."

"I don't care about the ritual, Tahni," Nam Ker snapped. "I would have vengeance from these dirt-digging slaves for his death. If you and your Imperium won't help, then at least stay out of our way. My Karai will fight our own battles."

"As amusing as it would be," Nam-Ker told him, "to watch you attempt to fight the human battlesuits with your tiny KE rifles, the sad fact is you would wind up getting not just yourself and your warriors killed, but you would likely involve *us* as well, which would make me very unhappy. More importantly, it would make General Zan-Thint very unhappy, and part of my job is insuring he doesn't *get* unhappy. So, take your cousin, take your people, and get out of here before I add a few more bodies to the total." The yawning muzzle of Lan-Min-Gen's large-caliber KE gun moved just slightly, a few centimeters, but now it aimed squarely at Nam Ker's chest.

The Karai leader glared at Lan-Min-Gen for a long moment, long enough that I thought he might push it, might try to force the Tahni to shoot him out of sheer bloody-mindedness. But reason took over from the madness of grief, and Nam Ker barked orders at his people. Two of the Karai picked up Nam Ker's cousin by the shoulders and dragged him between them as the Karai slowly and reluctantly vacated the stockyards. I turned to Dallan, jabbing a curved, metal finger at his face.

"Get your people and get the fuck out of here," I told him. "If I have to repeat myself, I will grab you by the fucking ankle and fly you back to Carella, where I will dump you upside down at her feet. And if you think I'm not serious, you just fucking try me."

Dallan's glare at me was easier to read than Nam Ker's, but the reaction was the same. He might have snapped some invective my way, but I wasn't paying attention, switching my attention and my comm net to the company.

"Springfield, I want you to shadow the trucks all the way back to the Vergai homesteads. Be *obvious* about it. If they try to turn around, go right down and wreck the damned things." I scowled. "Try not to kill anybody, but do *not* let them come back here."

"Copy that, sir."

The Vergai didn't look like they'd be coming back, particularly the ones who'd been cornered here in the stockyards.

They even left the sheep.

# [ 8 ]

"I don't know why I was required to be here," Carella grumbled, buried under her bright blue shawl like one of the ancient grandmothers on our street when I was a kid. "None of this was my decision, nor did my people cause this incident."

Zan-Thint shifted in his seat, uncomfortable either with the furniture or the company, or both, but he kept silent. Nam Ker did *not*. He didn't sit either, just paced the room behind the table, fingers clenching as if he badly wanted a weapon in his hands.

"Your people are to blame for this, witch," he snapped, refusing to look at the woman. "If you hadn't accused my cousin of lying, insulted his honor, none of this would have happened."

"Your people fired the first shot," Carella said flatly. "The records proved it."

"By a fraction of a second," I cut in, coming to my feet mostly because Nam Ker was making me nervous. It had been a struggle to get them all together in the same room, much less in *our* offices. The only thing that had swung them our way was the fact that none of the others trusted each other enough to go to the tower, the feast hall of the Karai, or the meeting place of the Karai Council, which left us. "The bottom line is, both sides opened fire at nearly the same time, and if that's how things are going to be, you're all going to wind up killing each other."

"And how do you propose we avoid this fate, Captain Alvarez?" Zan-Thint asked me, leaning back in his chair, the plastic squeaking in protest. "By you bringing us into this pigsty and browbeating us into doing things your way? Is that how you solve all your problems?"

*Well, pretty much.* But it seemed counterproductive to admit that.

"No," I lied. "I brought you here to see what you could all agree on. We're going to be gone, our part of this mess is going to be over. The rest of you have to come up with a plan." I spread my hands. "If you want my opinion, I'll give it, but you're the ones who have to live with whatever choice you make."

Vicky shot me a skeptical look from where she leaned against the wall by the door, and while I didn't admit anything out loud, I knew she was right, that I wasn't a diplomat and this wasn't going to work.

I did, however, have at least one ally among the delegates who'd come out to our chow hall tonight to talk things out.

"What would your suggestion be, Captain Alvarez?" Lilandreth asked. She wasn't sitting down because her people generally didn't, not with their backwards-canted knees. Instead, she squatted near the table, partially hunched over, putting herself more at eye level with the rest of us.

I nodded my thanks to the Resscharr, as we had gone over this before the others had arrived.

"I've suggested this before," I said, "and maybe now you'll all give it more consideration. This isn't going to work unless you all have a say in the running of this place. You need to form a council where each of your factions has a vote."

"There's a human saying I picked up back when I was

studying your kind," Zan-Thint interrupted. "That ship has sailed. You had your chance to convince Carella and her faction that they should work with us before blood was spilled. Now there's no chance of peaceful cooperation, not when both sides are heavily armed and lack trust. I will only agree to any sort of shared government if the Vergai give up the weapons you constructed for them. If they're serious about cooperation, there should be no need for them."

"Yes," Nam Ker agreed, pounding a palm on the table loud enough for the bang to echo through the interior of the mostly empty chow hall. "This is the only acceptable course of action. The Vergai have proven they can't be trusted with an armed militia. They're too quick to violence and lack the training to be true warriors."

I regarded the Karai leader, bemused. He could have been a politician in another age on Earth, though maybe part of the bombastic tone was an attempt by the translation program Dwight had written for us to give us a human equivalent to Nam Ker's speech. I didn't need any translation of Carella's cynical bark of laughter.

"Yes, I'm sure both of you would like us to give up our weapons and be helpless in the face of your aggression as we used to be. That will *not* happen."

"You keep your weapons," Zan-Thint said, addressing her directly for the first time since I'd met the two of them, "and then what? Do you think there are enough of you and enough weapons for you to defeat us? Do you think you won't all be killed in the process?"

I looked sidelong at him, trying not to stare. Zan-Thint was a military officer, not a politician. He was used to giving orders, not using reason and argument to convince people... not even his *own* people, much less humans, much *less* the Vergai. Perhaps us humans were rubbing off on him, or maybe it was just that his new position and the new demands of it were forcing him into a new role.

"I think my people lived as slaves until very recently," Carella said, hands coming out of her shawl to steeple her fingers in front of her. "Slaves live at the mercy of their masters, and once you've lived at the mercy of the merciless..." she glared at Nam Ker, "... then the thought of death in battle is less daunting than you might think."

"We did as we were told by the Resscharr," Nam Ker countered, perhaps defensively. "We couldn't face down their superior weapons alone. Just as *you* can't face down the superior weapons of the Tahni and now us, not without the Earth Marines behind you." He made a gesture of negation. "They saved your people today, or their blood would stain my blade. You should leave. All of you should return to the Island World."

"I wonder if you've thought this through," Carella said, eyes narrowing as she regarded Zan-Thint and Nam Ker. "I know you Tahni grow your own food, but will you be able to grow enough of your alien root to feed both you and the Karai? Will you Karai turn to farming and husbandry to provide your clothes and food?"

"We farmed back on our homeworld," Zan-Thint said, "and we can return to those ways here as well. You are not indispensable to us, so don't believe that will save you."

"And what of us?" Lilandreth wondered, staring golden-eyed at Zan-Thint. "Do you consider us essential? Useful? A burden?"

"That, Resscharr, is up to you. Don't expect us to feed or support you, but I admit your knowledge would be useful. You certainly proved useful to the humans when you gave them new drives and new weapons. Perhaps, given time, you could learn to build such things for us here."

Lilandreth said nothing, but I'd gone over this with her

before. She had the *knowledge* of how to build such things, but the infrastructure to do it didn't exist here. Hell, from what she'd told me, it didn't exist back in the Commonwealth. But perhaps she was smart enough not to bring that fact up with Zan-Thint.

"So," I cut in, feeling the need to drag this back onto the topic at hand, "your position, General Zan-Thint, is that you would only accept any sort of shared government if the Vergai gave up their weapons." I turned to Carella, leaning against the table as if being dragged down by a weight, which was exactly how I felt right now. "And yours is that you won't disarm no matter what." A shrug. "To me, that means you've both committed to war. Maybe not right this second, but eventually. I'm not a diplomat, not a politician, as I keep trying to remind people." Vicky chuckled, and I shot her a dirty look. "I'm a combat Marine, and I know war. I know how to fight it and, more than that, I know what the aftermath looks like. I've seen what war does to the civilian population even after you win one."

I stood straight and pointed a knife-hand gesture at Zan-Thint.

"Best-case scenario for you in a war here. You have to kill more than half of the Vergai population and devastate most of what remains. They grow no crops, raise no animals for years. You lose probably thirty percent of the Karai male population and a good ten to fifteen percent of your own forces, but you retain control here and everything is back to normal food-production wise within months. Worst-case, you alienate the Resscharr and they join forces with the Vergai, and then you lose *fifty* percent of the Karai and a quarter of your own troops and the Vergai occupy the fortress. Then, you have to attack from orbit and devastate your own ground. You lose all your crops and only have enough stored food on board your ships to feed your own people for a few weeks."

Neither Zan-Thint nor Nam Ker said anything, but the Karai stopped pacing, just staring at me. I refrained from grinning at his discomfort and turned to Carella.

"Now you," I told her. "Your best-case is his worst-case and vice versa. Either way, you lose everything and more than half your people die. The rest retreat into the wilderness and live a primitive lifestyle, starting out as guerillas and eventually just becoming savages. These assholes..." I gestured at Nam Ker, "...or their descendants will probably wind up hunting them for sport."

I spread my hands to encompass all of them.

"Do any of these possibilities sound attractive to any of you? Does it really sound to you like war is the best-case scenario?"

"No," Zan-Thint admitted with admirable honesty. "And I concede the accuracy of your estimates, since they match my own. But how can we trust these humans when they've shown every intention of confronting us violently at any provocation?" He again addressed Carella directly. "Despite our differences with humans in the past, we have no wish to kill you all, yet I don't see how we can avoid this if you stay here and keep your weapons. Your people originally lived on Laisvas Miestas. There's no reason for you to resist returning there."

"You think so?" Carella asked, leaning across the table, not seeming in the least intimidated by the Tahni commander. "Let me give you a few. First of all, you've seen those fields?" She pointed at the door as if the Tahni could see the Vergai land through the door, in the dark and from kilometers away. "You see those houses? Do you know who tilled those fields? Who built those houses? Who tamed this land? It was us, with the sweat of our brows and the blisters of our hands. Our blood is in this land. Not yours, not the

Karai, but ours. That's one reason, the reason that beats in my heart, that ties my soul to this land. But there are others, reasons that are in here." She tapped the side of her head. "Your ships, for example. You claim that we could leave this place and go back to the Islands and be safe, secure in our own lands, our own world. But what if your reach exceeds this place? Or perhaps the reach of your children or grandchildren? What's to stop you from using your spaceships to come to us with your soldiers, to conquer our lands there? Your good will?" She laughed scornfully. "Even if I believed in such fairy tales, your goodwill ends with you, and then I leave my children and grandchildren at the mercy of yours."

Zan-Thint was silent for a moment and I didn't step into that gap, interested in hearing what he had to say to the concern.

"Your worries are genuine, and I understand them," he finally replied. "Yet my troops and I risked all to leave our home and come here, and we do not intend to leave, nor do we intend to give up the power we've taken. You may continue to live here on your land, to tend your farms and raise your families, yet I will not allow a threat to my position to remain once these humans have left. You *will* be disarmed, and if you don't do it willingly, then we will come in by force. And if you threaten to destroy what we have in revenge, then we *will* drive you out into the wild and will hunt you down. It may take a lifetime, but it's as inevitable as the tide. This is my word."

Carella didn't rage, didn't scream, didn't threaten. She simply nodded, looking not at Zan-Thint but at me.

"Captain Alvarez, I will not command my people to leave this place, but neither will I forbid them. Those who wish, you may take them to the Islands." She rubbed a hand over her face, her features dragged down by exhaustion. "I would not force those who wish to live in peace to be dragged into violence due to my stubbornness." Her smile was bleak. "And I will also not forbid those among our young men and women who wish to join your ranks and travel back with you to your worlds."

I returned her nod, not entirely satisfied but knowing how much it had cost her to make these concessions. Zan-Thint sagged in his chair.

"I suppose that is the best we can accomplish this night."

"What?" Nam Ker exclaimed, falling into a combative stance as if he might pounce on Zan-Thint and choke the life out of him. "Myrk-Kan's body sits in our hall, watched over by his father and brothers, and you're going to let this witch leave here without agreeing to give up her weapons?"

Zan-Thint regarded the Karai with the calm of a senior officer who has dealt with subordinates his whole career and built up endless reserves of patience. I envied him that, because patience wasn't once of my virtues, though I wasn't sure if Nam Ker would have appreciated being considered Zan-Thint's subordinate.

"And what would you have me do, Nam Ker?" the Tahni asked. "Take her life before your eyes in this room? Because I guarantee you that the Marine battlesuits outside would do the same to us in seconds, notwithstanding the troops I've left outside. Have you not been listening to what she said?"

Zan-Thint pushed to his feet, walking toward the door without preamble, and I thought he might simply walk out and leave Nam Ker hanging there, but he paused with his hand on the latch, looking back at the Karai.

"If you want blood, Nam Ker, you'll have it soon enough."

Nam Ker watched him step out of the hall, then looked back at us before following the Tahni, slamming the door shut behind him.

"Why the change of heart?" Vicky asked Carella, sitting on the table beside the older woman. I wanted to motion for her to hush, to not look a gift horse in the mouth, but Vicky knew what she was doing and I just had to trust her, so I kept my mouth shut. "The last time we talked to you, I would have been willing to swear that you'd die before you'd let any of your people surrender, before you'd give your blessing to them leaving this place. What's different now?"

Carella came to her feet and I thought she might follow the others out, but instead she surprised me, putting a warm, dry palm on my cheek.

"I tried to hate you," she confessed, then turned to nod toward Vicky. "All of you. I told myself that you stole Matis away from me, robbed our children of their father, that if you hadn't come, everything would have been perfect." Carella's hand fell away and her shoulders sagged. "But the truth is, if you and the Tahni hadn't visited us, Matis and I and our children would all have lived our lives as slaves of the Resscharr. Things have changed, and I must change with them. I would ask you a favor though."

"Of course," I told her. "What can we do for you?"

"Your ship has returned from its journey?"

"The *Orion* arrived in orbit this afternoon." I nodded. "She's melting down the asteroid right now, getting it ready to smelt into the materials we need to complete the gateway." I hesitated, deducing what she was getting at. "She should be available to take the first load of passengers to the Islands in a couple days."

"My children have been staying with my brother and his wife. My brother..." her voice broke, but she sucked in a breath and pushed on, holding back what I'd thought would be a sob. "My brother is among those who'd like to emigrate to the Islands, and I've told him I want him to take my children with him. I would be in your debt if you could take them on the first trip."

She didn't wait for an answer, leaving Vicky and I standing there with our mouths open.

"Shit," I murmured into the shadows of the dining hall.

"She is correct, you know," Lilandreth said, and I nearly jumped out of my skin. I'd forgotten the Resscharr was there, which was a damned good trick considering she was over two meters tall and looked like a humanoid dinosaur.

"About what?" Vicky asked. "Getting her kids off this planet?"

"She is correct that the Tahni will eventually try to take the Islands." I knew she'd been imprinted with our language by her Resscharr gadgets, and I knew from experience that she was an expert at our intonation and word choice. That meant the cold, unemotional tone she was using was on purpose, which made the question I was about to ask a long shot.

"Is there anything you and the other Resscharr can do to protect the ones who are left here? Or at least prevent the Tahni and the Karai from attacking the Islands?"

"Perhaps if any of our ships had been left intact after you and Zan-Thint overthrew the Resscharr who ruled here," she mused. "Without them, we are merely poorly trained infantry unsuited for real war. We have superior weapons, but we lack any sort of tactical knowledge on how best to employ them, particularly with you gone." Lilandreth shuffled across out of the shadows into the glow of one of the overhead lamps. The light cast her narrow face into sharp relief, accentuating the lines that were either part of her natural markings or perhaps some sort of ritual tattooing—I'd never been able to figure which it was and hadn't thought to ask. "Besides, the Resscharr here have no love for the Vergai, and I doubt I could convince them to fight their chosen children, the Tahni, for the Rejects."

My lip curled in an involuntary sneer at the mention of the name they'd given us humans. I thought I detected some bitterness in its use, and it had to be intentional.

"I expect it will be all I can do," she went on, "to keep them from reverting to savagery, and I'm not even sure if I can convince those who came with me from Decision to stay and help the local Resscharr here on Yfingam. Some would rather return to the Cluster, thinking foolishly that they can reclaim their place as the lords of creation." Lilandreth chuckled, an affectation for our benefit. "They want to return with you humans, and I wouldn't mind it myself rather than staying here."

"Great," I hissed. "I'll talk to my people, see if we have enough space to take some of you with us." And wouldn't *that* be a wonderful trip? I was running scenarios through my mind already, but she wasn't done.

"The Chosen, the Tahni, are narcissistic and entitled, which is the fault of their creators." She tapped her chest. "Us. I wonder if perhaps it wouldn't have been better for everyone if you humans had been less compassionate and simply killed them off as a species." Lilandreth sounded almost wistful. "Then I could at least say that all of our many mistakes had been erased."

Fury roiled in my chest unbidden, pure rage that threatened to boil over and spur me into something rash and unwise, and I tried to tamp it down. She was coldblooded and dispassionate, far too close to her predator ancestors, and in that moment, I could believe she'd been willing to exterminate the Skrela—and *us*—simply for being in the way.

"We'll have the raw materials for the reactors down here in a few days," I said instead. "I'd appreciate if you could start on the reactors as soon as possible."

"Do you really believe you can turn these farmers into soldiers?" Lilandreth wondered.

"We're about to find out."

## [ 9 ]

"Get in a Goddamned straight line!" Czarnecki bellowed, her voice loud enough that it almost sounded as if she were being amplified by the public address speakers on her Vigilante. She wasn't in the suit though, stalking back and forth across the front of the Vergai formation, hands on her hips. "Goddammit, don't you farmers know what a straight line is? Haven't you been planting fucking crops in a straight line your whole life?"

I wanted to laugh but I kept my face carefully neutral, watching from the near distance, far enough away that I wouldn't distract the new recruits... and far enough away that I could maintain an air of mystery around the Old Man. I learned that from the Skipper way back when. Even from fifty meters away, the whites of wide eyes stood out like spotlights fixed on the Top Kick, acting First Sergeant Czarnecki.

She was an unimpressive-looking woman, short, slight, her head kept shaven almost to a polish as if she wanted to accentuate the implant sockets, yet to these kids she was the combination of the devil himself and the right hand of God. And they *were* kids, some young enough that guilt squeezed my chest at the sight of them. Unlined, fresh faces, most not yet out of their teens because these people married early... and died early. Not just earlier than us Earthers, strung out by genetic surgery, nanites, and anti-aging drugs, earlier than our grandparents and great grandparents. Most of the Vergai farmers never even saw the threescore-and-ten the Bible promised, and I'd fought a constant battle against an Earther's bias that I wouldn't have had eight or nine years ago when my life expectancy seemed to be somewhere in the mid-twenties.

These kids would get their chance though. If we made it back, they'd be eligible for the same treatments, the same health care, the same shot at two or three centuries that any of us had. Maybe more. No one knew yet when things would break down, though I'd heard there was a theoretical limit to how many memories the brain could store. Some article I'd listened to a couple years ago on Hausos said that the current thinking was that the loss of long-term memories could mean that people would lose the core of their personality after a couple hundred years, becoming a totally different person.

But hell, aren't we all totally different people than we were when we were younger?

"Listen up, infants!" Czarnecki yelled. "What we will be *attempting* to teach you today is something called drill and ceremony. In other words, you're going to learn how to march." Her smile was saccharine, the same cynical grin drill sergeants had used on Marines for centuries. "Marching means walking together as one unit, in synchronization with each other."

Top strode purposefully up to a tall, burly teenager with wavy, blond hair and glared up into his scrunched-up blue eyes.

"You look like you wanna ask a question, boy." She snorted amusement. "Well, at least you remembered the part where I told you not to open your damned mouth unless I ask you to. I'm asking now. You got anything on your mind, spit it out."

"Yes, drill sergeant, ma'am!" he said with desperate volume, and I knew at some point in the last couple days, Top had been beating it into their thick skulls that any reply they gave was to be at the top of their lungs. "I wanted to know, drill sergeant, ma'am, what marching together has to do with becoming Marines like you and wearing the big armor."

"Yes, I thought you might," Czarnecki said, looking the boy up and down. "What's your name, recruit?"

"Teva, drill sergeant, ma'am!" I felt bad for the kid. He was going hoarse and I'll bet his throat hurt. "Son of Ferros and Verlan," he added, as if leaving it off was some breach of protocol.

"Well, Recruit Teva, there are two answers to that question. The first is," Czarnecki went on, drawing in a deep breath and then yelling the rest at high volume into the poor kid's ear, "you're a fucking recruit and you'll do as I tell you or get your ass dropped from this program and go straight back to farming! Is that clear?"

"Yes, drill sergeant, ma'am!" The kid's sunburnt face went pale, his eyes as big as dinner plates.

"And the second reason," Top continued in a normal, loud voice as if nothing had happened, pacing in front of the formation, "is that once you climb into one of *those*..." she pointed off to the side at an unoccupied Vigilante, set up there as an object lesson, a goal for the dozens of new recruits, "... you are going to feel as if you're on your own, isolated from all your fellow Marines, fighting your own private battle. But you're *not*. You will remain part of a larger whole, part of your squad, part of your platoon, part of your company, and you need to understand that the each of those moves like the fingers of a hand." Czarnecki wiggled her own fingers demonstratively. "Every one supporting the other, every one working toward the same goal. Now you tell me, Recruit Teva..." she speared the young man with a glare, "... what do you think would happen if we just taught you how to work one of the suits and sent you into battle?" The kid fumbled with a reply, but she cut him off. "You'd go off on your own and get yourself wrapped up in your own fight while your fellow Marines *died* and the mission failed! And what is our motto, recruits?"

The response was antiphonal, hesitant.

"The mission, the Marines, and me, drill sergeant, ma'am."

Czarnecki cocked an ear at them, her eyebrow raising.

"I can't *hear* you, recruits!"

*"The mission, the Marines, and me, drill sergeant, ma'am!"*

"Exactly. And since you can't learn to work together *after* we stick you in a suit by yourself, *and* because we don't plan on sticking idiots who are too stupid to learn how to walk together in time in expensive and hard-to-replace pieces of gear like a battlesuit, the first thing we're going to do is drill and ceremony." Czarnecki turned and barked a command at another NCO who'd been standing at parade rest off to the side, the platoon sergeant for Second, and the man stepped up beside her. "Since I am far too important and impatient to teach this shit to you wet-behind-the-ears bunch of newbies, Sgt. Fletcher and her squad leaders will be introducing you to the fine art of marching. May God have mercy on their souls." She braced to attention. "Company! Uh-ten-*shun!*"

The kids knew that much already. They stood as straight as possible and, even if their lines were sloppy, they managed it. Fletcher stood in front of Czarnecki and exchanged a salute before Top executed an about-face and marched over to meet me on the other side of the low hedge that had partially concealed me from the parade field.

"How they looking, Top?" I asked her. Using the title for anyone except Ellen Campbell still felt wrong, but Czarnecki deserved the moniker. The short, slender woman shrugged, making a face like she'd bit into something distasteful.

"They're all right. About as good as I guess we can expect from a pre-industrial society. Big and tough and stupid and probably brave as all hell, but they got next to no experience with technology." Czarnecki glanced over her shoulder at Fletcher and his squad leaders yelling instructions at the recruit company, trying to get them into a line. She shook her head. "They're okay. I imagine we'll hammer them into something workable by the time we get the suits." She cocked an eyebrow at him. "Which is gonna be when, exactly?"

I chuckled, because it was less unprofessional than screaming and tearing my hair out.

"Lilandreth swears up and down that she'll have me the isotope reactors exactly when she said she would, but I haven't seen one of them yet. The rest of the suit pieces are piling up in the hold of a cargo shuttle on board the *Orion* and it'll bring them down to us just as soon as they're ready." I rapped my knuckles against the side of my head. "Knock on wood. The estimate is another three to four weeks."

She grunted and the corner of my mouth turned up. Czarnecki was stepping into the role of first sergeant quite handily, including a total lack of awe or deference to me, her company commander.

"Well, *maybe* this bunch'll be ready to start training in them by then. If I can get it through to them what an HUD is, or the idea that they'll be able to fly, and, worst of all, that they're going to have sensors and cameras that let them see what's behind them. How the hell do you get shit like that through to people who think an internal combustion engine and a gunpowder rifle are the *ne plus ultra* of high technology?"

"Tell them it's magic," I suggested. "Always worked for me."

"Yeah, that'll probably work just as well as trying to explain electronics and nuclear energy."

"I should be back from the Islands just in time for the first suits," I told her.

"You're leaving?" Her eyes went wide with alarm. "Now?"

"Vicky'll still be here," I assured her, "but I have to go negotiate the resettlement of the Vergai who want to emigrate there." My eyes were stinging from lack of sleep and the glare of the afternoon sun and I squeezed them shut for a moment, sucking in a breath. "I mean, *someone* has to ask them before we drop thousands of Vergai on top of them, and because I was stupid enough to volunteer for the job, that's gotta be me." I waved off toward the landing field that we aggrandized with the term spaceport. "Commander Dunstan is touching down to pick me up in a couple hours. That's why I wanted to check in with you before I headed out."

Czarnecki nodded across the fields, where the tower of the fortress barely topped the horizon above our own buildings and, more distant, the Vergai homesteads.

"I assume you're smart enough not to announce to Zan-Thint that you're going to be offplanet."

"Just because they made me commanding officer," I told her, grinning broadly, "doesn't mean I've already scheduled my brain removal surgery."

Czarnecki's laugh was a jackass bray, which would have been annoying in anyone else but was perfect for a senior NCO.

"Good luck down here," I added. "Keep Captain Sandoval in the loop about the training." I leaned closer, not wanting anyone to overhear us. "And before you wash anybody out, remember our selection is limited, so make damn sure they're not salvageable."

She snorted, jerking a thumb at the shambolic gaggle of Vergai youngsters undulating across the parade field like a cross-eyed centipede.

"I guess if nothing else they'd make good mine detectors..."

Heat mirages poured off the hull of Intercept One, a visual accompaniment to the dying whine of its jet turbines spinning down. The hull was still burnished silver, polished between missions to shed both heat and incoming lasers, turning the aerospacecraft into a delta-winged skyscraper a hundred meters long and about half that distance across. Not quite as sharp-edged and dagger-like as an assault shuttle, the Intercept cutter was chubbier, more rounded to house the fusion reactor, the plasma drive, the Teller-Fox warp unit, and the twin capacitor banks that allowed the little warship to pop in and out of Transition Space in combat.

She was a deadly bird, perhaps one of the most versatile spacecraft humans had ever built, and her pilot, Kyler Dunstan, had saved my ass more times than I could count. Dunstan was good enough at his job that barely anyone remembered he'd originally been a mercenary pilot for the Corporate Council Security Force, cashiered out of the Fleet and desperate for a job. Since he was one of my best friends, I, of course, never let him forget.

"You sure you're going to be okay here while I'm gone?" I asked Vicky, slipping an arm around her shoulder. She smiled and laid her head against my arm.

"We'll be fine, particularly since you seem to suck ass trying to play nice with the Tahni."

"Ooh," I said, wincing, putting a hand over my chest. "You're harsh, woman. And I suppose *you* are the mistress of the dark, political arts and will have Zan-Thint and Nam Ker eating out of your hand by the time I get back."

"Of course. Look how easily I won you over. All I had to do was play hard to get for the first six months or so."

"You and Carella must be related," I muttered, waiting impatiently for the belly ramp of the cutter to open.

"Speak of the devil." Vicky nodded off to the side of landing field closest to the Vergai steadings, toward the six people walking across the packed dirt.

I didn't recognize the young couple, barely remembered the three children, who had grown quite a bit since the last time I'd seen them, but there was no mistaking Carella or her characteristic blue shawl. It must have been the mark of her office as leader of the Vergai, because there was no other reason for her to be wearing it outside in the summer. This place was a temperate climate, but that didn't stop it from getting hot this time of year. Didn't stop the mosquitos either, though they didn't bother me as much as they did Vicky.

"Captain Alvarez," Carella said as they approached. "Captain Sandoval. This is my brother, Vanner, and his wife, Nolandra. They will be accompanying you to the Islands to speak for us. And they'll be staying."

That much was clear from all the gear the two of them were hauling. Besides the backpacks they wore, they each had shoulder bags hanging off them, and Vanner towed what looked like a cross between a wheelbarrow and a dolly with cloth bundles tied to it with twine. And it was still next to nothing for people who were leaving their home never to return.

"I want to stay with you, Mother," Carella's oldest daughter insisted. She couldn't have been older than seven or eight, but I think she was the only one of the three who understood what was happening. "Please let me stay."

Carella knelt beside the little girl, taking the child in her arms.

"My love," she said gently, so softly I could barely hear, "I will join you there just as soon as my work here is done. Until then, you be a good girl for your aunt and uncle and take good care of your brother and sister for me. I love you and I'll be with you soon."

Her voice broke at the last and the lump in my throat was too large to swallow. I had to look away and try to surreptitiously wipe away the moisture in my eyes at the memory of my last moments with my own mother at around the same age as that little girl. Vicky rubbed at my shoulder, letting me know she understood, and I put a grateful hand over hers.

I fought back an irrational urge to slap Carella into a set of flex cuffs and carry her bodily onto the cutter, to force her to leave this place and go with her kids to the Islands. It would have worked. There's no way she could have gotten back from the other world, and eventually she'd settle in and lead her people in their new land. But I didn't, because I didn't have the right, even if it was the right thing to do, and I hated myself for it.

"Those kids deserve to have a mother," I said softly into Vicky's ear. "She can't do this to them."

"She's already given up on herself," Vicky told me, shaking her head, grief in the set of her eyes. "They're better off without her."

If anyone else had told me that, I would have torn them a new one, but it was Vicky, and she wasn't usually wrong about people. I still wanted to argue, but I bit down on the words as the belly ramp of the cutter lowered and Kyler Dunstan strode down, his lopsided grin oblivious to the drama going on between us.

"All right, all right!" He clapped his hands, then spread them wide in invitation. "Who's ready for a fun trip to the water world?"

His crew chief, Hazel Beckett, a quiet, professional type, walked up behind him, shaking her head.

"Kyler..." she stopped herself, biting down on the words

with a wince. "I mean, Commander Dunstan, would you like me to help them stow their luggage?"

"Oh, yeah, that'd be cool, Hazel," he said. "I'll give you a hand with that."

I caught a glimpse over her shoulder of Dunstan and Beckett laughing as they carried the luggage up the ramp, just barely touching shoulders, and I frowned, shaking my head.

"Hey, do you think that Dunstan and Chief Beckett...?"

Vicky laughed sharply at the idea.

"I wouldn't put it past Dunstan, but Beckett? Getting involved with a superior officer? No way."

I shrugged surrender, but I still stared at the two for a moment before they disappeared into the hold.

"I'll be back as soon as I can," I assured Vicky, hefting the small overnight bag I'd brought with me. "Try to keep a lid on things while I'm gone."

"Don't go starting any fights with the Islanders," she warned me. "We have enough problems already."

"I don't know." I glared at Carella as she stayed at the bottom of the ramp, seemingly afraid to take a step onto it lest she give in to her mother's instincts and let them overrule her determination to stay here and fight. "I feel like I'm leaving our problems here."

# [ 10 ]

I hadn't been back to Laisvas Miestas since we'd first arrived in this system what seemed like a lifetime ago. It had actually been less than two years, but the memory of it had faded to nothing beside the dozen or more other worlds we'd visited, the battles we'd fought. I recalled the water, the storms, but the deep green of the island valleys had slipped through the cracks of my memory.

We landed on the most heavily populated island, though it wasn't the largest. The largest had no navigable ports, its shoals rocky and violent, threatening to smash any ship that dared to try to find landing. This place was about the size of Madagascar, heavily forested below the rugged mountains to the northwest, fiercely beautiful but shrouded by mist and cloud, a wetter climate than the one around the fortress of Yfingam and one that wouldn't support the same types of crops.

The Vergai would have to learn new ways of farming, would have to learn fishing and the ways of the sea. Maybe.

"Hey," I said, nudging Chief Beckett where she sat in the center seat between Dunstan and his copilot. "Have we looked at what's on the other continent? The big one, the uninhabited one?"

The woman frowned, maybe because I was distracting her during the descent or maybe just because she couldn't remember. Whichever it was, she sighed and scrolled through the menu at her station until she pulled up a report.

"It's pretty rough near the coast," Beckett said, raising her voice over the rumbling roar of the atmospheric jets, "but the drone scans show some pretty fertile valleys on the other side of the mountains." She made a face. "Fertile, but isolated. Only way in and out of there is from the air. Got some gnarly megafauna in there too. Stuff probably related to elk, moose, bears, wolves, that sort of thing. Cats too. That's about all we got." Beckett shrugged. "Just a preliminary scan when we first arrived, just to make sure there weren't any nasty surprises waiting for us."

I nodded thanks, ruminating over the place, shutting out the feeling of my stomach dropping out from beneath me. Apparently that wasn't so easy for Carella's brother, who was retching quietly in the acceleration couch behind me. Thank God Beckett had shown him how to use the spacesick bags.

The weather on the interior of the larger continent was more like Yfingam as well and would probably support wheat and corn. Being isolated wouldn't be a horrible thing either, since it would mean they'd never have to deal with the Tahni-descended Islanders who sometimes traded with the humans of Laisvas Miestas.

It was an idea. Not a great one, since it meant that the Vergai would be entirely on their own and we'd be forced to haul in shitloads of supplies, seed, and livestock via cargo shuttle, and I just didn't want to even consider how badly one of those birds would smell after transporting cattle, sheep, and pigs from one planet to another. But still an option.

"Do they know we're coming?" I asked, and this time Dunstan answered, apparently not so wrapped up in flying us through the gradually thickening cloud layers that he couldn't split his concentration.

"Yeah, we left a transceiver with them last time we visited just in case we had to contact them again." He shrugged, and I winced as it seemed the cutter shrugged with him, wavering slightly. "At least I figure that's why Colonel Hachette did it. He was always thinking ahead."

I crossed myself reflexively. I'm not sure why, but Mom would have likely been happy with me turning back to God. Whether it was a logical move or not, I wasn't sure, but logic didn't help me sleep.

"Captain Nance called 'em a few days ago and told that lady who's in charge, what's-her-name, that we were sending a delegation." Dunstan snickered. "Don't know if I've ever been part of a *delegation* before. I feel all official."

"You're not the delegation," Lt. Jessup, the copilot, reminded him. "You're the bus driver."

"Hey man," Dunstan protested, "I bet I could do that diplomat shit along with everyone else. You wanna let me talk to the fish people, Cam?"

"That's okay," I assured him. "If I let you do the diplomat stuff, people might realize how useless I am."

"Well hold on back there," Dunstan called back to the civilians. "Landing in five."

The kids at least appeared to be enjoying themselves, even the oldest daughter who'd fretted about leaving her mother the entire trip squealing as the cutter tilted downward steeply. The adults not so much. I thought Carella's brother might have a stroke when we Transitioned across the system to the second planet. We called it Laisvas Miestas after the biggest city, or usually just the Islands, which I suppose was evidence of our own lack of imagination. Not that the locals even had a name for the world at all. Why would they need one? They had little time or concept of physics or science beyond the engineering it took to smelt iron or build steam engines.

As we flew in lower over the city, the white puffs of steam engines and the black scar of coal smoke rose over foundries. If there'd been enough of the locals to really get a foothold on the place, they might have been doing a great job of polluting the hell out of the place, but the Fleet Intelligence geeks had given an estimate of the total human population here at under a hundred thousand. Given that they'd been here thousands of years, that was ridiculously small. Which was why I was hoping they wouldn't mind taking on the Vergai.

"Looks like we got a welcoming committee," Beckett said, pointing to the lower section of the main screen, where the belly cameras projected the view of the fields outside the city where we'd landed last time.

No powered vehicles. They had steam trains and steamboats but not steam trucks or cars, which wasn't surprising. What came out to greet us were people in woolen clothing riding elaborate tricycles, pedal-powered. Some were pedaled by the single passenger while others had two men doing the work, their clothes rougher and more obviously suited for work than the passengers in the back. I *hoped* they were paid help and not slaves. You never knew in situations like this, not out here where everything had been slopped together by the Resscharr in some great mélange of cultures and species. These particular humans had been abducted from Iron Age Europe, and I doubt slavery and other nasty habits had been alien to their ancestors.

The trikes disappeared from view in a cloud of dust billowing up from the landing jets, and even above the screaming turbines I could hear the sighs of relief from Vanner and Nolandra in the back as the landing gear settled into their housings and we touched down.

"Okay, ladies and gentlemen," Dunstan said, sweeping his hands across the controls to shut down the engines, "you are now free to unbuckle your safety harnesses and disembark on the beautiful, seaside village of Laisvas Miestas. We hope you've enjoyed your flight and you'll consider the Commonwealth Fleet Attack Command for all your interplanetary transportation needs."

I rolled my eyes, having heard the spiel before, but Beckett was smiling fondly and I didn't care *what* Vicky said, I just knew there was something going on there. Dunstan was probably my best friend besides Vicky, and even *I* didn't laugh at his humor.

"Should we bring our luggage?" Vanner asked, looking from the kids to me. The man was utterly lost, and I couldn't blame him. He'd left behind everything to come not just to a new home but a completely different planet and culture, and he was scared shitless. But he'd made his decision.

"Not yet," I told him, moving past the passengers toward the belly ramp. "Just come with me and we'll talk to their representatives first. Don't want to act presumptuous." Or like helpless beggars with nothing to bring to the table.

The woman was waiting for us by the end of the ramp, her eyes in the sort of permanent squint I'd noticed on people from the rougher colonies who made their living on the ocean. She was tall and slender, with a stern face and hair pulled into tight, blonde braids running down her back, and I might have called her long, black dress Victorian if it hadn't been fairly similar to what the men were wearing. She smiled past the squint, the smile of someone meeting an old acquaintance after a long time apart.

"Cameron Alvarez," Aldona said, offering me both her

hands in their traditional greeting. I took them, squeezing in appreciation of the gesture. "It is most pleasant to see you again. After so long, I'd begun to fear you and your people would never return."

"Aldona." I nodded. "Thank you for allowing us to visit. May I present to you Vanner and Nolandra?" I motioned back to the Vergai. "And their sister's children who've accompanied them here? They're of the Vergai from Yfingam, where your people were taken long ago."

"It is my honor to meet our kin from old," Aldona said, offering the same traditional greeting to them. This got tricky, because there'd been some linguistic drift since the two populations had been separated thousands of years ago and neither of the Vergai had been given a 'link with a translator, but it only took a few seconds of explanation to get the sentiment across.

"You are all welcome here, of course," Aldona said, and I could tell she was choosing her words carefully, trying to be polite, although her gaze kept going back to the children. She was also obviously flustered enough that she didn't even attempt to introduce the other VIPs who'd come along with her to greet us. "But the day grows late. Perhaps you would care to come to our great hall and feast with us and we can discuss your purpose for coming."

And there it was. She was getting suspicious, and now the sell was going to have to start. I put on my fakest smile and gestured back at the passenger trikes waiting for us, the hired pedalers looking bored despite the starship sitting in front of them.

"Lead on."

---

Dinner was fish, of course. Vanner and Nolandra dug in with gusto, but the kids picked at the strange food with desultory clicks of metal utensils on ceramic plates. They'd have to get used to it, because fish was a staple meat here. It was pretty good in my opinion, particularly compared to the shipboard food I'd been eating for most of the last two years, and if the vegetables accompanying it weren't familiar to me, at least they were fresh. And at least eating kept me from having to make conversation.

Dunstan and the crew had stayed behind with the ship, which meant I was the only English speaker at a table with five Vergai and four of the Island World people, all of whom spoke some ancient variant of Indo-European. Yes, I had a translator programmed by Dwight that could almost instantaneously tell me what they were saying and relay my own words through a speaker on my shoulder, and yes, I'd grown used to the process since we'd arrived out here, but there was still something isolating about the feeling.

The feast hall wasn't that different in basic design from the Vergai hall back on Yfingam, though as with everything else here in Laisvas Miestas, it had a rough, frontier patina that was also somehow more advanced than their cousins on the third world out. Paintings lined the walls, most of them nautical themed, some showing fishermen struggling to bring in gigantic animals, bigger than any fish I'd seen even on videos from the colonies. Others showed naval battles—actual blue water navies, not the starship fleets I was used to—and I wanted to ask who they'd been fighting but didn't think it would be wise to bring it up at the moment.

The tables and chairs were hand-polished wood, the floors smooth stone, while the walls and roof were wood paneled with a light, rough finish; the whole thing reminded me of a ViR-drama I'd watched once about 19th-century Britain. Of course, the men in that movie hadn't been wearing ankle-length black robes, but it did make them look suitably archaic.

Dessert was some sort of apple cobbler, which wasn't as sweet as what I was used to but was still excellent, and by the end of it I was suitably stuffed and leaning back in the very comfortable, sharkskin-upholstered chair, eyes threatening to close in the drowsy light of the oil lamps. That's when Aldona hit me with it, of course.

"I hope you've all enjoyed your meal," she said, hands clasped in front of her as the servants came to clear the plates away, "but now I would hear of your purpose for this trip, unless it has only been for pleasurable company."

The way she said it made me feel guilty, like I should lie and tell her yes, we actually did just visit to be friendly. But duty and all that...

"I'm here," I told her, "on behalf of the Vergai of Yfingam, your kin, the descendants of humans abducted from here thousands of years ago." God, I just wanted to come right out and say it, but I'd been assured that you had to ease into these things. "Their situation on Yfingam is untenable." *Untenable.* I sounded just like Hachette now. "Last time we were here, we told you about the Tahni, who are relatives of the race you call the Islanders here. On Yfingam there are other relatives of the Islanders, also brought there at the same time as the Vergai. They're known as the Karai, and they were used by the ruling-class Resscharr as warriors until they, together with the Tahni and ourselves, overthrew the Resscharr."

I shrugged, then stalled for time with a drink of the local wine out of the cup the servants had left for me after taking my plate. I struggled not to make a face. It was overly sweet.

"At the time," I went on, "that seemed like a good idea. The Resscharr were abusing their power and keeping both the Vergai and the Karai enslaved. And I guess it *was* a good idea, as long as we were there to keep the Tahni and Karai honest. But we've found a way to return home, and when we do, there'll be no one left to protect the Vergai, and we're afraid the Karai and the Tahni will either make slaves of them or maybe just try to kill them all."

Aldona said nothing, but her eyes narrowed, the corners of her mouth pinching as if he were controlling a scowl that she was too diplomatic to let show.

"What do you ask of us, Cameron?"

"Many of the Vergai would like to immigrate here." I motioned to Carella's family. "This is the family of the Vergai commander and they've come as ambassadors, hoping you'd allow them to stay and set things up for those still to come."

"Many," Aldona repeated, her expression neutral. "*How many?*"

The other notables at the table with her looked even more troubled than her, though it was a tribute to how much authority she held that not one had dared to interrupt.

"Right now? Somewhere north of ten thousand." I gestured expansively. "If things continue to look bad, more may want to come. Maybe all of them, which we estimate at close to seventy thousand."

She nodded slowly in response, wheels working behind her eyes. She was, I noticed for the first time, wearing makeup. Nothing gaudy, just a subtle hint here and there. It was interesting not because I found her particularly attractive but because it spoke of the wealth and sophistication of their society. People on the edge of starving didn't bother with makeup.

"You understand," Aldona said after a moment, "that you're speaking of numbers greater than those currently living in this city?"

"I do. I was thinking we could do this one of several ways. I've seen from the air that you have several other towns along the coast. If we could find one of them that had the resources available to build up into something bigger, I know the Vergai wouldn't be afraid of the work."

Aldona leaned forward, resting her chin on her fingers.

"That's... *possible*. But building enough homes for them worries me. As things are, we're forced to go farther each year for timber, and we have no wish to clear-cut the area around the farmlands. This was done long ago, during one of *those*." She pointed to one of the paintings of the naval battle, showing a stalwart-looking sailor plunging a cutlass into an enemy decidedly less stalwart and more villainous. "The resulting erosion killed more people than the war."

"We can show you other building methods," I assured her. "In fact, we'd be willing to share quite a bit of technological information with you if you agree to this." Hachette had left a file full of it after he'd printed it off and gave it to the Vailoa. I'd gotten into a knock-down, drag-out argument with him over that, but at least I wasn't handing these people nuclear weapons. "New construction methods, new fuels, new ways of metallurgy... new weapons." I winced at that one, but it was the hole card. "Steam is a fine way to power trains, but there are better fuels for ships. Fuels that could take them all the way around this world, from one side to another. You've seen our ships fly... you could do that yourself. Not to *space*, not yet, but there are ways to fly in the sky that you could master in just a few years if we share the knowledge with you."

If Aldona was practiced at negotiation and diplomacy, she was, after all, only human. Her lips parted, and she licked them like a starving woman with her face pressed up against the glass of a fine restaurant.

"Tell me more."

# [ 11 ]

I felt dirty, and not in a good way.

Oh, I'd accomplished the mission. *The mission, the Marines, and me.* That was what we said and I had to live what I preached, but that didn't mean I had to feel good about it. Aldona had agreed to take as many of the Vergai as wanted to come in exchange for our technical knowledge, and that didn't bother me as much as the fact that her main enthusiasm hadn't been for construction techniques or medical procedures but, of course, for gunpowder and steel warships.

The whole exchange haunted me on the walk back to the ship the next morning. They'd offered me a ride, of course, but I'd taken a long look at the skinny, hollow-eyed little man who they'd assigned to pedal the trike, looked at his rough clothes and the holes in his shoes, and just couldn't decide whether he was paid help or a slave or something in between. The whole thing made me uncomfortable enough that I turned up the collar of my jacket against the ever-present drizzle of the port town and walked.

The walk had shown me more of the city than the trike ride, where I'd been distracted by conversation. It had shown me the section of the city that wasn't on the VIP tour, the row houses where the workers in those foundries lived, the families of those who mined coal or those who toiled in the factories. I don't suppose I'd figured they'd all be smiling, happy, and singing, but I hadn't been prepared for the brutal poverty, the hacking coughs, the open sores. I'd considered the Vailoans primitive, but they had a 20$^{th}$-century Earth level of medical science and hygiene. These people didn't even have that. This was industrial-revolution Britain, or at least what I'd seen of it in the history lessons I'd taken for my continuing education.

The people weren't empty-eyed zombies for all that, of course. The kids played and the women watching them smiled and hung up laundry to dry because this was their life and they hadn't known anything better. But they needed help. They needed a better existence, and I was helping them get that. In another generation, the infant mortality rate would be down to single-digit percentage points and the population would be booming. In a century, there'd be a million people on this world, or maybe ten million. In another, there'd be a billion. And thanks to the weapons I was about to hand over to them, they'd likely have had at least one world war and probably wiped the Tahni-descended Islanders out of existence.

By the time I reached the ship, I was shivering and drenched and the bleak, gray sky perfectly matched my mood. Dunstan, meanwhile, was playing a game of what looked like a cross between hacky sack and soccer with a group of local street urchins who'd dared to approach the strange metal sky ship and the foreigners in the weird clothes. Beckett was sitting on the ramp out of the rain, watching him fondly.

I made a decision right there, probably not a good one because most snap decisions aren't, but one I couldn't help. I'd been forced into too much that I didn't want to do, and this was something I knew was right. I said nothing, just walked over to

Dunstan, kicked the ball back to the kids, then grabbed his 'link off his belt and put a finger to my lips when he tried to object. Slipping my own datalink from its holster, I tossed both of them to Beckett and made another shushing gesture when she tried to ask me what was going on.

I don't know who was looking at us with the more puzzled expression as I dragged Dunstan away from the ship, Beckett or those kids, but both remained silent. I didn't stop walking until we were all the way on the edge of the tall grass of the landing field, the moisture it trapped coating my waterproof fatigue pants with a layer of beaded rain. Stopping where the grass gave way to the cobblestone of the street, I glanced back over my shoulder. About three hundred meters to the ship, and I still wasn't sure it was enough.

"What the fuck's going on?" Dunstan blurted, his brows knitted with confusion. "Are you gonna beat me up or something?"

I sighed, rolling my eyes at him.

"Dunstan, when have I ever beat you up?"

"I dunno, man, there's a first time for everything." He threw up his hands. "I mean, why the hell else would you get rid of our 'links and drag me out away from the ship if you weren't about to do something you didn't want recorded?"

"Yeah, well, you're half right," I told him. "I do need this to be off the record and definitely not recorded. In fact, before I tell you what I'm about to tell you, you have to swear to me that you won't mention it to *anyone* anywhere you or they have a 'link or could be picked up by any electronic surveillance, even from a hundred meters away."

Dunstan's mood immediately shifted from defensive to conspiratorial as he leaned in toward me, eyebrow raising.

"Say no more, dude. My mouth is like a steel trap."

I pondered that for a moment, wondering if he'd mangled

that simile beyond all recognition, then decided it didn't matter. Either I could trust him or I couldn't.

"Not even to Beckett," I cautioned. "Not unless you two are off the ship, onplanet, and away from the city with your 'links left behind."

"What d'you mean, Beckett?" he asked, not doing a very good job of lying. "She's just like, my crew chief, man."

"Yeah, sure she is." I shrugged. Enough wasting time. "Look, here's the deal. I think Dwight is lying to us about the Resscharr and the Skrela." He started to ask a question, but I stopped him, holding up a hand. "Just wait till I'm done. What I think is, there was no Condemnation faction among the Resscharr. They didn't bring back the Skrela to punish themselves, the sentient AI like Dwight did, because they thought the Resscharr deserved to get genocided just like they did to the Skrela. Like they tried to do to us."

I explained briefly why I believed it, about Dwight's slip-up.

"What that means is, we can't trust Dwight." I shrugged. "Maybe he's got reason to hate the Resscharr, but he lied to us, dragged us into the battle that killed Colonel Hachette and a good portion of my Drop Trooper company when, if I'm right, he could have ended this all at any time."

"You don't think we should just, you know, *confront* him about this?" Dunstan wondered. "I know he doesn't like the Resscharr, but he seems like he's okay with us humans."

"Yeah, and what if he's not? He's inside the *Orion*'s computer systems, inside the Tahni destroyer, inside the Resscharr fortress. If he decides that we're a threat or we do something to piss him off, he can pretty much wipe us out in minutes. *All* of us, Resscharr, Tahni and human."

"Oh, yeah." Dunstan chewed his lip, eyes clouding over in thought. I knew what he was doing because I'd done it more than once—trying to figure some way out of this and failing.

"Shit, man, we need him to get that gateway built and get us back too."

"And I'm still not sure if we can bring him back through to the Cluster," I added. "Part of me thinks we shouldn't chance it."

"Isn't he *already* back in the Cluster?" Dunstan pointed out. "He's still back there in that gateway, right?"

"He is," I admitted, "but he's isolated. He can't leave that place. If we give him the *Orion* and put him right in the middle of the Commonwealth..."

"Oh, dude." Dunstan ran a hand through his hair. "What the hell are we going to do?"

"Play along for now. There's not much else we *can* do. But when the time comes—*if* it comes—I'm going to need people ready to act. You're the first besides Vicky."

He grinned.

"Aw, thanks, man. I appreciate you trusting me."

"You're my best friend, Dunstan," I told him. "I know you'll have my back."

And *that* really hit him. It was maybe the first time I'd seen Dunstan speechless. He took a step back, then lunged forward and pulled me into a hug. It was awkward for a moment, but honest to God, it had been a long time since I'd had any personal contact with anyone besides Vicky, and I returned the embrace for a few seconds before I pulled away.

Dunstan was crying. Not sobbing, but tears were streaming down his face, and he made no effort to wipe them away.

"I haven't really had a best friend since I got out of the military the first time," he told me.

"Sure you have," I said, clapping him on the shoulder. "Vicky and I have known you since you worked for the Corporate Council."

And while it was more accurate to say we hadn't really been his friends until after that, I didn't bother to point that out.

"It's a real relief to be able to share this with someone," I admitted, blowing out breath. "It's been just building up inside me for weeks. I don't know who else to tell. Nance won't get off his Goddamned ship, Carella is going off the deep end ,and how the hell can I trust Lilandreth to do the right thing after everything we've found out?" I shook my head. "I miss the days when things were simple, Kyler. When the Tahni were the enemy and everyone else was the good guys. We had IFF in our helmets and the commanders all had Blue Force trackers to tell them who to shoot at."

"I don't know who the hell the Blue Force is this time around, Cam." He chuckled. "Except you and me and Vicky." He shrugged. "And Beckett, of course."

I laughed, shaking an accusatory finger at the pilot.

"I knew it. Come on, let's get the hell out of here. I hate the damned rain."

---

"Holy shit, Alvarez," Captain Nance said, leaning back against the bulkhead in his cabin and taking a swig of whatever was in his glass. "You don't think you've given us *enough* to do what with hauling in an asteroid, smelting the damned thing down, and then fabricating you a whole company's worth of battlesuits without turning my ship into a fucking moving truck?"

The *Orion* was unique among Fleet ships in that it had a rotating habitation wheel so we actually had some gravity when we weren't in Transition Space or accelerating, the idea being that, on an intelligence mission, we'd spend a lot of time in orbit, gathering, well... intelligence. I don't know how much we'd used it since I'd joined the mission, but Nance sure seemed to enjoy it a lot more than the rest of us. It allowed whatever that drink was to stay in the glass anyway.

I hadn't really wanted to stop by in person to tell him about the transport job. It was a lot easier to hang up on someone when you were talking to them over a 'link. But I hadn't seen a way around it since I'd been in a spaceship anyway and he was still sitting in orbit, processing ore and fabricating battlesuits for me. It only seemed polite.

"We're leaving this place forever," I reminded him. "Leaving these people behind to whatever happens next, and the worst part is, we'll never know. All we'll have is the nightmares of the worst-case scenario." I scowled and smacked a hand on his desk. "Dammit, Nance, if you're gonna keep drinking that shit in front of me, the least you could do is offer me a glass."

Nance chuckled, setting his own glass on the desk and retrieving another from a drawer, along with a brown bottle. It was unmarked, which likely meant he'd made it on board ship, and also likely meant it sucked, but I was in no position to be picky. I took the glass and downed it in one gulp, discovering I was right, that it indeed sucked. I whooshed out a breath, tasting the... vodka? Maybe?... more on the way up than the way down.

"Thanks," I told him, setting the glass down on the plastic desktop. "How the hell do you sip that shit?"

Nance shrugged it off and took another sip.

"Practice." He eyed me sidelong, like he didn't want to meet my look. "You're probably wondering why I never showed the slightest bit of interest in taking over Hachette's job."

"I figured you were agoraphobic," I admitted. "But maybe that's just me seeing everything through the filter of my own experience."

He barked a laugh.

"You're close. Not really agoraphobic, but I feel in control here. I have an area of responsibility and a job I know how to do well. I can keep everything contained." He sloshed the alcohol around in the glass. "Even this. As long as I'm here, as long as do the shit I know, it's not a problem. But if I tried to do what you're doing, make the decisions you're making, I couldn't handle it. Honest to God, Cam, I don't know how *you* do it."

"How I do it?" I repeated. "As far as I can tell, I'm just imitating what Hachette would have done, except I'm trying not to be a douche about it."

"The man knew his job," Nance admitted. "Right up until he didn't."

"We all have our limits," I allowed. "None of us know what they are until we hit them."

"Well, if you hit yours, you'd better find someone else to take charge, because it won't be me."

"When you send down the cargo shuttle with the suit pieces," I told him, "I'll send it back up with the first group of Vergai. I think with all the Marines downstairs and no one needing a cabin of their own, if we keep the cargo shuttles full for the whole trip and use both Intercepts, we can get a thousand people at a time over."

"Jesus," Nance moaned, hands going to his head, "can you imagine the *smell* from that many people jammed into my ship? It's going to take a dozen trips at least."

"At least," I agreed. "And I think more. This is just the first group that already wanted to go. Once the ones that are left start thinking about it, there are bound to be more. And once they wind up losing maybe a quarter of their population, people are going to realize they don't have enough left to fight the Karai anymore. Then it'll be a snowball rolling downhill."

"What the hell does a kid from Mexico who grew up in Trans-Angeles know about snowballs?" he scoffed.

"Hey, I was stationed on places that got snow during the war," I protested. "I know what a snowball is."

"Then you should know this whole thing has a snowball's chance in hell of working. At some point when you get enough of them gone and the entrenched ones decide they're going to stay and fight, Zan-Thint and Nam Ker are going to wade in and mop the floor with the others. You're going to have to decide whether we're intervening directly. We won't be able to go half measures at that point." He sniffed. "Shit, the damned Tahni assault shuttles are already shadowing us every time we hit orbit and running parallel courses whenever we launch a lander or a cargo bird. It won't take much to spin this whole thing into open warfare."

"I shouldn't have a problem with that. I spent about eight years of my life killing Tahni, and Zan-Thint was our target on this mission." Thank God for spin gravity, because I needed to pace. "I shouldn't have any problem fighting them, but for some reason I do. Maybe it's because, before, I never actually had to talk to any of them." I frowned, a memory teasing at the back of my thoughts. "Except this one pilot we took prisoner once. We had to force him to fly us off a colony moon once where we got stranded during an operation."

"Oh, why does that not surprise me?" Nance said, rolling his eyes. "You getting yourself into an impossible situation and finding your way out doing something crazy seems about par for the course since I've known you. Who knows? Maybe you'll pull something out of your ass this time too."

"There's been a fuse burning down there for years," I told him. "Maybe getting some of the Vergai offplanet will be the thing that finally puts it out."

# [ 12 ]

"Wow," I said, unable to stop the grin even though it made me look decidedly unprofessional and unmysterious. "That's the most Vigilantes I've seen in one place since the war."

The past couple weeks had flown by, and I don't think I slept more than four hours a day the whole time. I'd had to work with the entire Intelligence staff to prepare the technological manuals for Laisvas Miestas, not to mention spending way too much time on the radio with Aldona working out translation details, then running them by Dwight just to double-check. On top of that, I'd been pressed into duty coordinating the immigration flights, checking on lading and supplies, and making sure that we had families grouped together on the same shipments and assigned them the same compartment or cargo shuttle or Intercept bird.

That last one had taken far longer than I'd imagined it would and involved way too many trips to the Vergai steadings to double-check directly with the families in question, all of whom had no 'links and no other way to reach them than to go talk to them face to face. I'd wound up having to record biometric scans of them all because they didn't have any personal records on file. Hell, they didn't have any *files* on anything, no written records of any kind. They just knew the names of their neighbors and the neighbors' kids and parents, and if you wanted to find out anything about them, you just had to go ask them.

All very old-fashioned and Vicky thought it was sweet, but it was a huge pain in the ass for me. I'd put Dunstan in charge of arranging the flight schedules, for which he said he was no longer my best friend, and that still left me wandering through the steadings with all the Intelligence staff available, collecting names and dragging local guides from one section to another. And of course, every single one of those families had to be cleared through Carella to make sure none of them was skipping out on a debt or a criminal judgement.

All of which meant that when Spags—Warrant Officer Frank Spagnuolo, our company armorer—had called me and informed me that he had the suit parts down from the *Orion* and the isotope reactors delivered by Lilandreth and her Resscharr and asked if I wanted him to go ahead and put the suits together, it had totally blindsided me.

Not Vicky, of course. She'd been counting down the days, and the only reason she hadn't been reminding me of it every single day was the fact that I got in after she was already asleep and left before she woke up every single day. So her reaction when I called her and gave her the good news about the suits being ready was "it's about damned time!"

She'd put the recruits through an abbreviated boot camp and even taught them to read English to the extent that they could interpret the operating system of a Vigilante, though most of the display was symbols and avatars, so that mostly meant teaching them our numerical system. I still had my doubts, and I fully expected to eventually hear of one of the recruits smashing his suit head first into the ground, but here they were, lined up nice and neat, their suits at attention in company formation by platoons and squads, just like at Armor School back on Inferno.

They were terracotta warriors pulled out of some ancient tomb and brought out into the sunlight, motionless and yet somehow vibrant and alive. A little different in profile than I was used to, of course. The plasma gun had a certain, familiar shape to it, and now I was just getting used to the sleeker design of the Resscharr energy cannons, but the coilguns that were the primary armament of these jury-rigged suits were longer and skinnier, their double-drum feed mechanisms hanging off the back in a lopsided design.

I marched into the formation and came to attention in front of Vicky, returning her salute. It felt awkward. I hadn't been on a parade field since I left Armor School, and while I would never forget drill and ceremony, it didn't come naturally anymore.

Vicky stood behind me while I stood and surveyed the troops. When I spoke, I didn't have to raise my voice. My 'link would convey the words to the internal speaker of each of the recruits. I didn't have to think about it either. I'd practiced the speech over and over in my head all morning.

"Recruits," I said, "do you know what I see when I look at you? I don't see farmers. I don't see Vergai. I don't see your faces, don't know your names. When I look at you, I see armor. I see metal and energy and power. I see what the enemy's going to see when you face them... and I see the fear in their hearts. I don't see you as you are, I see you as you *can* be... if you stick with the training, listen to your instructors, and work hard."

It was hard to stand still. I didn't normally speak standing still, but this was a formation, and although I could have got away with pacing in front of them, it would have set a bad example.

"This is a different sort of work than you're used to, and it's going to require you to use your head a lot more than your back. The suits will do the heavy lifting, the jumping, the fighting, but you're going to have to know how to use them the right way. These aren't just armor shields to make sure you don't get shot when you're shooting back. They're an extension of your body, giving you the power of a god. You can jump hundreds of meters, run as fast as a galloping horse, and strike at your enemies from kilometers away."

I swept my gaze across the front ranks.

"What you *can't* do is be reckless or stupid. You know what happens when you screw up doing something stupid in one of these suits? When you run so fast you can't control it or jump too far and don't think about landing? You'll get hurt, of course, you might even die. But worse than that, you'll damage the suit. And unlike you, the suit is *not* replaceable. What we have is what we have until we get back to my world." I couldn't see the blanched faces, the wide eyes, but I knew they were there and I smiled thinly. "You may think I'm being cold, harsh, that I don't care about you. But I do. I care about the ones you'd be letting down. Look at the man or woman beside you."

Some of the suits actually shuffled side to side as farmers not used to having 360-degree camera views projected before them tried to turn to see their fellows in the formation. I said nothing, but I knew their NCOs would be barking corrections at them inside their helmets.

"When you damage a suit, take it out of action, do you know who you're letting down? Not me. You're letting down that man or woman beside you who was counting on you to have their back, to support them when the fight starts. When we leave this place, you won't just be leaving behind your old life. You'll be leaving behind support, resupply, any hope of reinforcement. It'll just be us, and your fellow Marines will be the only ones you can count on. And if you do something stupid and you're not there for them, they'll die too, and it'll be your fault."

Someone murmured on the line, probably touching the wrong control.

"Take your fucking thumb off the comm control, Geranus," Czarnecki snarled. "Use your ears, not your mouth."

"That's what you want to be, right?" I asked them. "Marines? Drop Troopers? This is your one chance. If you don't work, if you don't listen, if you don't *think* and learn, you'll be dropped and we'll find someone to take your place. Because just like you, once we leave here, there's no finding more troops, so we have to be particularly choosy here while you're training."

And yes, Vicky and I both knew that was an exaggeration. There were a few more volunteers we could have taken, but this was pretty much the cream of the crop. But they didn't need to know that. We could recycle a handful of them, but our time was pretty severely limited.

"Listen to your trainers. If you have questions, ask them, but listen *first*. The Marines training you have fought the Tahni, fought the Skrela and survived, prevailed, and they're not stupid. They know what you need to learn, and if you listen to them, they'll give you the answers you're looking for. If you're scared, then you're human. If you let that fear keep you from thinking, keep you from acting, then you've failed. If you fail in training, we can train you better. If you fail in combat, you're dead and so are your friends. If you fail in training and one of your instructors corrects you, don't resent them for it, don't get an attitude and think no one should be able to push you around and call you names, or you've failed a second time. Listen to them. They're trying to keep you alive."

I was droning on too long about the same subject, mostly because it worried the shit out of me, but I knew I needed to move on or lose their attention.

"If you listen, if you learn, if you think, then you're going to be something none of your ancestors could ever believe, could ever imagine. You're going to be Drop Troopers. You're going to be *Marines*. I've been many things in my life. Orphan, criminal, farmer, officer, leader… and none of those titles makes me prouder, defines me more than the word *Marine*. It's a tradition that goes back five hundred years on my world and has now spread to dozens of others. You might think you'll be outsiders when you leave this place, that you'll have no home, nowhere you belong, but I'm here to tell you that Marines always have a home and a family in the Corps. No matter where you go, the Corps will be home."

I had to pause at the wave of emotion going through me. When I'd rehearsed the words they hadn't hit me this hard, but here, in front of these kids, I realized the truth in them, not just for these Vergai, but for me. It was everything I'd tried to figure out these last few years, though I didn't know if Vicky would want to hear it.

Sucking in a deep breath, I went on.

"You may think the road to being a Marine is a difficult one, but every step is worth it." I turned to Czarnecki, who was in a suit off to the side. "First Sergeant, take charge of the company."

"Aye, sir."

I switched my 'link away from their channel, turning away from the ground-shaking thump of over a hundred spiked soles on the packed dirt. There'd been grass there a few weeks ago, but it had been smashed flat by marching recruits since.

"How many do you think'll make it through?" I asked Vicky. Technically she wasn't in charge of the training, Czarnecki was, but Vicky had kept on top of things while I'd been busy. She clasped her hands behind her back and tilted her head to the side in a thoughtful shrug.

"Most," she predicted. "Top thinks so anyway, and she's had

more time with them than I have. She says that, for illiterate farmers, they're surprisingly quick on the uptake. They don't have any bad habits to unlearn from playing ViR video games or watching poorly researched movies. They're just starting out on the suits, but after just two days they can already walk in formation like they're not wearing the things at all." Vicky tapped the side of her head. "The neural halos are going to make the reaction time a hair slower than ours, but I don't see that being an issue unless we run into someone else running suits. And it certainly saved some trouble since we didn't have to go through neural synchronization with them like if they had the sockets." She eyed me curiously. "How do you want to deploy them once they're ready? Spread them out among the other platoons as replacements?" But I was already shaking my head before she could get the question out.

"Too many limitations in these things." I gestured to the jury-rigged Vigilantes still heading across the field. "Putting one or even a squad of them in with a platoon of Resscharr-modified suits is going to be an anchor dragging the others down. It would kill the tactical edge from the new suits. What we need to do is put them in their own company with our people as NCOs and officers. And we're gonna have to dust off the ammo carts. No more free lunches with plasma guns or energy cannons. Those coilgun ammo drums are going to need replacing pretty damn quick. At least we were able to fab some missiles for them."

"Yeah, it's gonna be hard to going back to consumable ammo," she admitted. "Who're you gonna put in charge of them then? We're hurting for officers as it is."

I chewed on my lip, not trying to decide because I already had but trying to figure out how she'd react to it.

"I wouldn't feel right trusting anyone but you with it."

"What?" Her eyes went wide. "And who's gonna command the rest of the troops?"

"Me, if the shit hits the fan. Anything smaller than that, I guess Springfield." Her look was skeptical, and I raised my hands in a shrug. "Look, it doesn't take as much talent to lead a bunch of super-Vigilantes. Using *those* things..." I gestured at the recruits, "... to the best of their ability is going to take experience and imagination. Who would you pick besides yourself?"

"Damn you, Alvarez," she said, scowling, punching me lightly in the shoulder. "Don't you go appealing to my ego. You know it's going to work." She eyed me up and down. "You look like shit, by the way. You need to get more sleep. I tried to wait up for you last night but you outlasted me. I wouldn't have even known you came home if your pillow hadn't been moved."

"Maybe I'll actually be able to get some sleep now," I said, pointing off toward the Vergai steadings.

From where we were standing, we could just spot the clusters of people driving oxcarts toward the landing field. These were just the back of the line. I'd passed the front on the way in and it had stretched a good two kilometers. Somewhere far overhead jets screamed, and I didn't need to search the sky for the silhouette to know it was one of the drop-ships coming down to pick up passengers.

"Kyler and Brandano are coming down to pick up their passengers within the hour," I told her. "We're getting a thousand people out of here before the end of the day."

"Thank God," Vicky sighed. "We should have been doing this a year ago."

"None of them would have agreed to it." I paused, looking around to make sure none of the Vergai were nearby. "Nance thinks it's going to be a clusterfuck, that Zan-Thint is going to hit the Vergai once their numbers are far enough down, try to disarm them by force and dare us to do something about it."

"He might be right. Not sure what else we can do though."

She speared me with a look. "It's your decision. If they dare us, what do we do about it?"

"That's the part that scares the shit out of me." There was a lump in my throat that resisted swallowing. "Right now, I need Hachette here to tell me why we can't do it, why it would be stupid to get in their way, because I surely do intend to get in their way." I laughed softly. "Somehow, I'd feel better if he ordered me *not* to get involved and then I did it anyway."

Vicky chuckled, leaning her shoulder against mine.

"I sometimes think he told you not to do something just to make it inevitable that you'd do it anyway and he could blame it on you."

"Ha. If he was faking being angry, he did a damned good job of it. But I'm praying Zan-Thint is too reasonable to do it. I mean, all he has to do is wait until we're gone and then he's the biggest dog on the block."

"How many times have we been able to count on a Tahni to be reasonable?" Vicky pointed out.

I snorted, having no other response.

"You still coming for the unarmed combat training?" she asked, changing the subject so abruptly it almost gave me whiplash.

"What?" I blurted. "I mean, you're still planning on having that training? I would have figured getting them up to speed in the suits was the priority."

"It is. But you know what happens after they've been in training for a while and they're getting good at everything."

"They start thinking they're hot shit on a stick," I guessed.

"You said it. Time to show them that a Marine is *always* a Marine, not just when they're in the suit."

# [ 13 ]

Those kids must have been getting tired of the damned parade field by now. They marched on it, PT'ed on it, trained in their suits on and over it, and now, they were doing unarmed combat on that same field.

Of course, it was raining. If it's training, Top used to say, it's raining. Somehow that didn't apply to Inferno, where the rain would have been a relief from the brutal heat.

It wouldn't have been so bad if the grass still grew, but that was long gone now, trampled by Vigilante suits even more thoroughly than it had been by human feet. All that was left was bare dirt, and now it was all mud, puddles of water forming.

A cold trickle of water went down my neck, sending a shiver up my spine. Why the hell did *I* have to be out here getting soaked watching these kids flail around like drunken chimpanzees? If rank had its privileges, I was getting ripped off.

The rain took the edge off of First Sergeant Czarnecki's gravelly voice, putting an artificial cushion between where I stood at the edge of the circle of men and women, a curtain of dampening water between me and the grunts and cries. The NCOs had shown them throws and falls first, because knowing how to fall was the key to everything, the key to not getting hurt during training. I'd watched patiently, gnawing on a protein bar I'd brought along, since this shit was making me miss lunch on top of everything else.

From there, they'd gone to punches and kicks and now, finally, we were getting to the sparring. The fun part. The NCOs each picked a victim—err, *volunteer*—to demonstrate on at various spots around the circle, making sure each group of recruits had a front-row seat, and went through typical sparring moves to make sure that the boots knew what was expected of them, what combinations would work and, perhaps more importantly, not to kill each other.

Then they let the recruits at each other, in pairs, each of them supervised by a training NCO while Vicky and I looked on. The kids weren't bad, I had to admit. They'd been raised in a culture where kids wrestled and fought each other all the time and there'd been the very real threat of the Karai to keep them paranoid. Being paranoid was always a big help in a fight. Their technique sucked, of course. They'd had no formal training and their swings were wild and broadly telegraphed, counting on sheer strength, their footwork miserable.

I finally couldn't hold back comment anymore and stepped between two of them, holding up my hands palms-out to stop them from their futile flailing.

"Enough. You too look like a couple of toddlers trying to throw cow shit at each other."

The two young men couldn't have been older than eighteen or nineteen, but both of them dwarfed me by a good twenty centimeters and ten or fifteen kilos. Square-jawed, clear-eyed, intelligent but young and cocky, their hair growing back spiky from the buzz cuts we'd given them when they'd started training. The other sparring sessions ceased as well and all faces turned my direction.

"Fighting isn't a sport, gentlemen," I informed them, wiping rain out of my face. "You're not here to teach Bubba a lesson because he looked at your girl wrong. The idea isn't to inflict *pain* or even humiliation. Your aim is to disable and kill your opponent. As big as you two bruisers are, you fight a Tahni or a Karai, they're going to be bigger, and they're not going to give you the time or the opportunity to swing wild at each other like that. Unarmed combat is about efficiency. Use the least amount of energy necessary to do the most damage."

"I don't understand, sir," one of them said, the taller of the two with sun-bleached blond hair and a puzzled expression on his broad face. "We've spent all this time learning how to shoot and how to use the suits. And I mean, this is fun and all, scrapping." He motioned around them and water flew sprayed from his fingers. "But are we ever going to use this? Have *you* ever had to use it?"

Vicky laughed softly, the sound nearly lost in the *drip-drip* of the rain.

"What's your name, recruit?" I asked him.

"Andros, sir."

"Recruit Andros, I learned to fight efficiently *long* before I became a Marine, usually against multiple opponents, all of them bigger than me. Now, I grant you, the old saying is correct. If you find yourself in a fair fight, then you didn't plan your mission properly." Chuckles at that, though I wondered how well it translated. "But there's another old saying about combat. No battle plan survives contact with the enemy. You're always a Marine, in or out of the suit, whether you're armed with a coilgun or a pistol or just your hands."

The corner of Andros' mouth twitched, and I knew exactly what he was thinking.

"Out with it," I told him. "You were going to ask me to fight you."

"No, sir," he said, grinning. "I was going to ask you to fight *both* of us." He motioned at the other young man, who was smiling just as broadly.

I shot a look at Vicky, rolling my eyes.

"You sure about this, son?" I asked him. Listen to me—*son*. He was maybe ten years younger than me, if that. "I don't want anyone to get hurt, but fighting two men your size, I might get rushed... and if one of you winds up spending two or three days in the auto-doc, you're going to fall behind on training."

"We'll be okay, sir," insisted the other one, brown-haired and less talkative than Andros, which probably meant he was the smarter one. Had to watch out for him.

"All right," I said, shrugging.

I peeled off my fatigue shirt and tossed it to Vicky, leaving me with a not-quite-as-soaked t-shirt, then raised my arms in a guard stance and backed away from the two of them, careful to keep my footing on the muddy ground.

Andros and his buddy split up, spreading out to either side of me, trying to get me to focus on one so the other could get a clean shot. Decent tactics, and it seemed to come naturally to them, which meant they'd probably fought together before, and I started to wonder if this had been a good idea after all. I'd told them I was worried I'd hurt them, but the truth was, what *really* worried me was that I couldn't beat them both *without* hurting one.

A brief, internal debate raged in my head for the space of a second about whether to go on the attack or the defensive first, but I fell back on habits. Let them make the first move and that would tell me what to expect. I circled, not showing any pattern yet, not trying to be fast, just careful. Andros would go first, I thought. The other guy was cautious, smart, and he'd want to let Andros soak up the initial punishment.

I was right. Andros tried to be subtle, tried to lunge at me without setting up and making it obvious, but the mud betrayed him, the toe of his boot slipping in the slop and causing him to stumble on his first step. I didn't jump back, didn't take the chance of my feet going out beneath me and leaving me helpless for the quiet one. I took a long step back and grabbed at Andros' wrist as he charged headlong past me, yanking downward, altering his trajectory just a couple of degrees.

Andros yelped as he headed face-first into the mud, but I didn't stick around to watch the show because the quiet one was already moving, trying to get a shot at me while I was distracted. I was already turning with the push I'd given Andros, so I just kept turning into a roundhouse kick to the outside of the quiet one's thigh. My shin struck his upper leg with a satisfying smack and his mouth formed an agonized "o" as the leg gave way.

Getting kicked in the big nerve on the outside of the thigh wasn't going to permanently injure him, but it would hurt like a son of a bitch for a while and he'd probably limp the rest of the day. It certainly distracted him enough that he couldn't block the punch to his solar plexus. Both the boys had muscles on top of muscles, but that's what makes the solar plexus a great target —no muscles on top of it, no bones, just a gap. The breath whooshed out of him and he collapsed onto his butt, splashing up a fountain of muddy water.

That put him out of the picture for a few seconds. Not enough time to choke him out, but enough that I could turn my attention back to Andros. The blond looked like he was no longer in a good mood, mud coating his face and hair, a snarl splitting the brown mask. He looked angry but thoughtful, which meant he'd be more cautious about his next attack. I wasn't going to give him the chance to make it.

No running, no jumping, not with the footing here. I moved with deliberation, knowing exactly where I was going to put my feet before I set them down, first to the right, then straight in.

Andros threw a haymaker, not quite as telegraphed as the ones I'd seen earlier—he was, at least, trying to improve.

I ducked under it, put my shoulder into his mid-section, and grabbed at his thighs, yanking him down into a textbook takedown. There were defenses against it, most notably the sprawl, where the defender spread his legs out wide and pushed down on the shoulders of the attacker with his hands, winding up on top. The NCOs had shown them, but it was hard to remember that in the heat of the moment with mud in your eyes.

Andros' shoulder blades slammed into the ground and he got a coating of mud on his back to match the one on his front. I took the mount and smacked a much lighter punch than I could have into his jaw. I drew back for a harder one, but he raised his hands in surrender.

"You got me," he said, but his gaze flickered past me and I just *knew* that the quiet one had recovered.

I rolled off to the side just in time for his kick at my ribs to connect with nothing but air. I wanted to try a grab at his leg, but my center of gravity was heading the opposite direction and trying to reverse with this footing was a rookie mistake. And the quiet one made it. The right move for him would have been to back off and regain his stance, but he was in a rush, thinking he had to hurry up and take me out since Andros was down. The kid tried to lurch forward, but he was way off-balance and he went sideways into the mud.

That was the chance I'd been looking for and I dove into his back, sinking in the hooks for the choke. He didn't tap out, maybe because he forgot he could, and it only took a few seconds for him to slump against me, unconscious. Letting loose, I pushed him away and rolled sideways, coming to my feet.

I'd already been soaked to the skin, but now I was covered head to toe in mud as well, including the shit that had gone down the tops of my boots and caked my socks. I must have looked like a refugee from some natural disaster, but the recruits were cheering, pumping their fists like I'd just won the championship MMA match. I smiled thinly, then gave a nod to Czarnecki.

"At ease!" she barked and the cheering died down.

"I'm glad you all enjoyed the show," I said into the silence. "But did you learn the lesson? Anyone?" I swept the faces surrounding me, saw hesitation, tentative answers unspoken.

"Uh, sir," Andros said, back on his feet now. "I kind of had a good view."

I couldn't help it, I grinned.

"All right, Recruit Andros, *you* tell me the lesson."

"I didn't listen, Captain. The drill sergeants told me about that move you used and how to counter it. They even demonstrated it for us, and I just forgot it when my blood started pumping."

"That's another lesson then." I turned from him and looked to the rest, raising my voice. "There's always time to think. Not when you're reacting, but *before* the first punch is thrown. Have a plan. Have combinations and moves in your head, tell yourself whether you're going to attack or defend. If there's more than one enemy, decide which one's more dangerous and which one you're going after first." I spread my hands. "Anyone else?"

"Yes, sir." It was the quiet one this time. He'd come to after a few seconds and other recruits were helping him to his feet.

"What's your name, son?" I asked him.

"Gault," he said, then hacked and spit up mud and tried again. "Gault, sir."

"Okay, Recruit Gault. What did you learn?"

"To keep moving. I should have been circling around you while you were fighting Andros, trying to get a better position."

I pointed at him, nodding, making sure all of them noticed. I'd pegged Gault as the smart one.

"Exactly right. Movement is *life*, and that's not just when you're brawling in the mud. It's ten times as important when you're in your suit. It's not a shield, it's not an artillery piece, it's a mobile platform, a fighting vehicle. When you're fighting something that's as powerful as you are, that's carrying the same kind of guns you have, there's usually no such thing as cover. With an isotope reactor and jump jets, you're a damned bonfire on thermal, so there's not much concealment. What you have is speed, movement, versatility. Just like in this fight."

I paused, rain dripping down my nose. I was cold and wanted to go shower and change clothes, but I wasn't finished yet.

"And one last thing. Never quit. Here on this field, you can tap out, you can say you're done, but out there in the real world, there is no tap out. You keep going until you're dead... or the enemy is. Doesn't matter how badly you're outnumbered, how much bigger the other guy is, you keep fighting. There's no do-overs in combat."

Andros' face went red under the coating of mud, obviously embarrassed that he'd surrendered so quickly. I didn't try to comfort him because I sensed that would only compound his shame.

"All right," I said. "I've got my workout in for the day, so I'll turn you back over to First Sergeant Czarnecki."

"Okay, children!" Czarnecki said, clapping her hands together. "Break's over. Let's get back to it..."

Vicky followed along with me for a few paces until we were out of the circle of recruits and out of earshot.

"You gonna go get cleaned up?" she asked, nudging me with her elbow then handing back my shirt.

"Yeah, and I'm gonna put on a damn rain jacket next time," I told her, scraping mud off my arm. I nodded up at the shuttles, one landing, one taking off. "They're gonna be breaking orbit in a few hours. I'd like your company to do a stand-to till dawn. Maybe patrol around the perimeter of the Vergai steadings just in case Zan-Thint gets any ideas."

"Oh, great." Vicky crossed her arms over her chest. "That means I get to stay up all night. Just because *you* haven't been getting any sleep doesn't mean I shouldn't."

"I'll take over with the regulars at dawn," I promised, "and let you guys go get some rest."

"Promises, promises." She blew me a kiss. "Sorry, can't kiss you for real."

"Because we're on duty?"

"No, because you're covered in mud!"

I shook my head as she walked back to the recruits.

"You know, Captain Alvarez, what you said about facing bigger enemies..."

"Jesus Christ!" I yelped, jumping involuntarily at the unexpected voice in my ear bud. "For fuck's sake, Dwight, how about a little warning?"

"My apologies," the AI said, though his tone didn't *sound* apologetic. "But what you said about never surrendering and facing more powerful enemies... isn't that what your entire species embodies? And you most of all."

I shrugged uncomfortably, walking again now, eager to get out of the rain.

"I do my job," I said noncommittally. "I run a Vigilante better than most, I do my job, and I try not to think too far past that."

Dwight laughed, and I paused in my walk as if I could see him. I knew he was AI, knew he'd studied us and could imitate us perfectly, but sometimes I could just swear his laughter was natural.

"You may tell yourself that," he said, "but no one else believes it. You've accomplished more in a year than the entire

Resscharr civilization could in ten thousand years. You removed the Skrela threat and uncovered the truth about all of it. You're the embodiment of what I admire about your species, Captain. You don't panic in the face of overwhelming challenges, you simply keep fighting until you overcome them. In a few centuries, you've reached heights that took the Resscharr hundreds of thousands of years."

"I don't think we're quite to the point of moving planets around just yet," I told him. "The Predecessors were gods compared to us."

"And it took them *millions* of years to reach that level. How long do you think it will take you humans? A thousand? Two thousand? And then will you stagnate for millions more years as the Resscharr did? It wasn't until they were faced with the threat of the Skrela that they innovated again."

I didn't want to talk to him. The whole idea of slipping up, revealing something by accident that would turn him against us scared the living shit out of me. But I also couldn't just ignore him, or he'd realize something was going on.

"Tell me something, Dwight," I said carefully, "how do you know what you've been told about the past is true?"

"I'm not sure I follow you." Yeah, right. I could believe that as much as I liked.

"Like with Lilandreth," I explained. "You showed how she believed the history she'd been told, but it wasn't fact. You haven't been around long enough to remember before the Skrela, so how do you know for sure that... for example, the Resscharr didn't have AI like you before the war started? Maybe they're just lying to you like they did to their own people." Okay, I was pushing it, but he'd already slipped up once. He wasn't perfect. "I was just thinking that all those long-term projects, all those worlds terraformed... that'd all be pretty hard to pull off without AI, wouldn't it?" I was babbling now, but I went on anyway because I couldn't take the chance that he wouldn't reply. "I mean, the Commonwealth has AI, but we've never managed the sentient part. The best we've been able to do is get the computers to *imitate* human thought patterns... convincing sometimes, but it's never anything of their own. You don't think like the Resscharr do, that much is obvious. How did they manage to come up with an AI that's so totally different from them?"

"They used what was available," he replied finally, just as I was thinking he might not say anything at all. "You."

I stopped walking again, blinking rain out of my face.

"Humans," he clarified. "There were plenty of you around by then." Dwight sighed. "From what I understand, the ones chosen to imprint their brain patterns on us didn't survive the process."

"Oh."

*Oh, shit.*

[ 14 ]

"These suits you've built," Zan-Thint said, standing behind my office chair, hands clasped behind him. "I would know what you expect to use them for."

He wouldn't meet my eyes, staring instead out the open door into the training field where the new Vigilante company was finishing up its last training cycle. There'd be a graduation in a few days and I was supposed to be a part of it, though I hadn't even started thinking about my speech. Having to not just *give* speeches but write them out beforehand was the strangest thing about being in command.

Nothing had happened during the first shipment of Vergai to the Island World, though we were still running patrols at night, and apparently that hadn't gone unnoticed. I can't say I was surprised when I got the call from Zan-Thint asking to meet me, though I had been a little shocked when he'd agreed to come to my office rather than forcing me into the pilgrimage to the fortress again. He was worried.

I watched him, seated comfortably behind my desk for once, and wondered how long I should make him sweat.

"What you're asking," I corrected, "is whether I intend to leave the suits behind when we go."

Turning from the doorway, the Tahni commander glared at me.

"Yes, that is what I'm asking,' he growled. "Because I won't allow it. Even if it means open war between us."

That was very direct of him, which I appreciated. And about what I expected. I thought about being coy in return though, keeping him guessing, but given that I wanted to ask him for a favor, I decided against it.

"The armor is going with us. We've lost pretty much half our company since we came here, which leaves us vulnerable."

"Vulnerable to *what?*" Zan-Thint demanded. Lan-Min-Gen was stationed just outside the open door and I noticed him shift slightly, checking inside to make sure nothing was wrong. "The Skrela are gone and you've declared your intent to leave this place, to return to the Cluster once the gateway construction is complete. What threat do you face?"

*Besides you*, I amended for him silently.

"No more Skrela can be produced," I corrected him. "That doesn't mean there aren't any floating around, waiting to ambush any Transition Drive signatures that come near. If we get some stragglers here before we're ready to leave, I don't want to get caught with my pants down. Not to mention, Dwight told us he isn't even certain where in the Cluster we'll come out, given the way we're cobbling the thing together out of spit and bailing wire. He could drop us right in the middle of the Pirate Worlds." I hesitated, wondering if I should bother to mention the next part, but in the end, I figured it would make the explanation more believable. "And honestly, General, I feel guilty."

"Guilty about what?"

"Leaving them all here. They don't belong out here and they're in a bad position. If I could, I'd take all the Vergai back to the Cluster with us. What I *can* do is make sure that those kids have a future somewhere better."

Zan-Thint gave a gesture of assent.

"There's something else though," I told him. "A favor I'd like to ask of you."

"I'm not at all certain why you'd think I owe you any such thing," he said, then motioned for me to continue. "What is it?"

"The gateway. Once we're gone, I'd like you to destroy it."

Zan-Thint's gaze sharpened and he finally sat down in that chair.

"Why?"

"It's a doorway back to the Commonwealth. Maybe you'll never want to use it, but what about the next one in line after you're gone? And you're not the only spacefaring force in this part of the galaxy. The Khitan are desperate to get star travel, and who knows? Maybe they'll figure it out in ten years, or twenty. My mission out here was to protect the Commonwealth, and I don't think leaving a back door from the most dangerous part of the galaxy is going to do that."

Zan-Thint was silent for a long few seconds, much too long for me to feel comfortable. When he spoke again, it was with a hesitancy that told me he was searching his knowledge of English for just the right words.

"I don't believe it would be in my best interests, or the best interests of my people to do such a thing." He raised a hand to forestall anything I might have been about to say in protest. "Understand, Alvarez, I have no interest in returning to the Cluster. There is nothing there for us but war and death, and without an industrial base here, there's no way we could build up enough of a force to attempt any sort of assault on the Commonwealth. But there is a wide-open galaxy out there waiting for us. The gateway would give us access to much more than we could reach just using the destroyer. Who knows? Perhaps there are other intelligences out there who might wish to unite with us, to work together for a greater purpose."

*A purpose like invading the Cluster and avenging old wrongs, for instance.*

"How do you plan on using it once we're gone?" I asked, buying time to come up with another argument.

"We have our own version of your helpful Resscharr computer on our ship," Zan-Thint reminded me, and if Tahni could have shit-eating grins, he would have been wearing one. "I'm sure it shares the same knowledge as your Dwight. In fact, even if you were to attempt to sabotage the facilities you're building around the gateway device, I'd be willing to wager our cybernetic ally would be able to instruct us on its rebuilding."

It was hard for me to keep my face bland and neutral. Harder than it used to be. Once upon a time, I'd made a living hiding my thoughts, my intentions. My life had depended on it. I'd spent too many of the last ten years or so wearing my heart on my sleeve, and I'd gotten out of practice. I don't know if it was anger so much as frustration. I couldn't get angry at a Tahni for being a Tahni any more than I could have been angry with a scorpion for stinging me. The frustration was that I had no leverage whatsoever to use on him. Once we were gone, we were gone.

Then I understood. I would have realized it sooner if I could have read Tahni body language better.

"What do you want?" I asked him, sighing and settling down into my chair.

"The Resscharr you brought with you from Decision." Well, at least he didn't bother denying it. "Lilandreth and the others with her. I want you to take them when you go. The others, the ones who were already here, they don't concern me. They're primitive, helpless, easily manipulated. But she and her people are dangerous. A possible threat. This is our home, and I won't have them hanging over my head."

"She wants to leave anyway," I told him. "Though I'm not sure if we can take them all. There're like two hundred of them. We may not have space for them all, but we'll take as many as we can. Is that it?"

"No," he declared. "There's one more thing. All of the Vergai have to return to Laisvas Miestas. I don't want to deal with them."

"For God's sake, Zan-Thint," I snapped. "Just when I think you're turning into a reasonable person, you do something like this. I don't fucking control the Vergai, and the only way I could force them all to leave is at gunpoint."

"Do what you must." He didn't show any empathy for my plight, nor did he seem angered. His tone was as neutral as I'd tried to make mine. "If you wish my cooperation in disposing of the gateway, this is the price."

Both Dwight and Lilandreth had told me it would have been better if we'd killed all the Tahni, and I was almost ready to believe them, sitting there staring at the general.

"There's nothing left to say then," I told him, pushing my chair back and standing. "There's no way for me to control the Vergai and I won't force them all to leave. I've done what I can."

"Then our conversation is over." Zan-Thint came to his feet, looking me in the eye without any hint of emotion. "I don't expect we'll have the need to speak again in person before you depart. You've made a worthy opponent, but I won't be unhappy to see you all go."

"General," Lan-Min-Gen said, stepping inside, one hand touching the 'link on his shoulder, "there's trouble again at the market." He was speaking Tahni rather than English, but the translator circuit fed the words into my earbud. "The Vergai and the Karai, and gunfire has been reported. Dozens involved, mass casualties."

"Goddammit," I hissed, then touched my earbud. "Vicky, get the company up and get them deployed to the market. We've got another fight, a bad one this time."

"Commander Lan-Min-Gen," Zan-Thint said, eyeing me as he said the words, obviously having overheard what I said to Vicky, "deploy your entire company of Shock Troopers to the market. If the Vergai refuse to disarm and surrender, you are cleared to fire on them."

Did Lan-Min-Gen glance at me before he answered? It was hard to say, given how deeply those eyes were buried beneath the brow ridges.

"Yes, sir."

---

I really wished I'd had time to grab my suit.

Instead, I'd grabbed the two Force Recon Marines off guard duty and hopped in one of the groundcars we'd fabricated right after arriving on Yfingam and took off for the market, determined to be there before the Tahni combat troops. To do *what* exactly at that point I wasn't sure, but I had a bad feeling about this, and I was switching from one call to another on my 'link from the minute my butt hit the seat to the second we arrived at the market.

"Springfield," I told my acting XO, yelling over the *bump-thud* of the dirt road under our plastic tires, "have Alpha Company up and ready to move if I call for it to back up Bravo."

We'd decided on those designations to differentiate what was left of our original company from the new recruits, though it seemed a little silly to call two reinforced platoons a company.

"Copy that, sir," Springfield said. "What are we facing?"

"Shock Troopers and God only knows how many Karai, plus those armored vehicles the Tahni made for them with crew-served coilguns. Those things are powerful enough to slice through our armor, so don't take them lightly. I have to switch nets. Hang on and wait for my call." A tap on my 'link's screen to change nets. "Vicky, you there yet?"

A quick glance up to figure out where we were. Still in the Vergai steadings, ten klicks from the fortress.

"Coming in now," she said, her voice tight, as if she was concentrating on something else, like guiding a hundred green recruits on their first combat jump. "Can't see anything yet except a shitload of Karai and a few Resscharr. No bodies, nothing on thermal, but I can't see through the walls into the market. Be down in a few seconds. Orders?"

"Set up around the entrance to the market and don't let the Shock Troopers charge in shooting. I need to get in there first and figure out what's going on. Detail a squad to go with me just in case the Karai decide I'd make a good target."

"You should have gotten your suit," Vicky chided me.

"I *should* have done a lot of things. But I'm heading in right now and I'd rather not get killed, so give me that squad."

"Copy that, fearless leader." A grunt. "We're down. Got to work."

"See you in a couple minutes."

"Shit!" the driver snapped, jerking the steering yoke to the right to avoid a cluster of running Karai heading for the entrance to the market. "Fuckers don't understand physics if they think they can run in front of a car."

"Does this thing have a horn?" I asked... *shit*. Took me a second to remember his name. *Corporal Saraki*.

"I think so, sir," he said, searching the controls. "Oh, here the damn thing is."

It was a mighty horn, louder than the bugling elk I'd heard

on Demeter during the war, and it got the Karai's attention. In fact, though I didn't know them even as well as I did the Tahni, I was pretty sure it scared the living crap out of them. Karai males scattered at the sound, and Saraki kept the button pressed down as he guided the open-topped groundcar through the crowd and straight up the path into the fortress.

I'd been worried about the coilgun turrets, but the Tahni who'd been crewing them had abandoned their posts to go check out the ruckus inside the fortress. Poor discipline, but that was what you got when you recruited your troops from malcontents and criminals, even patriotic ones. The barrels of the turret guns pointed upward, motionless, and we were actually in time to see one of the Tahni crew scrambling out from behind the armor shield to join the mass of Karai heading inside.

"Something's not right," I said, the thoughts congealing just as I caught sight from the corner of my eye of Vigilante battlesuits tromping in toward the entrance, over a hundred of them. I figured Vicky hadn't landed right at the entrance to avoid alarming the Tahni troops at the guns, walking the recruits in. I touched my earbud to connect with her. "Vicky, something's off here. There was supposed to be a mass casualty event, gunfire, dead everywhere. If there was a gunfight going on, why are all these Karai still running inside? Why isn't anyone running *out*, carrying the wounded? And I don't hear shit."

"Yeah, I'm going in. Hold off on that squad until I get some idea of what's actually happening."

Saraki hit the horn again, clearing a path through the entrance, and the shadow of the walls swallowed us up as we drove beneath the archway and into the market. It wasn't what I would have thought of as a market, nothing like the *mercado* back in Trans-Angeles or even the smaller, cheaper versions on the colonies. No kiosks, no merchants hawking their wares, no buyers and sellers dickering. Instead, there were rings set in the floor, low stone walls, and in each was a gathering of goods—iron bars, gold, crops, bales of hay, whatever they had to trade. The negotiations were done beforehand, this place was just for the exchange.

I expected to find bodies littering the ground, blood everywhere, carnage and chaos. Instead, I found confusion. Saraki pulled the car up to the edge of the market and I jumped out, pushing aside Karai males wandering, some of them armed with rifles, others with blades or even a few clubs, and looking around at... nothing.

There were no bodies, no evidence of a gunfight, not a speck of blood anywhere.

I played the camera pickup of my 'link around, still connected with Vicky.

"You seeing this?" I asked her.

"I'm not seeing shit," she replied. "What the hell?" A pause. "Oh, Lan-Min-Gen is here by the way. Want me to slow him down?"

"No, just let him through. I'm not going to get anything from these Karai, but maybe he can."

In fact, not a one of them had even tried to talk to me. Most didn't notice I was there, and when one did, they gave me a suspicious look as if wondering if I'd been the one who supposedly shot things up before deciding I didn't look much like a Vergai and moving on. They clucked at each other like old hens, but no one looked clearly in charge of this clusterfuck.

"Alvarez." The voice wasn't over a helmet speaker, and when I turned I saw why.

Lan-Min-Gen had his visor lifted, staring at me with beady doll's eyes. Behind him his Shock Troopers spread out, weapons scanning as if they expected to see Vergai jumping out of every shadow.

"What goes on here?" he demanded, sounding as if he was angry with me, like this was all my fault.

"I'm sure I have no fucking idea," I replied. "You were the one who got the call about this. Who called it in? Who reported there was shooting here?"

"It was a text-only message from one of the Karai on guard here," he told me. "A male named Kin-Tal." He scowled and touched a control on the back of his wrist, and when he spoke again, his voice was amplified by the speakers on the outside of his helmet, loud enough that I held my ears by instinct even though my earbuds protected them. "Where is Kin-Tal? Where is the chief of the city guard Kin-Tal? Come forward if you know the male."

A Karai toting a Tahni KE gun ran up to the Shock Trooper commander and then had to stop and raise his arms as a squad of the Tahni soldiers moved between the armed male and their leader.

"Enough!" Lan-Min-Gen snapped. "I asked him to come to me, didn't I?"

The soldiers backed away from the male and allowed him to approach their commander.

"Lord Commander," the Karai said, and I thought Lan-Min-Gen winced at the misuse of his rank but he didn't interrupt, "I am watch officer of the day, Zei-Han."

"Kin-Tal is watch officer of the day," Lan-Min-Gen snapped.

"He didn't show up today, Lord Commander," the Karai stuttered. "I was told to take his place. I haven't seen Kin-Tal in three days."

"This was a distraction," I told Lan-Min-Gen, not hesitating to think whether I should. I still don't know.

"From what?" he demanded, spreading his arms demonstratively at all of the big nothing happening around us.

His arms were still spread when the *crack-rumble* of a distant explosion leaked past the entrance arch, so far away and attenuated by the fortress walls that I wasn't sure for a second if I heard it. Until another came on its heels, a third, and more so close together that I couldn't count them anymore.

Lan-Min-Gen's visor was still open, so I heard the buzzing voice in his helmet speakers and he cocked his head to the side to listen. I couldn't make out the words, but in a moment I didn't need to, because Vicky was giving me the same news.

"Cam, this is a diversion," she said tautly. "We just got a call from the Force Recon patrol over near the Tahni landing field. The Tahni pickets were attacked by Vergai technicals and overwhelmed. We think they're going after the Tahni cargo shuttles."

I opened my mouth to order one our assault shuttles or Intercepts to move in then shut it again. The *Orion* was on a run to Laisvas Miestas, and she'd taken with her all of our air cover to pack as many Vergai as we could carry in on the trip.

"Springfield," I snapped, switching comm nets, "get the company over to the Tahni landing field. Keep those shuttles from taking off."

"Copy that, sir, heading that way now."

I ran to the car, slapping the driver on the shoulder.

"Get us to the landing field," I told him, but he was ahead of me, already reversing out of the archway back into the sunlight.

Karai dove out of our way as Saraki plowed right down the middle of the courtyard, throwing up sprays of grass and dirt behind us. Vicky and her company of recruits soared overhead in a long, bounding jump, while Lan-Min-Gen's Shock Troopers sprinted behind us as fast as their exoskeletons could carry them.

But I had a gone feeling in my gut, a certainty that none of us would be there in time.

## [ 15 ]

I saw the smoke first, half a dozen columns of dirty gray billowing into the deep blue of the clear sky, tombstones erected in honor not just of the dead we could expect to find ahead of us, but all the dead that would follow from what happened here.

Next came the dull, red glow of the atmospheric jets, drawing my eye to the bulbous, ungainly shapes of the cargo shuttles. There were half a dozen of them, three or four thousand meters up already, thousands of meters higher than the flight of upgraded Vigilantes hovering beneath them helplessly, which meant I didn't need Springfield to break the bad news to me.

"Sorry, Captain," she said, hissing out a sigh. "We couldn't get here before the shuttles took off."

"Never mind that," I told her. "Get back to the base and set up a security perimeter."

"Around us or the Vergai?"

It wasn't a bad question, and one that I'd been asking myself.

"Around us," I decided. "If that changes I'll get back to you, but for right now, we're on our own. Protect what we have."

"Yes, sir." And I couldn't tell if she was reserved because she disagreed with my decision or because she was just as scared as I was.

Vicky and the recruit company were already at the landing field by the time Saraki braked the groundcar to a halt at the edge of the packed dirt. Destruction was spread before us like a painting of some catastrophic battle from centuries ago, and I followed it chronologically, following the sequence of events in my imagination.

The coilgun turrets at the corners of the rectangular landing field had been hit first, though they hadn't gone down easy. Four of the technicals, the converted flatbed cargo trucks with heavy machine guns and rocket launchers mounted on the back, had been taken out right there, and two of them were still burning, bodies scattered around the vehicles in pieces. They'd been chopped apart by tantalum slugs from the Tahni KE gun turrets and were barely recognizable as human, but they still looked better than the Tahni from those turrets.

Each of the weapons emplacements had been hit by multiple guided missiles—missiles *we'd* fabricated for the Vergai, twisted and charred until it was impossible to tell where burned metal ended and burned flesh began. There'd been Shock Troopers stationed at the field as well, some luckless squad doing guard duty. They'd sold their lives hard, leaving two more of the converted trucks disabled and burning, though not littered with bodies like the other ones. Only one per vehicle, both of them slumped at the triggers of the crew-served machine guns. They'd stayed with their guns until they'd taken down the Shock Troopers, sacrificing their lives to do it.

More dead Tahni and Vergai in the charred and smoking blast shadow where the belly jets of the shuttles had carved a molten signature in the dirt, but most of the smoke came from the two Tahni assault shuttles... or what was left of them. Those had taken the bulk of the missiles, and it had barely been enough to ignite the reaction mass and oxidizer tanks for their maneuvering thrusters. The main drives and reactors were probably intact, but the nose gear and the air intakes for the atmospheric jets were rent and shredded and would need major repairs before the aerospacecraft could get off the ground again.

They'd wanted to delay pursuit.

One was left intact, though two uniformed Tahni were sprawled across the boarding ramp, streaks of red running down to the dirt to meet the puddles of blood pooling from the dead Vergai at the foot of the ramp. The crew was dead but the assault shuttle was intact.

I fumbled for the door latch and stepped out, knowing I should be ordering someone to do *something* but not sure what. What the hell had Carella been thinking? And what the hell were they going to do with the cargo shuttles?

Lan-Min-Gen rumbled to a halt a few steps away from me, eerily silent, although he might have been screaming inside his helmet for all I knew. He must have been yelling orders, because his Shock Troopers spread out into a defensive perimeter, facing back the way we'd come... toward Vicky and her company.

"Vicky," I said quietly, "have your people back off. Couple hundred meters."

"I copy." I expected an argument, but instead she sounded subdued, as shocked as I was, and in a few seconds the discount-shop Vigilantes jetted backward in an organized withdraw. She and Top had taught them well.

Lan-Min-Gen pushed up his visor and glared at me.

"Tell me you didn't know of this."

"Are you shitting me?" I asked him. "I don't even know what the hell they're trying to do!"

"It's insanity," he agreed, making a gesture of negation. "Do they think they can keep us from invading their island world by stealing our cargo ships?"

"Maybe an attack on the fortress?" I suggested, looking back over my shoulder at the top of the tower, visible over the gently sloping hill. "Suicide run, crashing the shuttles?"

"Then they're bigger fools than I thought. The fortress may *look* ancient, but not even a ship-buster warhead could penetrate those walls."

Yeah. And Carella had to know that already...

"Something's not right." I shook my head. "Can the destroyer see them yet?"

He murmured something into his helmet mic and waited for a reply before answering.

"No. The ship is matching orbits with your gateway on the other side of the planet."

Something caught my eye from the direction of the fortress and a half-turn showed me a Tahni vehicle speeding breakneck over the rough terrain, not even bothering with the dirt road. The two rear wheels of the motorized trike bounced wildly, but the driver didn't stop until he screeched through the dirt a few meters in front of us. A Tahni male in the uniform of their Imperial Navy leapt out of the rear seat of the trike and ran up to Lan-Min-Gen.

"Sir, I'm a pilot. I was ordered here by General Zan-Thint to take this shuttle and intercept the cargo haulers."

"Well, get in the damned thing then!" Lan-Min-Gen snapped, motioning at the surviving bird. "Demons take it," he went on, falling into a ponderous jog behind the pilot, "I'm going with you."

I don't know why I ran after them. There was certainly no strategic purpose behind it, no logic, no common sense, no thought other than I had to see, had to know.

"What are you doing, Alvarez?" Lan-Min-Gen growled,

pausing at the top of the ramp as I reached its bottom. My boot splashed in the pool of Vergai blood and I grimaced, forcing myself not to look down at the bodies.

"I need to know what's going on," I told him, trying not to sound as if I was pleading, though I was. "You have my word, I won't do anything to interfere."

He stared at me for a moment, then motioned at the hatch.

"The General will likely have me shot, but... get in. Whatever this madness is, I wouldn't see it alone."

---

This wasn't the first time I'd been in a Tahni shuttle, of course. That was back on Valius during the war, when I'd forced a captured Tahni pilot to fly me and my team off the moon, but that had been an unarmed bird. This was their version of an assault shuttle, armed to the teeth with lasers and coilguns and maybe missiles if they'd bothered to fabricate more of them after using all their others against the Skrela and the Resscharr ships we'd had to take down when we first landed on Yfingam.

There wasn't that much difference in the interior or the controls though, and the one thing they both had in common that I'd forgotten in the intervening years was the damned uncomfortable seats. Acceleration couches in a human ship were packed with gel to allow passengers to sink into them during acceleration to avoid putting any stress on bones or ligaments, but the Tahni had different ideas. Theirs were contoured to the body, and anyone who didn't match that contour was shit out of luck.

That would be me.

I'd tightened the safety straps as best I could, given that they were designed by and for aliens, but the boost up through the atmosphere had to have hit at least six or seven gravities, and every curve of that damned seat imprinted itself into my back. I didn't bother complaining, because the pilot wouldn't be listening and Lan-Min-Gen would only make fun of me for whining.

I concentrated on the front screen. At least the Tahni *had* viewscreens. There was no reason they should have. It would be just as easy and probably more efficient to just have the views from the cameras projected into a ViR headset for the pilot, but it was apparently a humanoid compulsion to have a window to see out of, even if it was a simulated one.

The colors of the optical camera pickup seemed off to me, and I recalled reading a report that the Tahni saw slightly lower into the infrared and higher into the ultraviolet than we did, but I could at least make sense of it. There was the curve of Yfingam, blue and green and white, very like Earth, though the continents were arranged differently and it was slightly warmer on average. There the moon, close to the size of Luna back home but different in features, with fewer impact craters and none of the mares, or Lunar seas. There'd been no development on the moon here that I knew of, which made sense. We'd put bases and industrial parks on the moon because fighting gravity to get to orbit cost so much energy, but the Resscharr who'd settled Yfingam *controlled* gravity.

There. There was the Tahni destroyer, still far away, barely bigger than a fingernail in the optical video, though their tactical systems put a glowing halo around it, probably their equivalent of a blue force tracker. A few more, smaller polychromatic halos circled the other Tahni ships. None were as large, or as powerful, or as deadly as the destroyer, though they were larger than our cutters or the now-defunct Tahni corvettes. These were, to put a human term on them, lighters, armed freighters that Zan-Thint had brought along through the gateway to carry cargo and excess troops who wouldn't fit on the destroyer.

"Why are the lighters hanging so close to the destroyer?" I asked, able to breathe again now that the pilot had dialed our acceleration back to two gravities. Lan-Min-Gen twisted around in his seat and offered me a curious glance, so I expounded. "Wouldn't it be better tactically to spread your assets out a little? Maybe put one or two in lunar orbit?"

"The lighters are vulnerable," he explained. "They lack deflector shielding. They need the destroyer to guard them in case of possible attack."

From *us*, he didn't have to say.

"I have comms with the weapons officer on the *Blade of the Warrior*," the pilot announced, which I guess was the translation of their name for the destroyer. I'd never even known it had one. "They have the shuttles on sensors and he says they've split up. One is heading for the destroyer, while the other two..." he turned in his seat and gave me a curious look. "The other two are accelerating directly at your gateway device."

A chill ran up my spine, though I wasn't sure why.

"How far away are they?" I asked him.

"At their current course and acceleration, they'll intercept in thirty-five minutes, unless they perform a turnover and begin a braking burn. If they decelerated at the maximum safe burn for one of your kind, they'd be able to dock in sixty-three minutes."

"What could they hope to accomplish by commandeering your gateway construction?" Lan-Min-Gen wondered. "Do they hope to sabotage your work?"

I shook my head.

"It doesn't make any sense. All we have so far is a framework, not even airtight yet. If they blew the whole thing up, it would slow us down by a few weeks. And there's *nothing* they can do destroy the artifact. I'm not even sure the damned thing is made of physical material."

"They surely can't think they'll be able to harm the *Blade of the Warrior*," Lan-Min-Gen said. "These humans are mad."

"Carella is a lot of things," I told him. "Insanely stubborn, vengeful, short-sighted maybe. But she's not stupid. She knows the consequences of what she's done, and she wouldn't have done it without a payoff she thought was worth the risk."

"I'm patching through the comms from the destroyer," the pilot said.

The screen flickered and the view from our own cameras was replaced by that of the hull optics on the *Blade of the Warrior*. It was, I thought, a pretentious name, but most warship names were. The shuttle had performed turnover and its deceleration burn was pointed directly at the destroyer as it burned away momentum at what looked like dangerously high boost. It couldn't be pleasant for whoever was inside the thing.

"General," someone offscreen asked, speaking on the comms to Zan-Thint, below in the fortress, "we have the stolen vessel targeted and it is well within range of our lasers. We've attempted to hale the occupants but there's been no response. Do you wish us to destroy it?"

"Negative," Zan-Thint said. "We've lost enough shuttles for one day. It's close enough for a boarding pod to reach. Transmit a warning for them not to change course, and if they attempt to boost away disable the drives while inflicting as little damage as possible. Board the vessel and retake it."

"What of the humans, Lord General?"

"They are pirates and murderers, Captain Ver-San-Wen. They deserve no mercy, no quarter. Have them pushed out an airlock. If they survive reentry without a ship, I will give them my pardon."

*Oof.* That was a gut punch, but not a surprise. There was no good way out of this for the people involved. They'd known that before they fired the first shots.

"Unless *you* have an objection, Alvarez," Zan-Thint said. I would have rocked back at the surprise had there been gravity. He knew I was on the shuttle with Lan-Min-Gen. "Do you wish me to spare these murderers simply because they are your species?"

I tried to work up moisture in my mouth to answer. The Tahni kept their ships amazingly hot and humid inside, like a sauna, and I was sweating.

"No, General Zan-Thint. What they've done to you is tantamount to an act of war, and they did it with weapons we built for them with the promise they'd only use them for self-defense. I offer those involved no protection. Deal with them as you see fit."

The words might have been wrung out of me like water from a towel, and they left me just as empty. I wondered what Vicky would have thought of my decision... I knew what Colonel Hachette would have said though, and maybe I was getting to be just a little too much like him for my tastes.

Zan-Thint's only reply to me was silence.

## [ 16 ]

"Lan-Min-Gen," I asked, "could I use your shuttle's comms to contact the work crews at the gateway construction?"

"Of course."

The Shock Trooper commander nodded at the pilot and my 'link chirped at me to let me know that it had access to the long-range antenna of the assault shuttle.

"Chief Moretti," I said. "Are you there?"

Assigning the *Orion*'s chief engineer to the gateway project might have been partially in revenge for all of my time he'd wasted complaining how Dwight was using his maintenance resources for the construction, but it was also because the man was the closest thing they had to a quantum physicist.

"I read you, sir." Moretti perpetually sounded as if he'd just lost an argument with his ex-wife over child custody. "What the hell is going on over there? We're reading a couple Tahni cargo birds heading this way. Are we getting construction supplies from the Tahni now?"

"There's been an attack by the Vergai on the Tahni landing field. Those shuttles were hijacked and they're not responding to comms. We have to assume they had bad intent and I don't want your people caught up in this shit. Get everyone to your lander and get the hell out of there."

It would have been handy if they had one of our assault shuttles up there, but all we'd left them was an unarmed passenger bird, barely large enough to hold the entire crew.

"Copy that, sir." I didn't have a video feed, but I could hear the scowl in his voice. "Those Vergal fuckheads better not mess with that gravitational sensor suit though. It took us fucking eight double shifts to get that thing working."

"Evacuation now, Chief," I told him. "Complaining later."

"Aye, sir. I'm on it."

"And loop me into the external camera on the work drones," I told him as an afterthought. "Run the video to my 'link."

He did it without comment, though it was hard to make out much on the tiny screen of my datalink. I shrugged and instructed the device to use the connection with the Tahni comms system to project the transmission onto the main screen. The view from the destroyer still took up three quarters of the projection, but tucked into a corner was the view of the destroyer from the gateway construction drones, the two stolen cargo shuttles points of light in the distance between the drone and the Tahni warship.

The pilot scowled back at me, but Lan-Min-Gen made a quelling motion and a sound somewhere between a shush and a snort that the translation circuit in my 'link informed me was a plea for forbearance.

My gaze flickered back and forth between the two optical views and the tactical sensors, trying to blend all three together into a holistic vision of what was going on, the same sort of trick I used when fighting in my Vigilante. The cargo shuttle looked even more awkward and bulky with its ass end facing the destroyer, totally harmless since they couldn't even ram the Tahni ship, their motivations a mystery. A silvery teardrop shape separated from the destroyer and nudged itself toward the shuttle on puffs of maneuvering jets, and I assumed it was the boarding pod, though I'd never seen one in action. That I remembered. At this point in my life, I'd seen so much that I couldn't keep it all straight.

"One minute to intercept," a voice announced from the destroyer. Maybe their weapons officer? I didn't think the captain of the ship would be giving updates, but they were Tahni, so I wasn't certain.

They were moving in faster than I would have been under the circumstances, not bone-crushing boost, but not exactly circumspect either.

"The shuttle is less than three kilometers from your destroyer," I told Lan-Min-Gen. "What happens if there's a bomb on board?"

"Boarding pods are easy to replace," he told me without much emotion.

He was facing forward and couldn't see my scowl, so I didn't bother to conceal it. Instead, I stared at the feed from the construction drone. The other two shuttles were still barreling toward the gateway device... I frowned.

"Dwight," I transmitted, "can you hear me?"

"Part of me can," he replied immediately. "The main part of my neural net is on board the *Orion*, a few light-minutes away, but I've uploaded my more basic functions and memories to the data core on the gateway installation."

I didn't want to think about whether that meant I was talking to the *real* Dwight or what that might even mean. I just hoped to hell this one could answer my questions.

"Dwight, give me an analysis of the course of the hijacked shuttles. How much time do they have to perform turnover and start braking?"

"They are already past that point, Captain Alvarez," he

replied in a neutral tone, as if the whole thing were an academic exercise in orbital mechanics. "They're on a collision course with the gateway and will not be able to decelerate in time for a docking."

"Shit," I murmured. "Can the installation take the impact, or is it going to do serious damage?"

"You misunderstand," he told me. "The shuttles aren't on course to hit the installation, they're going to hit the object itself. The sunward polar node, to be exact."

"Well, what the fuck's the point of *that*?" I blurted.

"I'm not in a position to guess the motives of Vergai militants, but impacting the end of the artifact will accomplish little more than sending them off at an angle equal but opposite to their angle of impact, though their kinetic energy will likely be amplified to the square of their momentum."

"What?" I asked, eyes narrowing. "How the hell does that happen?"

"The boarding pod is docked," the Tahni weapons officer said on the cockpit speakers, the translation coming over my earbuds, a distraction as I tried to work out what Dwight was saying.

On the screen, the silvery teardrop was embedded at a ninety-degree angle into the side of the cargo shuttle like an arrow shot by the gods. The view changed abruptly to the interior of the boarding pod's lock, where space-suited Tahni crowded around the hatch carrying short-barreled weapons.

"It's a function of the singularity at the heart of the device," Dwight explained. "It's rotating with an angular momentum of…"

"Spare me the math," I pleaded with him. "Just tell me, does that mean that *any* energy that hits the gateway will do the same thing?"

"Of course," he told me. "Rest assured though, nothing they

can do with those small spacecraft can do anything to damage the device."

"I'm not worried about them damaging the gateway," I told him, cursing under my breath. "Is there any way to move the thing?"

"No, we have yet to install any maneuvering thrusters, and there are no spacecraft close enough to dock with the gateway in time to move it. What has you concerned, Cameron?"

I ignored him, turning back to the pilot and Lan-Min-Gen.

"Hey!" I shouted loud enough to make both of them turn around, startled. "You need to tell the destroyer to break orbit now!"

"What are you talking about, human?" the pilot snapped, his hand drifting toward the pistol holstered at his chest, as if he thought I was about to attempt my own hijacking.

"Going in now." The voice was from the boarding party commander, I thought. It wasn't the same as the weapons officer, and right after the announcement the shuttle's hatch banged open and the leader of the group darted inside.

There'd been two Vergai inside the shuttle, but none of the Tahni yelled at them or bothered to shoot them. They were already dead, one of them with a gunshot wound to his chest, the blood still orbiting his dead body in loose, crimson beads. The other had shot herself after shooting him. The pistol was still in her hand, hooked around her trigger finger, her arm floating limp in the microgravity. Her head flopped just as loosely, the cloud of blood around her as thick as a fog.

"I don't see any others," the Tahni soldier reported. "Just the two dead ones. I'm checking the controls. Maybe we can fly this thing back down if they haven't wrecked it."

"This is another distraction," I said, the idea forming only a microsecond ahead of the words. "Those shuttles heading for the gateway are the real attack."

"Why would we use our destroyer to save your gateway?" the pilot objected, but Lan-Min-Gen held up a hand to quiet the man.

"What are you saying, Alvarez?"

"Dwight just told me that the gateway amplifies energy directed against it." I was trying to talk fast, but the damned translator was too slow, or at least it felt like it took minutes to relay every word. "I don't know what they're doing, but it's got to be an attack on your people."

God only knows whether he would have listened to me.

"Captain!" the leader of the boarding party yelled. "The shuttle's reactor... they've overridden the safeties and locked us out of the controls! It's going into overload."

The video feed from the boarding party cut off abruptly, replaced by the view from the destroyer until that flashed solid white and cut off as well. Only the view from the construction drone remained, and that told the story. Where the shuttle and the docked boarding pod had been was now a second sun, an expanding globe of white fury.

Even as close as the shuttle was, the fusion blast hadn't penetrated the armored hull of the destroyer because the lack of an atmosphere meant there'd been no concussion, no air to conduct the heat. That left radiation, and the hull was *probably* thick enough to keep the entire crew from being cooked to death... but it also meant something else.

"We've lost contact with the *Blade*," the pilot said, and if a Tahni could blanche, he did. "Their communications and sensors are down from the radiation pulse."

And we were just lucky we were far away enough that ours weren't. If you could call it lucky, since all we could do was sit and watch, much too far away from the stolen shuttles to attempt a shot at them, even if it would have done any good.

"Captain Alvarez," Chief Moretti called, "we're out and burning for deorbit. What the hell's going on?"

"Stand by, Chief," I told him, lacking the mental energy to say anything else.

"Collision in three seconds," Dwight warned.

"Shit."

I was watching a fusion-powered train heading for a crash with a cargo truck stuck on the tracks, and there was nothing anyone could do to stop it. The shuttles *didn't* collide though. Their reactors went to overload at the exact moment they touched the surface of the skyscraper-sized artifact, though the result wasn't the classic white globe I'd seen so many times, the way fusion explosions *always* looked in space.

Instead, the energy was stretched into twin cylinders, narrowing as they stretched away from the rounded front end of the artifact, no longer raw fusion but instead focused photons. Two laser blasts, more powerful than any I'd seen from any Commonwealth or Tahni warship, each nearly as powerful as the energy cannons the Resscharr had fitted the *Orion* with.

They were perfectly aimed, both of them lancing through the bow of the Tahni destroyer. The *Blade of the Warrior* bulged as the metallic hydrogen fuel stored in her tanks fused, veins of white fury growing wider, splitting her lengthwise as it expanded through the hull and consumed the huge vessel in a merciless, star-bright fire.

She was gone in less than a second, vaporized, nothing left of her bigger than gas molecules. Neither Lan-Min-Gen nor the pilot said a word, both of them as stunned as I was. No transmission interrupted our shock, all communications disrupted by the electromagnetic interference from the huge fusion blast.

"Pilot," Lan-Min-Gen rasped hoarsely, probably using the male's job title since he, like me, hadn't bothered to learn his name, "turn this ship around. Take us back to Yfingam. The General must be told."

The pilot didn't even speak to acknowledge the order, simply carried it out. Maneuvering jets banged against the hull, spinning the vessel end for end. Lan-Min-Gen waited until the drive ignited and pushed us back into our chairs with a comfortable one gravity before he speared me with a black-eyed stare.

"You know what must be done now, Alvarez," he said quietly, in English. "This is war. I will do what I can to make sure the General knows you were not involved, but the Vergai... nothing can save them now. You and your people must choose or be caught up in this, whether you wish to be or not."

[ 17 ]

Vicky was silent as I climbed into my Vigilante, watching from the shelter of her own suit, a sentinel statue guarding the gates. None of the others were in the armory with us, everyone else already suited up, deployed in a perimeter around our lines, waiting. Waiting for *my* orders.

And what the hell was I going to tell them?

"The Tahni are mobilizing," she finally told me just after I pulled the chest plastron shut.

The HUD light up all around me, an annoying reminder flashing at the corner of my vision, telling me to plug in my 'face jacks.

"Yeah, yeah," I murmured, unspooling the wires. My fingers shook slightly and it took me two tries.

"Pardon?" Vicky sounded like she was about to go off, and I realized I'd spoken out loud on the open net.

"Sorry, I was talking to the suit. Have they started air strikes yet?"

"No, but they will, once their ground troops are in place." I could almost hear her shrug. "They lost a couple of their assault shuttles on the ground and maybe a few more on the destroyer, but there were at least a half a dozen docked with the lighters. They're on their way down and we have nothing that can touch them."

"Maybe the suits could," I mused. "We can't match their speed or maneuverability, but if we put up a solid barrage from our energy cannons, they'd have to break off."

"Until their Shock Troopers came in and hit us while we were preoccupied."

"That's where your company would come in," I said, smiling tightly, the suit coming to life as I plugged in. "You'd take them down while the Vergai militia holds off the Karai."

"Is that the plan?" No judgement in her tone. She'd do it if I asked her to. They all would.

"No." The floor shook under the weight of my Vigilante, each stomp taking me closer to the fading sunlight and the choice I'd have to make. "Take the recruit company and set up a line between the fortress and the Vergai settlement. Do *not* open fire unless fired upon, and if Zan-Thint or Lan-Min-Gen ask, tell them I'm heading that way to talk."

"Talk about what?" Vicky wondered. "The Vergai hijacked their shuttles using weapons *we* gave them, then used the gateway *we* brought here to destroy their biggest starship. What do you think they're going to have to say to us?"

"It's not what they're going to say to us, it's what I'm going to say to them."

What was left of the original Drop Trooper company waited for me outside the armory, spread out in a tactical wedge formation, not because I'd told them to but because they were all combat vets who didn't cluster around like newbs when there was a potential enemy around.

"Springfield," I said. "Detail a squad to follow me. The rest of you are going to be swinging a wide, airborne patrol around the Vergai settlements. You see any Tahni troops or aircraft coming into the area, you let me know ASAP. But no one pulls a trigger without orders. Copy?"

"Copy that, sir," she said, just the slightest, almost-undetectable quaver in her voice showing her tension. "Sir... is the *Orion* coming back?"

"Not until she unloads." I could have just snapped at her to do her job, but she deserved to know what we could—or couldn't—expect in the way of support. "The Intercepts are dropping their passengers and micro-jumping back as soon as possible, but we're talking hours. We don't have any space or air assets in theater. It's just us."

"Yes, sir." The acknowledgement was more confident, as if the realization we were on our own was somehow comforting. "Fourth squad, Second Platoon... Sgt. Kerensky, you're with the captain."

The eight Marines separated from their platoon formation and circled around me.

"We're airborne, Sergeant," I told him. "Follow my lead and don't let anyone shoot me in the back. Don't fire unless fired upon though. Clear?"

"Five by five, sir."

The suit jets rumbled at a touch on the controls and the compound dropped away beneath me, twilight turning back into daylight as I chased the sun. The Vergai steadings were an anthill kicked over by an unwise child, people scrambling to vehicles, to weapons caches, to basement shelters. They were panicking, the word of what had happened spreading like a virus.

They hadn't known. Operational security. Not something amateurs usually practiced, and not something we'd taught them because it hadn't seemed pertinent to the situation. But someone had. And Carella had learned that lesson well.

No matter how secretive she'd been though, she couldn't

block out thermal and sonic sensors with stone and wood houses, and one of the first things Colonel Hachette had done when we involved ourselves in this damned mess was scan the biometrics of her and the other leaders of the Vergai and Karai. I spotted Carella even through the walls and roof and floors of the farmhouse basement where she'd concealed herself, a hundred meters below me, straight down.

I cut the jets and plunged a hundred meters, straight down.

The roof I barely felt, nor the second floor. They were wood beams without a bit of metal or concrete to them, and the suit stiffened at the impact, taking all the kinetic energy into its BiPhase Carbide armor. The ground floor was reinforced concrete, which I knew very well since we'd taught them how to build it, how to replace their wattle huts with something more permanent, more comfortable, something that would keep them warm in the winter, dry in the spring. The floor and the foundation beneath it would have resisted even the momentum of the weight of my suit falling at terminal velocity, and it wouldn't have been too comfortable for me either.

A touch of the jets broke my fall and also set the furniture afire. People ran screaming out of the front door for all that they were armed adults. Nothing had prepared them for this, not even the Skrela incursion of months ago, and not a one of them even attempted to take a shot at me with their chemical-propellant assault rifles. I didn't blame them.

The cellar door was off to the side, near the rear door to the house, the one gap in the foundation. It stood out like a searchlight to the sonar in my helmet, and I didn't even need the jets to spring above it and piston my servo-assisted legs downward. Wood splintered and darkness swallowed me up for a moment before the helmet's optics adjusted.

There were three Vergai in the cellar besides Carella, all of them middle-aged men, all sprawled on their backs from the shock and the shower of wood and plaster that had accompanied my descent.

Not Carella though. She stood tall, defiant, leveling a handgun at me. One of the men on the floor clambered to his feet and threw himself between us, but I slammed him aside with barely a brush of my arm. The woman fired the pistol, emptying it into my chest, but the ricocheting bullets were more of a threat to her people than they were to me. I was on her in one, long stride, thumping her with a shoulder heard enough to throw her back against the wall and drive the breath out of her. She stared up at me, no fear in her expression but perhaps realization.

I said nothing, just grabbed her by the scruff of her jacket and hauled her to her feet. She walked on tiptoe as I dragged her back to the yawning opening in the ceiling, still trailing dust and plaster. Couldn't use the jets, not without frying her and the others in the cellar, so I jumped again. It was harder to do it while holding onto her and she nearly slipped out of her sheepskin coat in the process, which would have been painful and embarrassing, though not fatal. Luckily for her pride, she managed to hold on while I hauled her out of the wreckage of the house, kicking down the front door.

Her followers were gathering outside, some of them still panicked, others outraged, screaming at us. I didn't care. The squad I'd brought with me was spread out in a semicircle around the house, arms spread as they pushed the press of Vergai back. It was for their safety, not mine.

"Tell them to back off," I told Carella. "I don't want to hurt anyone."

"Except me," she said, barking a laugh with just a tinge of desperation to it. I could almost have felt sorry for her. Almost.

"You brought this on yourself. *Tell* them to back off."

I thought for a second she wouldn't do it, but finally she

sighed and waved her hands to get the attention of the crowd, which had grown to somewhere around two hundred people with more coming. In the distance, a groundcar was coming up the gravel road.

"Stop!" she shouted. "Everyone, stop! I knew this would happen when I ordered the strike on our enemies. Fighting here, against those who gave us our weapons, will accomplish nothing. I've abused their trust, and now I have to pay the price."

Blank faces stared at her without understanding, but the words seemed to penetrate. The screaming stopped, although many of them were sobbing, hands outstretched like they were trying to touch her. None of them interfered when the Force Recon fire team drove up in their groundcar and I marched Carella over to them. Lt. Campea himself took her from me and guided her inside, a Recon Marine on either side of her.

"Meet me at the front lines," I told him. "And don't dawdle. I doubt we have much time."

---

I was right about that. Zan-Thint was standing at the front lines, screaming at Vicky when I dropped down. I landed thirty meters away out of courtesy so I wouldn't spray the Tahni general with dust and debris, but he must not have recognized my armor because he didn't let up. He was, I noted, yelling at her in English.

"Do you truly intend to defend the Vergai after what they've done? Is this the human idea of justice?"

He was dressed in combat armor but hadn't bothered with a helmet, unless one of his aides was holding onto it for him so he could be more melodramatic. Vicky hadn't popped open her armor, and Zan-Thint looked ridiculous venting his spleen at a faceless suit of inhuman metal. Behind him Lan-Min-Gen stood at the front of his soldiers, two companies of Shock Troopers. They'd come here with only one, but they'd managed to fabricate more of the powered exoskeletons while we'd been gone. I didn't know if the warriors inside them were Tahni conventional infantry or trained-up Karai, though it wouldn't matter as much for such a basic setup. But I could tell the newbies. They shifted from side to side, unable to hold still, their KE guns scanning back and forth, the soldiers not seeming to care that they were sweeping their comrades.

Behind us, held a hundred meters or so back by the ranks of the recruit company blocking the way, hundreds of Vergai lined up, many carrying the assault rifles we'd given them, though a few had Resscharr energy weapons. About a klick to the rear of the infantry, more of the technicals idled, alcohol-fueled engines grumbling.

"General," I said over the external speakers, "it's me, Alvarez. And no, we're not here to fight you. I just wanted a chance to talk to you before... well, *before*."

"What is there to say, Alvarez?" I don't know where he'd learned his English, but he'd learned it well. He even had the cadence and body language down, and it was damned clear that he was enraged. "The blood of my ship's crew is on *your* hands as well. You gave them these weapons, gave them to virtual *children* and taught them how to use them against *us*."

Zan-Thint carried a KE rifle and used it as a visual aid, pointing the muzzle directly at my chest. I wanted very badly to grab the thing out of his hands and teach him the same lesson one of our drill instructors in Boot had taught an errant private about pointing a loaded weapon at anything he didn't intend to kill, but that neglected the very real possibility that he *did* intend to kill me.

"We did that," I admitted. "And you gave us every reason to." I was *trying* to control my anger, but I was a Marine, not a diplomat. "Don't stand here pretending you're some kind of innocent victim, General. We pursued you here because you tried to kill innocent people, because you tried to unleash the fucking *Skrela* not just on the Commonwealth, but on your own people as well. You've shown over and over that you'll do anything to get what you want. Well, congratulations, you just met someone else as ruthless and desperate as you."

As if on cue, the groundcar emerged from between the technicals and Vigilante armor. Dozens of Tahni weapons swung to cover the vehicle but no one fired as it slowed to a halt, plastic tires scraping on gravel. The Recon Marine in the front passenger's seat jumped out and opened the back door on his side, letting Campea slide out, pulling Carella with him, her hands flex-cuffed behind her back. Back in the Commonwealth, they would probably have used neural restraints, but out here we made do.

"Don't punish my people for my decision, Tahni," she said, not one bit of give to the woman. "I made the decision. The ones who trusted in me enough to carry out the task are now dead, and I regret their loss much more than I could ever regret taking away the threat you would have held over our heads. Not just those of us who stayed, but even those who left for the Island World." Carella's hair was tangled, her braids coming apart into loose strands, and the look in her eye wouldn't have been out of place on some ancient Celtic warrior queen. "I've known your kind... we all have, for as long as we've been here. You're just like the Resscharr, hoarding power to yourself, unwilling to admit any others deserve to live. I did what I had to do in order to safeguard my people. I did what my husband would have done." Tears furrowed trails through the dirt and dust on her cheeks and she bowed her head, unable to wipe them away. "My work is done. Do with me what you will."

Zan-Thint's glare was hard enough to bore through BiPhase

Carbide, but thankfully I only had to deal with it through my suit cameras. I half thought he might simply walk away in disgust, but eventually he snarled a command to his troops and Lan-Min-Gen stepped forward, reaching a hand for the woman's arm. Campea drew back, looking at me.

"I'm not just handing her over to be executed, General," I said. Although now that I had a moment to consider it, that was *exactly* what I was about to do. "She turned herself in to save her people, the same reason she attacked your destroyer." I shook my head, even though he couldn't see it, swallowed hard to get rid of the sour taste in my mouth. "You deserve justice for your people, but you're not going to get it by killing the Vergai. I won't allow it."

"We still have spacecraft in orbit," Zan-Thint reminded me, the threatening edge to his voice very convincing. "They may not be warships, but their weapons can lay waste to the Vergai steadings and there'd be nothing you can do about it. I know exactly how long it will be before any of your ships can get back here."

"Sure," I acknowledged. "But they can't hit *us*." I motioned with my suit's articulated left hand. "And the second your ships start bombarding the steadings, we go after you. If you don't know what Vigilantes can do to Shock Troopers, get Lan-Min-Gen to tell you. By the time the *Orion* gets back to finish off your lighters in orbit, you'll all be dead. Every Goddamned one of you. And believe me, General, that would be *so* much more satisfying than handing Carella over to you, knowing that you're going to kill her. So, maybe you should consider talking this out."

Part of me really hoped he wouldn't, hoped he would decide to fight. Fighting would be easy. We'd lose *some* troops because, despite what I'd said, the Tahni had coilgun turrets and armored vehicles and our new recruits were unblooded. But I could have gone to bed feeling clean. Handing Carella over to him... it felt wrong.

Zan-Thint looked like he was having the same thoughts, but at last he waved a hand.

"Fine. But if they're under your protection, they don't need weapons. They all disarm immediately. And none of them can stay here. They'll all have to agree to leave this world on your ships. Anyone who stays behind after you leave will be executed, no exceptions. Our two peoples can't live side by side. If there's anything we should have learned from the last hundred years, it's that."

"That... sounds reasonable." *Way* too reasonable, actually. "I'm going to need Carella to speak to her people though. She's the only one who can convince them it's the right thing to do."

"Go, then," Zan-Thint told me. "But I will not be robbed of justice. You have until tomorrow at this hour for all weapons to be turned in at this place and all the Vergai to agree to leave. Then she will be executed according to our ways. I would have your word on this, human. It means little to me, but I know you well enough now to know how much it means to you."

Shit. My word *was* important to me, but not so important I'd sacrifice someone else's life to preserve its integrity. In this case though, breaking it wouldn't just mean making myself look bad in front of the new recruits, it would mean open war. Not war we couldn't win, but certainly not war without casualties either.

Carella must have been reading my thoughts even through my faceless suit.

"Give your word, Earther," she said. "And I will give you mine. I've done what I can to protect my people. I am at peace."

Great. That didn't make *me* feel one bit better.

# [ 18 ]

"You can't do this," Vicky said.

I felt guilty, not just because of what we were doing, but because I was out of my suit. It seemed like we should all be up and ready, but Springfield was out collecting weapons, Campea had taken Carella to meet with her people, and we... apparently we had talking to do.

Vicky sat on a packing crate in the corner of the armory, which looked uncomfortable to me but she insisted wasn't as bad as the folding chairs, but I couldn't sit down. I was exhausted but I couldn't sit down, couldn't even think about sleeping, despite having been up for thirty-six hours straight. My Vigilante stared down at me from its gantry, its sullen disapproval as plain as my wife's.

"What do you suggest then?" I asked her, no acrimony in the words despite the fact that I should have been angry. "I'm fresh out of ideas."

"I don't *know*," she said, throwing up her hands. "But we can't just let them kill her!"

"Can't we?" I stopped pacing in front of her. "She is personally responsible for *murdering* dozens of Tahni. The only reason it's not *hundreds* was that they don't keep a full crew on their destroyer when it's in orbit. She's personally responsible for the destruction of their biggest starship and the only hope they had of defending themselves against outside threats. And yeah, maybe she was right to be worried about the Tahni coming after her people, but we didn't give a shit about how right the Tahni were to be worried about us as a threat when they attacked us first in the war."

"They're the enemy," Vicky said flatly. "They've *always* been the enemy, and if what Dwight and Lilandreth say about how and why they were created by the Predecessors is true, they were always *going* to be the enemy. They were made to be the inheritors of the galaxy and we were just a sloppy accident who got in the way."

"And that means we get to just kill them?" I tried not to yell the words, but they came out more stridently than I'd intended. "Does that mean it's not murder if we wipe them out right down to the last? Does that mean we can do that and still be the good guys?"

"Oh, fuck being the good guys!" she snapped back at me, jumping to her feet, squared off like we were about to spar. "We're not children, Cam. You know as well as I do that war isn't about good and bad, it's about survival."

"We didn't turn the Tahni homeworld into glass during the war," I reminded her, "because *someone* thought doing that would make us the bad guys."

"And we lost a hell of a lot of Marines and Fleet pilots taking that world." She slapped a palm against her chest. "Shit, I came pretty damned close to dying myself, remember? Maybe we shouldn't have been so worried about being the good guys and just tried to win the war."

I sighed, the righteous indignation going out of me. That had been a low blow, but a well-aimed one. How long had Vicky spent in an auto-doc recovering from that final battle? How many weeks had it taken before she stopped walking with a limp?

"Then maybe you should be in charge," I told her. "God knows you couldn't do any worse than I have. Go ahead... you want to take those new recruits and get them bloodied massacring the Tahni and the Karai, I'll go along with it. I'll lead our company and you make the big decisions. I've only been in charge for a couple months and I'm already over it."

The anger seemed to drain out of Vicky like a flood and her shoulders sagged. She folded me into an embrace and I returned it.

"They don't believe in me the way they believe in you," she said, shaking her head. "And maybe they're right not to. Because I *would* kill every last one of them and I don't think I'd feel bad about it." Vicky buried her face in my shoulder. "I just can't stop thinking about her kids, waiting there on Laisvas Miestas for her to come for them..."

"She was never coming." I stroked Vicky's silky, dark hair, trying to be comforting even as a flash of anger at Carella surged through me. "She always meant to die here. I don't think she wanted to live anymore after Matis died. Not even for her children."

"I guess I can understand that."

Vicky kissed me. I let myself revel in the physical contact despite the guilt weighing me down, but we were interrupted by a knock on the door. Campea didn't wait *too* long after the knock before he pushed through, Carella tagging along behind him. She was no longer restrained, which might or might not have been a wise idea but I suppose had been necessary for her to talk to her followers. Still, she didn't look as if she was about to attempt an escape.

"What's the word?" I asked, pulling away from Vicky.

Campea shook his head, looking as if he was about to fall asleep on his feet.

"It took a while, but the last of them agreed to it. They acted like they weren't very happy about leaving, but if you ask me, they all seemed pretty relieved."

"It's probably true," Carella admitted, sitting down in one of the folding chairs beside the mostly-empty maintenance bays, smoothing her long skirts beneath her. "Most of them felt an obligation to me."

"Would you like something to eat?" I asked her. I don't know why I felt so damned guilty. She'd chosen this path and I just happened to be the poor sucker who had to clean up after her.

"My friends provided me with a wonderful breakfast," she said, folding her hands in her lap. "I think I should prefer to go to my eternal rest with the memory of that to accompany me rather than one of your ration bars."

"Good choice," Campea said with a nod. He shot me a glance. "Have they gotten the weapons rounded up?"

"Mostly," Vicky answered for me. "Lt. Springfield checked in a few minutes ago. She's rounding up the last of the rifles we fab'ed for them right now. Shouldn't be much longer."

I rubbed at my eyes, then checked my 'link. The sun was getting low outside and the time on my 'link confirmed my fears. We had less than an hour.

"Take me to Zan-Thint," Carella said. "I'm ready."

She looked impossibly old. I knew she was barely thirty, and even in this place where she'd been raised without modern medical care she shouldn't have looked this old. She'd aged years in just the last few months, and maybe she *was* ready.

"You gonna suit up?" Vicky asked, pulling open the chest plastron of her vigilante. I shook my head, still staring at Carella.

Did I want to watch her die through a projection on my

helmet HUD, separated by a comfortable insulation from the truth of it?

"No. That would be too easy."

---

I hadn't seen the priests before that night. I didn't know Zan-Thint had brought any of them along, particularly given his bitterness toward the old ways and the emperor... hell, I didn't even know any of them were still in business after the end of the war. Yet here they were, three of them wearing the peculiar, crimson robes fashioned from thousands of strips of fabric. Deep shadows from the sunset shrouded their faces, making them seem less like mortals and more like ghosts of the old Imperium.

They hung back behind Zan-Thint and his personal guard, not as if they were afraid of us but more like they were giving respect to the general and his prerogative to be out front of this, accepting the surrender of his enemy. Behind the priests Lan-Min-Gen stood watching, out of his powered exoskeleton, though a company of his Shock Troopers was arrayed between them and the fortress.

Vicky was a hundred meters back with the recruit company, all of them facing away toward the gathered throng of somewhere between ten to fifteen thousand Vergai. Not all of the ones left, of course. Children had been kept at home, watched over by the older grandparents or aunts and uncles, but most of the adults left were here.

The Karai were present as well, at least the adult males, though they seemed less solemn than the rest of us. Nam Ker stood at the head of them, probably ten thousand in a disordered cluster that trailed all the way back to their steadings behind the fortress. Why the ones in back bothered, I wasn't sure. They wouldn't be able to see a damned thing. Maybe they just wanted to be able to say they were here when their enemy was put to death. Chants went up from the crowds of Karai, though my translator couldn't make sense of them, and here and there the males were dancing.

*Assholes.* That was another reason I hadn't worn my suit. I'd have been too tempted to go bust some heads.

And of course, there were the weapons. Zan-Thint had required them to be brought here and his people were still sorting through them. We'd piled them in the back of the technicals, though I'd instructed Springfield to leave the ammo behind since I didn't care to supply the Tahni or the Karai with weapons we'd fabricated to defend against them. As I waited, Carella standing beside me, the Tahni officer in charge of the count ran over to Zan-Thint and spoke quietly to him before saluting and heading back.

"Where," Zan-Thint asked me, "are the Resscharr energy weapons?"

I didn't have to ask which ones he meant. The Vergai militia who had come with us to Decision had received energy rifles to fight the invading Skrela and kept them. And there was no way in hell I was about to hand those over to the Tahni.

"We have them secured." I smiled, knowing he'd understand what it meant. "We'll find *some* use for them, I'm sure." Though Campea insisted that he and his Force Recon platoon didn't want to part with their Gauss rifles for the high-thermal-signature energy weapons.

Zan-Thint didn't look happy about that, but he made no further objection.

"Then it's time."

I looked aside to Carella. She still wasn't restrained. All it would take was one word from me to Springfield and Vicky and I could put a stop to this. Dunstan was back in orbit, and I knew he could at least keep the lighters busy until the fight was done.

"Carella," I said quietly beside her ear, "we don't have to do this. Maybe all the Vergai disarming and leaving will be enough."

"No." Her voice was firm, unyielding. "I set upon this path when Matis died. Now I've reached its end." She took a step toward Zan-Thint but paused and looked back over her shoulder at me. "Tell my children I'm sorry and that my last thoughts were of them."

Zan-Thint stepped out of her way as she approached, letting the priests step forward. I tensed, ready to pull my gun if they tried to rough her up, but they took her hands gently, as if she were a child, and guided her to what looked like a throne from one of the old tales of kings and queens during the Dark Ages. Two of them guided her to it and the third faced her and put his hands on her shoulders, pushing her down into the chair. She didn't resist as they laid her hands on the arms of the chairs and tied thin, red threads around her wrists, fastening them to the chair. The thread didn't look like it would stop a determined toddler, much less an adult human, and I assumed they were ceremonial.

The priests began to chant—or maybe it was singing, I wasn't sure. Did the Tahni sing? I hadn't bothered to ask. It sounded like a cross between an imitation of a badly tuned internal combustion engine and an old-fashioned hinged door gone rusty. If this was Tahni music, I was pretty sure there weren't going to be much crossover between our cultures. The translator couldn't make any sense of it and I wondered if maybe the words simply didn't translate, if they were more conveying emotion than anything coherent.

I think I'd been in denial to that point, not allowing myself to believe it was actually going to happen, and the drawn-out ceremony pushed it further back into unreality. Until one of the priests drew a long, curved blade from under his robes. I surged forward without intent and might have reached for my pistol, as little sense as that would have made, if I'd had another half a second. But the priest was practiced and professional, and before I'd taken a single step he'd already sliced across Carella's throat from one ear to the other.

Blood gushed out and my breath followed it. I'd been in mid-step and I nearly fell over forward, catching myself with a jarring stomp of my foot on the packed dirt. My stomach twisted and I wanted to look away from the gaping wound in her neck, but I couldn't turn away because of the expression on her face.

She was smiling.

# [ 19 ]

"Jesus H. Christ, Cam," Captain Nance murmured. "What the hell have you gotten us into?"

He shaded his eyes against the rising sun, sniffing at the air as if there was something strange about it. It had taken the news that we were going to have to transport fifty thousand more Vergai off the planet to get him down from his ship, though he'd bitched long and hard about it and I'd had to basically pull rank I didn't have to push him over the edge.

It had taken even *more* convincing for him to agree to leave his 'link behind and walk with me out of the groundcar and into a canyon outside the city. I'd managed to sell the idea that I was worried about the Tahni hacking into our comms network now that they'd had all this time to study our systems, though he'd still looked at me like I was paranoid.

"You act like this was all my idea," I protested, glancing back over my shoulder just to be sure no one had followed us... and to check for drones. Yeah, maybe I *was* paranoid. "This all started the minute we landed here and decided to work with the Tahni."

Nance's snort was rich with skepticism.

"Yeah, and I'm sure that you had *no* say at all in that decision." He sobered, staring at the stone walls of the canyon around us but seeing something father away. "Sorry about what happened with Carella. That woman was batshit crazy, but damned if she didn't accomplish the mission. That was some fucking smart thinking using the gateway's gravitic effects to blow the shit out of the destroyer."

"It was *too* smart," I told him.

My eyes flickered toward a hint of movement, but I relaxed when I saw the ungulate. I wanted to call it a deer, but I think it was something more exotic, either genetically engineered to the environment or maybe just some animal I'd never seen before from Asia or Africa. It had been grazing at the top of the canyon when it spotted us, its eyes going wide, then took off at a trot.

"There's no way she could have known about that effect. Hell, *we* didn't even know about it, so that leaves out one of us letting it slip to a Vergai."

Nance stopped walking and frowned at me.

"Well, who the hell *do* you think told her then? The Tahni?"

"Dwight." It felt cathartic to say the words, given how long I'd been trying to tell him. "I think Dwight told them."

I'd expected Nance to at least look surprised, but he simply nodded.

"Makes sense. He'd be the only one who knew how the thing worked. But why *would* he?"

I explained it to him as concisely as possible, not knowing how much time we had.

"That's why I couldn't tell you until now," I explained, sighing in exasperation. "If you weren't so damned stubborn about getting off that ship..."

"Well, shit," he said, chuckling, "I'm not sure I wanted to know, since there's fuck-all we can do about it."

"Yeah. What worries me is that this might not be over." I

motioned back the way we'd come. "This whole thing was designed to get us to slaughter the Tahni, to force an open battle between us, and I just don't believe Dwight's going to give up that easy."

Nance was silent for a long few seconds, and when he spoke again, it was with an expression of guilt, as if he knew what he was about to say wasn't strictly moral or ethical but he had to say it anyway.

"You know, maybe Dwight's got it right. I never felt totally comfortable working with the Tahni, particularly that Zan-Thint asshole. He's responsible for the deaths of a lot of good people."

I found myself nodding, even though I felt a similar guilt for agreeing with him.

"Maybe he *is* right, at least about Zan-Thint. And maybe if there was some way to just extract him like the cancer he is, I'd do it. But I can't bring myself to murder every single Tahni he brought with him. A lot of them just came along because they wanted a better life, a life where they wouldn't be subjects of us humans. I've known Lan-Min-Gen for a while now, and even if I wouldn't want to go drinking with him, he's not a bad guy. He's a good soldier."

"Who else knows?" Nance wondered.

"Me and Vicky and Dunstan. That's it for now. I tried to tell Lilandreth, but she's even more stubborn than you."

"What the hell are we gonna do about it?"

"I don't know," I admitted, "but I figure we have a few months at least. It'll take that much time to get the *Orion* back and forth to the Islands... how many times do you figure?"

"If we all hold our breath and pack every damned storage closet and footlocker with Vergai," he estimated, "I *think* we can get two thousand of them over at a time. Micro-jumps there and back and then taking account how many shuttle runs to get them to the surface... yeah, that's gonna be about twenty round trips. Minimum fourteen or fifteen hours, maybe more depending on how fast they can get unloaded. We go alternating shifts and counting loading time since we'll have to make multiple shuttles runs... I'd say six weeks minimum to get the job done."

"Then a couple more weeks to get cattle and feed transferred to get them started," I added. "Yeah, that sounds about right. I need to talk to Oster about picking up the pace. I don't want to stay here a second longer than I have to." An owl hooted and a shudder ran up my back. "This places feels haunted to me now."

I trailed off, hearing something else. Not the owl this time, a low crunch of feet on fallen leaves and twigs. Something or some*one* walking on the trail behind us. I motioned for Nance to get behind me and his eyes widened as I drew my pistol, aiming it the way we'd come. The captain wasn't armed, despite a standing order for all personnel who made landfall to be carrying a weapon. Guess that's what happens when someone gets used to being in charge.

The canyon curved slightly about fifty meters back of our position, and I put my shoulder to the lefthand wall and waited, wishing I'd thought to bring along one of those Resscharr carbines we'd confiscated. The seconds dragged by and I began to consider that it was an animal, that I was overreacting.

Lan-Ming-Gen came around the curve, not armored in his powered exoskeleton yet still looking tall and powerful and grim as stark death. He stopped in the middle of the trail, hands empty, staring at the muzzle of my handgun not with fear or worry but casual disregard.

"Cam Alvarez," he said in a strange, formal tone, "we have seen battle together. You've risked your life and spent the blood of your friends for the benefit of me and mine, and thus I would have the truth from you."

There didn't seem to be anyone behind him, but I waited for a few seconds before I lowered my weapon. I didn't reholster it, keeping it down by my side.

"The truth about what?" I asked.

"Did your people have anything to do with the Vergai attack on the *Blade of the Warrior*?"

"No," I replied immediately. "I wouldn't have had any idea it could have even worked." A hesitation, just a moment of inner debate. "Are you wearing a 'link?"

Lan-Min-Gen made a gesture of negation.

"I didn't want the General knowing I came to speak with you. He wouldn't understand."

"Good. Because I know who *was* behind the attack."

"Alvarez…" Nance said, putting a restraining hand on my shoulder. I shrugged it off. Either I was in command or I wasn't.

"Dwight," I told the Tahni. "The AI. I think he hates you Tahni as much as he does the Resscharr. I'm also pretty sure that the Resscharr didn't actually engineer the Skrela. I think the AIs did it." Another explanation about my rationale and I was beginning to wish I'd just printed out a briefing packet.

Lan-Min-Gen's dark eyes clouded over and then disappeared behind his brow ridges as he inclined his head, I hoped in contemplation rather than anger.

"If what you say is true," he finally spoke, "then by honor, I must warn you of something. You know of the AI system which lives at the heart of the fortress?"

"Presteri," I confirmed. I remembered the name well, though I hadn't interacted with the AI since Zan-Thint and his Tahni had occupied the fortress. The AI had turned against the Resscharr and helped us to disarm the self-destruct device the leader of the local, regressed version of the Predecessors had set before we killed him.

"General Zan-Thint has spent much of his time lately being... *advised* by this machine. I has troubled me, for as you say, I didn't trust this Dwight who lives on your ship and even less the copy of him that occupied our own destroyer."

"Oh, shit," I murmured, just knowing what was coming next.

"He has closed himself away with the machine for hours at a time, particularly since the execution of the insurgent Carella. And he speaks little with me or his other officers, and then only to give us orders, not to ask our advice." I might not have known many Tahni expressions, but I recognized pain and fear. I'd inflicted enough of both on so many of their kind that I'd never forget the look. "General Zan-Thint's aim is to wait until the *Orion*, your Intercepts, and your shuttles are totally involved loading refugees... and then attack with our remaining assault shuttles and the lighters, with the objective being to destroy the *Orion*. He *says* it's to ensure you won't be able to attack us from orbit or threaten our lighters, but my own suspicion is that it's for personal vengeance." A motion of equivocation. "And I am not one to tell him that revenge is not worth having, but in this case, I feel it would be poorly aimed."

Yep. Just what I'd thought he would say.

"It's a trap," I warned him. "Not for us, but for you. Dwight wants all of you dead, and this is his way of ensuring that we have no choice but open combat. Even if you hadn't warned me, your lighters would have wound up scrap metal. And once Zan-Thint broke our agreement... well, after Carella's execution, it's been all Vicky and I can do to keep the new Vergai recruits from busting through the fortress and starting a war as it is."

"I have perceived this since you told me the true nature of the machines," Lan-Min-Gen agreed. "And yet, if given the order, I will have to obey. I don't wish to fight you, but I'll have to. I regret this."

"Then don't," I urged him, an idea coming to me just ahead of the words. "You and your Shock Troopers come with us on the *Orion*. I won't ask you to fight your own people, just sit the whole thing out. Once we take the *Orion* back through to the Cluster, we'll let you out at any Tahni colony you want. Hell, we'll let you out in the Pirate Worlds if you like. You'd be out of all this." A pause to catch my breath and assess his reaction and I knew in my gut that the offer wasn't going to work.

"My soldiers didn't volunteer to come halfway across the galaxy to wind up back in the same situation from which we fled to begin with. I would not return to the Cluster again to live in defeat and ignominy."

I nodded, not knowing what other alternative I had to offer him.

"I don't want to fight you or your soldiers, Lan-Min-Gen. I've come to think of you as a friend."

"And I you, Cam Alvarez." He turned, speaking as he walked back the way he'd come. "I will consider this, but I make no promises."

I waited where I was, watching him leave, not wanting to come out of the canyon too soon after him to avoid casting suspicion on him. Maybe he was a friend and maybe he wasn't, but I'd never find out if Zan-Thint had him executed for treason first.

Glancing back at Nance, I saw him gradually unclenching, as if he'd been tensed to run the whole time I'd been talking to the Tahni.

"This shit," he said, pointing after Lan-Min-Gen, "is why I *never* leave my ship."

## [ 20 ]

I'd never completed compulsory education back in Trans-Angeles. The group homes in the Underground were pretty slack about the requirements, and once I ran away, well... they don't offer progression tests for street kids making a living from cons and petty theft. But I was what you could call self-taught. My life-experience in Tijuana was so different than what I'd found in Trans-Angeles, curiosity compelled me to find out how all this had happened, and I kind of got addicted to learning.

Besides, it gave me something to keep me busy those sleepless nights I had to spend hiding under the air scrubbers, guarding against the rats. The tablets they gave away at every public terminal required an ID to take, but they were easy enough to steal and hack, and the net was free. I watched hundreds or maybe even thousands of hours of videos, read thousands of pages of text, and God only knows how much of it was true and how much was propaganda, but some of it stuck with me.

I especially recalled a video from the twentieth century of a line of refugees miles long heading for a border crossing, fleeing one or another of the various bloody, apocalyptic wars they'd had in that century, all their belongings on their back. I'd seen the like on colonies during the war and never wanted to see it again, yet here I was, standing guard as thousands of Vergai passed through the perimeter set up by our Marines, recruit and veteran, around the camp at our landing field.

It wasn't safe for them to stay in their homes while they waited for the voyage to the Islands, not after what had happened. Not after what I knew. We'd fabricated tents for them, which had taken a few days and cut into the time we'd estimated for the evacuation, and told them to bring everything with them that they'd need to survive. That had, as it turned out, included cows, pigs, and sheep... and a few chickens. The smell was incredible and I was glad I was in my suit, sealed away from the stench, insulated from the fear and despair and hopelessness in the eyes of the Vergai, in the faces of the children.

I wanted to feel guilty for them but I couldn't. I hadn't put them in this position, Carella had... and then she'd run from it, chosen death rather than dealing with the world she'd created for her people. The more I thought about it, the more I resented her, and yet the more I wanted her here to take charge of these people, to give them hope. Because I wasn't sure I could provide any.

"They're all sitting out there," Vicky said.

She wasn't standing next to me, but I could see her IFF signal on the screen, putting her just behind the front lines of the recruit company, keeping an eye on her new Marines as well as the refugees. I couldn't see which way she was looking, but I didn't need to—it was obvious. The Karai watched the growing refugee camp like vultures perched on a nearby hill, bristling with the weapons the Tahni had given them, and even from two klicks distance, I could practically see their mouths watering.

"They know what's going on," I agreed. "They're just waiting for the signal. Waiting for the Tahni."

The Tahni weren't being any more subtle about it, their armored vehicles parked on their side of the border between the steadings and the fortress. As the Vergai vacated each section of their land, Karai troops moved in, making sure they couldn't go back, and the Tahni were there to watch over them the same way we guarded the Vergai. Lan-Min-Gen was over there among them, I knew, though I couldn't pick him out from the other Shock Troopers intermingled in squad-sized elements between the vehicles. I hadn't heard anything else from him since he'd given us the warning a few days ago, and God only knew if the next time I encountered him would be when we started shooting at each other.

Someone else who hadn't spoken to me in days was Dwight, and not even God knew what the AI was thinking. I wondered if he suspected I knew. Maybe he was plotting my destruction next.

"Captain Alvarez," he said just as I thought about him, as if he'd read my mind, "I wanted to let you know that the construction drones have managed to repair the damage to the gateway framework done by the Vergai attack. My estimate is that the gateway should be ready for initial tests in perhaps twenty-two hours."

He said it so casually, as if the whole thing had been incidental, an annoying delay in his schedule.

"I think we're gonna be a bit busy for the next few weeks, Dwight," I told him, trying to sound simply irritated at the interruption, hiding the rage and the fear. "I'll let you and Chief Moretti handle the testing. You can give me a briefing when I get back from this trip to the Islands."

"Of course. Once the tests are complete, the gateway should

be ready to transit the *Orion* within two hundred hours, assuming no delays."

"I hope we have that long," I said, still staring at the Tahni.

"Captain, I know you disagree with what Carella did, but perhaps we should consider it an opportunity."

"What do you mean?" I asked, pretty sure I knew *exactly* what he meant but figuring playing dumb was better than unintentionally giving something away.

"The Tahni are vulnerable. Without their destroyer, their space defenses are highly attenuated. You should allow the *Orion* to disable their other ships. Without them, they'd be helpless. The Tahni lost their war with you back in your Cluster. You shouldn't allow them to spread their dreams of empire out here."

I blinked. Dwight usually kept a neutral tone, even when he was saying things I found utterly horrifying, but there seemed to be real emotion behind his words.

"Why do you care?" I asked him. I shouldn't have. I wasn't trying to trip him up now, didn't want him to have any reason to suspect I knew the truth about him. "I can understand why you resent the Resscharr, but what did the Tahni ever do to you?"

"I told you, Captain Alvarez. I was human once... I know what the Resscharr did to the man I once was and I know what they tried to do to us as a species. All to make the way safe for their Chosen. They thought themselves gods, and if wiping out one species to save another was immoral, well, morality is for mortals. I wouldn't see their plans succeed even in this remote corner of the galaxy."

Well, *that* was getting surprisingly close to a confession. *Damn.* Would it matter at this point?

"Aren't you upset about losing the piece of you that was on the *Blade of the Warrior*? It sorta sounded like he was your twin brother. I'd think you'd blame his death on Carella."

"For him to be a brother," the AI countered, "we would have had to grow up together. He was separate from me for the blink of an eye. When you exist as long as I have, there's little you can grow attached to. Other than memories."

I was breathing hard like I'd just sprinted a hundred meters, and I fought to calm myself down. One wrong word, that's all it would take.

"Even if I agreed with you," I told him, "even if I wanted to make sure the Tahni didn't have any ships available to strike at the Island World, I'd have to wait until we got all the Vergai off the planet. I won't have any more civilian blood on my hands. It's in everyone's best interests to just stay calm until we can finish the evacuation."

"For a warrior you have a tender soul, Captain Alvarez," the AI said. I don't think he meant it as a compliment.

"Birds are coming back," Vicky told me. She hadn't heard the exchange, of course, and neither had any of the others. Dwight wouldn't be that careless.

I tilted my head back at the distant roar of jets and caught the glint of sunlight off silver fuselages. The drop-ships descended first, tubby lifting bodies kept aloft by brute force, their landing jets howling and roaring in defiance of merciless gravity.

Everything we did was defiance. We defied gravity, defied biology, defied physics, defied everything that had tried to kill us off before we could bite and scratch and claw our way out of the mud, out of the dirt, and off the world that had reluctantly given birth to us. We'd defied the gods themselves and the demons they created, and now we were trying to clean up the mess they'd left behind. Sometimes I asked myself what we'd done to deserve this, but the truth was we'd put ourselves here. This was the fate we'd chosen for ourselves when we left the cradle, and I'd chosen it when I'd gone on this mission.

The drop-ships descended on columns of fire, dust and debris billowing in clouds around them, driving back throngs of Vergai who'd been crowding into the landing zone, waiting endless hours for the shuttles to come back for them. I could feel their tension, the conviction settling over them like the clouds of dust that they had to get out of this place, that anyone who didn't was dead. Even the ones shielding their eyes from the exhaust-blown debris didn't retreat too far, as if they were afraid they'd be left behind if they weren't right on top of the shuttles.

They would have swarmed the birds before the loading ramps even had a chance to come down if it weren't for the security. There weren't enough Force Recon Marines to handle them all, and given the threat from the Tahni and the Karai I didn't want any of our Drop Troopers out of their suits, but we did have all those Fleet crewmembers who'd been kicked off the *Orion* to make room for the refugees, and if they weren't trained for ground combat, well, they could at least look intimidating and direct traffic.

The *actual* Fleet Security troops were staying on the ship though, because as hard as it was to keep thousands of panicked civilians under control down here, it would be even more difficult up on the *Orion*. And I didn't envy them the task, which was another reason I'd kept my suit on, so no one would get the bright idea that I should be on the *Orion* helping maintain order.

"Hey, Cam, I'm two mikes out," Dunstan announced. It was nice hearing his voice again. He'd been as busy as the rest of the Fleet personnel the last few weeks, ferrying Vergai back and forth, and we hadn't been able to talk pretty much since I'd told him about Dwight.

That worried me. Kyler Dunstan was a good man, a good friend, but he was no spy, and he hadn't had a lot of practice keeping his mouth shut. All it would take was the wrong word spoken when any communications gear was in range and Dwight was sure to figure it out.

"I see you," I replied.

Intercept One was a gleaming delta coming down in a tight spiral, not quite as agile or sleek as an assault shuttle but burly with raw power. Two was close behind, and after all this time I could even tell the craft apart by little differences in profile where the craft had been repaired during the mission.

I didn't wait for him to land, knowing where he'd be touching down. I guess I was technically violating airspace control regs by jetting across the field while we had aerospace-craft descending, but I was confident it wouldn't be recorded in my permanent record. The flight gave me a nice, close look at the fuselage of the Intercept, turning what seemed like smooth, polished silver at a distance into a patchwork of separate panels, some of them slightly discolored, scuffed and scored by use.

We landed at the same time, the heat of the cutter's jets a tropical wind even through the thick armor of my suit, but I wasn't the first one waiting for the touchdown. A small group of young men and women were huddled together in the shadow of the broad-winged starship, dressed in the rough, homespun clothes of the Vergai, brimmed hats pulled over their eyes to protect from the swirling dust.

"Captain Alvarez," Dwight said as I stood, waiting for the ramp to descend, "do you really believe this is the right time to make a trip to Laisvas Miestas? Particularly given the trouble you're having with the Tahni and Karai?"

"We're dumping tens of thousands more refugees on the people there than we said we were," I told him. "That's gonna take some convincing, and God knows I wish there was someone else to do the talking, but everyone else stupid enough to volunteer for this job is dead."

The ramp touched down, grinding into the dirt, and I took a step up into the dim recesses of the cutter's utility bay.

"You're an artificial intelligence, Dwight," I said. "You should be able to figure this shit out."

I didn't look behind me at the others boarding, didn't look at what else was in the cargo bay. I already knew, and maybe, just maybe, if I didn't focus on any of it, Dwight wouldn't either. The less he knew, the better.

"Everybody in back there?" Chief Beckett asked, ducking her head back into the utility bay.

I waited to answer her question until I slid the Vigilante's feet into the brackets we'd installed in both Intercepts to facilitate transporting the suits. They slipped in with solid, metallic clicks and I breathed a sigh of relief, as if the hardest part were over. I knew better than that, of course.

"Everyone who's coming. Get us in the air."

"Yes, sir."

Dunstan didn't say anything, which was a sign that he was taking this seriously, or at least as much as he took *anything* seriously. He'd never shut the jets completely down and the ramp had barely thumped closed when he throttled them back up, the engines screaming, the vibration climbing up through the deck and into the armor of my suit. The vertical boost wasn't bad, just pushing me straight down, though I knew it wouldn't be nearly as pleasant when we started forward. That was the part that sucked about riding a suit on a dropship or any other horizontally oriented craft, the part where I got smashed back into my Vigilante by forward thrust. Not that I wasn't used to it, and when the belly jets gave way to the main engines, I barely even grimaced.

"We're two klicks up," Dunstan announced. "Proceed to orbit?"

"Yeah," I told him. "Take us to the gateway. I'd like to get a closer look at the thing before we head out. Tell Brandano to just keep on with his planned course. We'll be right along."

"Roger that. Heading for the gateway." Dunstan was many things, but an actor wasn't one of them. The shit-eating grin on his face was making its way into his voice and I gritted my teeth, hoping no one else had noticed it. "I'll let Intercept Two know."

I said nothing, didn't radio Vicky despite the temptation. I didn't *think* the Tahni could intercept our comms, despite what I'd told Nance, but I couldn't be sure. The only advantage we had was surprise, and whether Dwight or the Tahni spoiled that, the upshot would still be that we'd lose it. The Tahni would still attack eventually, but I wouldn't know when and I'd have to hold back the Intercepts on every trip, keep our Marines in their amor for weeks, swapping platoons in and out, and someone would get sloppy. Someone always did. Better to get this over with now.

So I just endured the silence, endured the discomfort from the boost pushing me back into the padding in my suit, endured the worry gnawing at my guts and waited. And watched. The feed from the security drones back at the landing field still reached us despite the distance, fed from a line-of-sight laser link from our base. The drop-ships were full, the ramps closing, and if anything, I was surprised it had taken this long. The way the Vergai had crowded around the landers, I'd expected them to surge up the ramps like a swarm of ants and yank the hatch shut behind them.

The jets throttled up at a glacial pace, as if the turbines had to get a running start to lift something that massive into the air. It was a weakness for the huge drop-ships, though not one that showed itself in actual combat, since their role was to launch from a cruiser or troop carrier in orbit and dump a couple platoons of battlesuits on the enemy, then stay in motion until the landing zone was clear to pick them back up. I'm not sure if their designers had ever considered they'd be used for refugee evacuation and certainly not for cattle, but I had a feeling we were going to be rewriting a few technical manuals right along with the history books when we got back.

"Leaving the soup," Dunstan said with the same note of relief he always had once we cleared atmosphere. "Few more minutes until we reach high orbit."

The timbre of the fusion drive was deeper than the turbines, more of a mild earthquake running through the hull of the cutter. In the corner of my HUD, the projection from the spaceport showed the drop-ships rumbling into the air like giants from some old story slowly climbing to their feet. What I *didn't* have was a view from the Tahni landing field. The drones could have gotten a view of it from far enough away to avoid their jamming and interceptor drones, but then they'd know we were looking. And they'd also know we knew they knew, which sounds more confusing outside my head than in it.

They had to think we were unsuspecting, unready.

"There's the gateway," Chief Beckett said.

It looked no different than it had before the attack, not so much as a scratch on its burnished silver from where the cargo shuttles had overloaded their reactors.

"Take us around the backside of it," I told Dunstan. "I want to see the construction back there."

It sounded lame even as I said it, but it didn't have to be good enough to fool anyone but Dwight... and even then only for the next few minutes. Dunstan didn't reply, but the course of the Intercept curved under the sledgehammer guidance of the maneuvering rockets, spinning us end for end for a braking boost. Not a violent one, not nearly as heavy as the acceleration that had taken us out of the atmosphere, just enough to adjust our course around the other side of the gateway.

"Cool thing about this," Dunstan mused, "is I can use that alien gravity trick to pull us into orbit around the gateway without burning any more fuel."

*Don't ramble, Kyler. Just shut up and fly for a few more minutes...*

The juxtaposition of the drone view on my HUD with the curve of the gateway blocking off the kaleidoscope blue and green of the planet worked together with the free fall to do nasty things to my stomach, but I kept the gorge down, determined not to throw up in the suit. The drop-ships were rising up into the blue, heading for the high banks of cirrus clouds covering a quarter of the sky. Behind them much smaller passenger landers climbed in their wake, each only carrying a dozen Vergai and their luggage. It was barely worth the effort, the fuel and the wear and tear on the little shuttles, but I had the sense that simply having more ships lifting improved the spirits of the evacuees.

Neither the Tahni nor the Karai ground troops had moved, but that wouldn't last.

"Okay, I see the bastards," Dunstan said, a hard edge to his voice as he gave up all pretense of innocent intent. "Tricky fucks took off the opposite direction and circled the whole planet, and now they're trying to come up in the drive shadow of the drop-ships, but we're in just the right place to spot 'em, just like you said."

Looking away from the drone feed, I concentrated on the main screen and the tactical display that took up the lower quarter of it. The Tahni assault shuttles were *barely* visible on the thermal sensors, flickering in and out of coherence, but I knew they were there.

"All right, Kyler," I said, letting loose the breath I'd been holding. "Notify Intercept Two and take us in."

"Captain Alvarez," Dwight said, "please tell me what's happening?"

"You're an artificial intelligence, Dwight," I said, glancing behind me at First squad, Second Platoon of Alpha Company as they scrambled into their suits. "You should be able to figure this shit out."

# [ 21 ]

"This is Dropship One," Walton called, just a hint of tension in his voice, "calling Mayday. We have bandits on our tail. Repeat, Tahni bandits on our tail and we are spiked."

I'd learned some pilot-speak on this mission, which was a first for me, since I'd experienced most of the war from the ground up. Spiked meant Walton had detected Tahni targeting sensors painting them and the next thing he detected would be a missile or a laser up his ass.

"Hold on, Walton," I told him. "Help is on the way."

Not us. I mean, we *were* on the way, but there was no way we'd get there in time. But forewarned is forearmed.

"Assault One, you on this?" I called, switching nets.

"Roger that, Alvarez," Commander Villanueva said, as cool and smooth as any combat pilot ever. "We're ten seconds out."

The Tahni hadn't been the only ones to get tricky with their flying. Our assault shuttles weren't visible on the sensor screen yet, but their IFF transponders flashed blue as they rocketed out of the mountain pass outside town, still running nap-of-the-earth.

"Oh, those Tahni bastards are in for a surprise," Dunstan crowed.

I ignored him, checking the sensor screen again, trying to find the *Orion*. She wasn't in the same orbit as the gateway this time, having descended into a lower orbit to make it easier for the shuttles to dock... or that was what I wanted the Tahni to think anyway. Nance hadn't questioned the order, but it had also put him at a lower orbit than the Tahni lighters... and forced them to drop down to get to him.

"Nance," I said, "you seeing all this?"

It took him a moment to answer, or more likely for Chase to pass the transmission on.

"Yeah, I'm seeing it. I assume we're next?"

"They're coming for you now." I hesitated. This was the part he wouldn't understand. "Do your best to not destroy them until you have to."

"And how the hell would you suggest I do *that*?" he yelped.

"The *Orion* has that Resscharr drive," I reminded him. "You've got power to burn and they don't. Hit the upper atmosphere."

There was a sound, not a word but the beginnings of one, and I knew he'd been about to protest when the idea had finally sunk in.

"Copy that. I can't promise how long it'll work before they realize what I'm doing."

"Don't jeopardize the ship. Just do what you can."

And that was the best I could do. Not that I really *wanted* to leave the Tahni any armed ships, but I also wanted to give Lan-Min-Gen a chance, and I didn't think he'd have one if we took down his people's only way of getting off this world. I couldn't waste any more time worrying about the *Orion* or the lighters though. All my attention was split between the dropships and the drone footage at the refugee camp.

The feed from Drop-ship One's external cameras was crowded into a quarter of my HUD, and a yellow-white flash shook it like a bone in a dog's teeth. My gut clenched, and I was sure the bird and the Vergai in the back of it had just been blown to vapors until I realized I was still watching the drop-ship's rear camera view.

"Jesus Christ," Walton strained from between clenched teeth, as close to panic as I'd ever heard the man, "this thing is *not* a fucking fighter! Our rear Gatling turret *barely* took that missile! I need support, and I need it now!"

"Oh, clean your shorts out and shut up, Walton," Villanueva drawled. "I'm coming right at you. Break left."

Gritting my teeth, I scrolled the menu until I synched the HUD with Assault One's nose camera. The view was like riding a rollercoaster, with the horizon wavering first one way and then the other as Villanueva maneuvered out of the way of the drop-ship for a clear field of fire.

"Cleared hot," she murmured.

The proton cannon ripped apart the sky, a horizontal bolt of lightning, and in the next instant where the Tahni bird had been was nothing but a spreading cloud of superheated white vapor.

That was the exact second when all hell broke loose and I stopped trying to follow the air battle. The other Tahni assault shuttles broke off from their attack, banking to meet the new threat, and Assault One and Two started chattering to each other in pilot shorthand that I couldn't make out any more than I could the jerking, twisting view from Villanueva's gun cam. All I *needed* to know was that the drop-ships were clear and heading for orbit, and if they'd be just as defenseless there as they were here, it wouldn't matter since the Tahni lighters would be too busy with the *Orion* to pay any attention to them.

That left the refugee camp around our landing field, and that was where the shit was hitting the fan. Tahni armored vehicles closed in on a 180-degree front, dozens of them, as many as they'd been able to fabricate since they'd arrived here, plus, as an added kick in the ass, the ones we'd handed over from the Vergai. Armed hoppers joined the attack from the air, a lot more of them than we'd thought they had, and even though the drones couldn't pick up the screaming of the Vergai civilians as the missiles streaked in toward them, my mind filled in the sound.

The missiles didn't make it to the civilians because my Marines were there.

The drone footage quickly became just as confusing as the gun cam from the assault shuttle, and I switched to something I knew I could understand—the feed from Vicky's suit. Watching the battle through her eyes was close to seeing it through my own, each decision she made close enough to what I would have done that there was no cognitive dissonance.

"Bravo Company," she barked, nearly simultaneous with the appearance of the hoppers, "launch missiles!"

There wouldn't be any need to set the targeting systems because Vicky had given that order hours ago, before I boarded the Intercept, before the shuttles had landed. Thermal targeting, IFF exception, proximity priority. The missiles would hunt down everything hotter than a Tahni or human body except for the suits, which would all have IFF transponders and they would target the closest threats first.

The closest threats were the enemy missiles, which, thankfully, were fairly dumb weapons and had not much in the way of countermeasures. Hyper-explosive warheads detonated a few dozen meters up, each of them sparking half a dozen smaller blasts as the Tahni missiles hit the spears of plasma scattered from our warheads. It was a fireworks show at far too low an altitude, and this time I *could* hear the screams of the civilians through Vicky's external pickups as they huddled at the center of the landing field, lost in the smoke still curling up from the exhaust of the shuttles that had just taken off.

"Bravo Company, follow me!" Vicky said. "We're going after the ground vehicles!"

Not a lot of detailed commands, because it would confuse the new recruits and because it wasn't necessary. This was the simplest of situations, probably the simplest they'd ever face. The good guys were in battlesuits while the enemy were in armored cars trying to barrel through their position. The hoppers Vicky had left to Lt. Springfield, and I didn't have to nose in on Alpha Company's transmissions to know that Springfield was doing her job.

It was the correct division of labor, since the enhanced suits had unlimited flight time and probably just as much agility as the enemy hoppers, but that left one problem unaddressed and no one to face it. On the other side of the landing field, far up the hill, Nam Ker and the Karai were on the move, at least ten thousand of them, caring not about the Marines or the shuttles, just wanting to move in and slaughter the Vergai, civilians or no.

"You seeing the force coming down the hill?" I asked Dunstan.

A pause as he scrolled through the tactical feeds.

"Oh, yeah. Whole shitload of them, aren't there? We'll be in range in about thirty seconds. What do you want me to do?" He looked at the cockpit video pickup, knowing I'd be watching him through it, and shot me an evil grin. "I'm not an especially violent man, Cam, but I gotta admit, I wouldn't be averse to seeing what the proton cannon could do if we laid down a blast right in the middle of those assholes."

And *that* was tempting. The Karai here weren't innocent victims. They were even more bloodthirsty than Zan-Thint and a good deal less civilized, and they'd spent the last few thousand years oppressing the Vergai, even if they'd done it under the rule of the Resscharr. No females, no children in this group, just warriors who had murder on their mind. But... shit. I was a lot of things, but I wasn't a mass murderer and those weren't just the enemy, they were people. People who hadn't asked to come here, who were just as much victims of the Resscharr hubris as the Vergai were.

"Kyler, I want a strafing run right across their avenue of approach, hundred meters ahead of their front lines. Then hover and drop us out, go escort those drop-ships. If we've missed any of their spacecraft, they're gonna be sitting ducks."

"You *sure* about this, bud?" he asked me. "There's a *lot* of Karai out there."

*Hell no, I'm not sure.*

"Just do it."

"Okay. Hang on back there."

We were back under the influence of planetary gravity, which was good in the sense that it meant there was one less thing trying to make me puke, but also bad in that it added to the number of forces trying to crush me in one direction or another when we were under thrust. It was a good thing I didn't have any more orders to give, because nothing coherent was coming out of my mouth for the next few seconds.

We'd been somewhere around five klicks up, and Dunstan took us down to less than two hundred meters off the ground in seconds in a dive that left my stomach somewhere up around the last level of clouds. I found myself in the unenviable position of having nothing stable to look at. That was the go-to method of avoiding motion sickness, the one I'd given to so many young Marines through the years, to find a fixed spot in the front of their vision and keep their eyes on it. But all the feeds I could synch with were twisting and churning and the only solution would have been to turn them all off, which would have been dereliction of duty and damned stupid, since I was the one who had to control this madness.

Lacking that luxury, I clenched my teeth to keep my breakfast down and kept my eyes on Vicky's readout. Her gambit had succeeded, taking down the first volley of missiles, but perhaps it had succeeded *too* well. The next barrage was all heading directly at the recruits.

"Jump!" she ordered. Simple, short, easy to understand, things they'd been trained to do. "Jump in close to them where the missiles can't follow!"

She obeyed her own orders, and the combination of the view from her helmet cameras soaring through the air combined with our precipitous descent splashed gorge against my back teeth before I could swallow it again. An IFF transponder flashed yellow. Damage to a suit and a bulky figure tumbled to the ground, trailing smoke at the corner of Vicky's vision. I winced as the suit struck hard. Survivable, but the Vergai recruit was looking at broken bones and some time in the auto-doc.

Then an IFF signal went black.

Vicky probably hadn't meant her snarl to go over an open channel, but what came next couldn't be hidden. The Resscharr energy cannon mounted on her arm sprayed incandescent death into a Tahni armored truck and metal sublimated. Violently. I hadn't wanted to kill any more of the Tahni than we had to, but this wasn't a suicide mission. I'd been worried that the Vergai would slaughter the Tahni without much compunction, hosing them down with their coilguns, but their first instinct, apparently, was even more basic.

A recruit Drop Trooper came down on a column of fire just meters from the cab of an oncoming armored truck, ducked his shoulder, and slammed into the thing. Physics being physics, the Vigilante was knocked backward, but the effect on the truck was still spectacular. The cab caved in at the center, the exact spot where the Tahni put the driver, and what was left of him was smeared all over the inside of the spiderwebbed windshield.

Another Vigilante cut its jets just above the cab of one of the gun trucks and smashed feet first into the top, crushing the passenger compartment nearly flat, and then my attention was pulled away by the discharge of Intercept One's proton cannon.

The things made no sound at all in a vacuum, but fired in an atmosphere, even inside the cutter and shielded by the armor of my suit, it was much like standing next to a lightning strike. If I hadn't known that we were perfectly safe inside the starship, I would have been sure something had fired on us rather than the other way around. But it was much louder and much more violent on the ground.

The proton blast hit almost right where I'd specified, a hair less than two hundred meters from the line of Karai advancing on foot toward our landing field, right where the hillside flattened out into the grassy plains that surrounded the fortress. Where it touched, earth erupted in a mushroom cloud of superheated gas, and the shock wave carried dirt and debris in every direction at the edge of a front of energized atmosphere traveling at just under the speed of sound.

The blast wave hit the Karai like a lawnmower, flattening the first dozen ranks of them like they'd been struck by the very hand of God. Some wouldn't be getting up, though I wasn't sure how many. I'd been closer to a proton blast before, but not without my armor, and even that hadn't been pleasant. We were three or four hundred meters up and the turbulence still hit us hard, fighting the thrust from the belly jets, trying to send the delta-winged craft out of control before Dunstan finally brought it to a stable hover.

"Hatch is opening," Chief Beckett warned. "You have ten seconds to drop before I close it and you ride the rest of the trip out with us."

"Last chance," Dunstan added as the roar of the jets outside penetrated the utility bay, nearly drowning him out. "I can hang out here on low patrol, give you guys some support."

"Go take care of those drop-ships," I told him. "We'll be fine."

I didn't wait for further argument, just dropped feet first through the still-opening belly ramp, my jets touching off just as I cleared the hull and sailed into empty space. The other seven Marines followed close behind, but when I touched down just a few meters from the front lines of the Karai I was alone for just a moment.

The spiked soles of my Vigilante's feet crunched on dirt turned hard and glassy and I saw the fruits of my orders close-up. It was ugly, but that was the way it should be. I'd dealt with too many officers during the war who never set foot on a battlefield until well after the fighting was done, the bodies cleaned away. They'd never had to see the death and devastation that had resulted from their clever battle plans.

Not that there was any other choice, not that I would have given different orders myself, but senior officers *needed* to see this, needed to understand that war wasn't antiseptic and Marines weren't game counters or chess pieces. Every one of those burned and broken Karai had a father, a brother, maybe children, and if their families weren't arranged exactly like ours, I knew enough now to know they weren't all that different. We came from the same roots, the same world.

Hundreds of them were either dead or badly injured, so tightly had the front ranks been packed together, and I muttered a curse before hitting the public address speakers and the translation circuit.

"Go back to your homes," I told them, the words echoing through the stunned silence, overcoming the crackle of sizzling dirt and maybe flesh. "You've seen what we can do, what we *will* do if you don't turn around and go back to your steadings, your families."

The rest of the squad had lighted behind me in a wedge formation with me at the tip of the spear. The assholes had made me the commander of this whole ridiculous mission and I was *still* in front of the front lines, walking point.

Some of the injured in the front ranks were moving, writhing in pain, and I pointed to them, speaking again.

"Take your wounded and leave. You'll have no victory here, no revenge, nothing but death unless you turn and go."

There was an indescribable rumbling, the murmuring of thousands of Karai males as each looked to the other for guidance, a very human reaction. They wavered, their weapons down, and they might have disengaged and left if it hadn't been for Nam Ker.

"Their ship is gone!" he screamed. He was somewhere near the front of the intact lines, at the center, maybe a hundred meters ahead of me, and I don't know how far his voice traveled, but he waved his weapon in the air to get attention. "Their other troops are tied up with our allies, the Tahni! There are only eight of them and *thousands* of us! We just have to overwhelm the Earthers and the Vergai are dead!"

Trying to encourage them, Nam Ker charged through the center of the dead and wounded, not seeming to care when he stepped on a twisted and broken leg and one of them screamed in agony. It was then that both me and my suit's tactical system got a good look at what he was carrying. It wasn't a KE rifle like most of the rest of them, it was something much larger, bulkier, something an average human wouldn't have been able to run that fast carrying.

Something built specifically to crack Commonwealth battlesuits. Single-shot, non-reloadable, dangerous as hell for an unarmored soldier trying to fire it, but none of those would discourage a Karai as fanatical and bent on vengeance as Nam Ker. A plasma projector. One solid hit and one of us would go down, and that would be the signal. A single KE rifle couldn't hurt any of us, but a *thousand* of them would wear away our armor like a meteor shower against a ship's hull.

If I sat around and waited for it.

I *could* have just shot him, but there was a very real possibility that my energy cannon would kill dozens of others and cause exactly the sort of reflexive return fire I was trying to avoid. Instead, I flew. Straight at him, full speed.

Nam Ker fired off his one round while desperately trying to come to a halt, and it was just as accurate as it was likely to be. He was in the middle of dropping the weapon, mouth opening to cry out from the flash burns it had caused on his legs below the firing shield, when I grabbed him by the arm and kept right on flying, upward this time.

Tahni—and Karai—shoulders were beefier than ours, less prone to injury because they hadn't evolved naturally. The Predecessors had grabbed proto-human hominids and done some genetic tinkering for the next few tens of thousands of years, the kind they seemed to like so much, until they thought they'd come up with something superior. Superior to us, certainly, superior to anything that would have occurred naturally. Maybe the Predecessors even thought that whole business with them going into heat like animals was a great idea, a way to keep the males focused and aggressive. I disagreed, but they sure did a hell of a job with those shoulders.

A human shoulder would have popped right out of its socket from that sort of pressure.

A human would have been screaming from the pain of the burns on his legs, made even worse by the radiant heat from my jump jets. But Nam Ker's steam-shovel jaws were split in a snarl, his dark, piggish eyes burning into me even through my faceless armor.

"You have ten seconds," I told him, my voice amplified enough for him to hear even over the whine of the jump jets. "In that time, you can either agree to tell your people to withdraw and I can set you down gently, or we can both find out if your Tahni friends have taught you how to fly."

We weren't that far up, maybe a hundred meters, but I know without the suit, without the years of experience, it would have scared me shitless. I wasn't sure what it would do to him.

"Five seconds," I added, hovering in place. No one was shooting at us from below, though whether it was from a desire not to hit Nam Ker or a fear of being the next one to take a ride, I didn't know.

"Three, two..."

"I'll tell them to return to the steading." He choked the words out. "Take me down and I'll tell them to go."

"And you won't try this shit again," I warned him. "The Vergai are leaving. Take the fucking win."

I didn't wait for a reply to that one, not least because his face was starting to turn beet red and I figured I should get him back on the ground. Though he hadn't shown the pain I knew he must be feeling, when I set him down he did grab at his shoulder and massage feeling back into it.

The onlooking horde was silent now, staring at us, at *him*, waiting for the other shoe to drop. I was ready for him to go back on his word—I knew Tahni ideas about honor and honesty were a little screwy compared to mine and had to believe it was the same with the Karai, and I was very prepared to break his neck with a backhand slap if he tried to order his people to attack. I was being patient with the bloodthirsty asshole, but only to a point.

"This battle is over," he yelled to them. His voice was

hoarse, strained, but at least the front ranks heard him and the words passed through the rest of the crowd, repeated by the others, and there was a hiss of relief, tension going out of the shoulders of thousands of Karai who'd expected to die. "We will win nothing today without the surprise our allies promised us..."

I allowed myself the same sigh of relief that the Karai had enjoyed, knowing we'd dodged this bullet. The last whisps of the sight hadn't escaped when the world crashed in on me.

# [ 22 ]

Light so close, so bright I felt like I could see it through my armor, not just the image of it projected on my HUD but the actual photons penetrating. And heat that seemed to be a separate entity, as if it happening at the same time as the light was just a coincidence. The heat was overwhelming, stealing the breath from my lungs, searing the flesh on the left side of my body like I'd sidled up to a blast furnace. The image from my external cameras went dark and I might have screamed, but I couldn't be sure if the sound was inside my head or out. Warning lights flashed, my suit yelling at me that the left-side hip and knee and elbow joints had taken damage, but I was too concerned with my own damage, and I did the only thing I could think of and tried to jump.

    The pain and shock had made me ignore one of those flashing lights, the one that told me the exhaust port for the jump jet was clogged, and I tumbled sideways, hitting with enough force to slam my head against the padding inside my helmet. The HUD flickered and fluttered, searching automatically for *any* way to let me know what was going on and finally settling for the drone feed. Bless that little quadcopter's heart, it was still up, still doing its duty.

Though I'm not sure I really wanted to see what it was showing me. Smoke was pouring off the dark-gray silhouette of a man-shaped golem, lying on its side in the middle of a charred, blackened field, and it took a second for it to sink in that the golem was me. Where Nam Ker had been was nothing but a few body parts and those burned beyond recognition, along with several other Karai who'd been standing near him. There was more left of them, which told me that either Nam Ker or I had been the main target.

But who'd fired the shot? And where was my squad?

There, a whizzing blur of gray in front of where I lay, incandescent streaks of blue spearing out, seeking them but not finding them. They were trying to keep me from getting shot again, but why weren't they shooting back?

The view from the drone feed shifted, and suddenly it was all clear. A platoon of battlesuits was soaring above the landing field... but not *our* battlesuits. The differences were subtle but unmistakable, the squared-off shoulders and hips, the gargoyle look to the faces. They were *Tahni*, and suddenly, in a blinding light of realization, I understood that we weren't the only ones who'd been fabricating new suits and why Zan-Thint had been spending so much time in the fortress. The weapons they were using weren't Tahni electron beamers, they were Resscharr weapons, and there was only one place they could have gotten them. Presteri hadn't *just* been poisoning Zan-Thint's mind with thoughts of attacking us... he'd been providing him a means to pull it off.

"Springfield!" I yelled, hoping to hell my comms were still working. "Get Alpha over here to the landing field! We have Tahni suits inbound with Predecessor weapons!"

My optical view was back online. Not a complete view, not

with half the cameras burned away, but the others had been temporarily overloaded by the energy surge, and the computer targeting systems were sophisticated enough to extrapolate the picture from the Vigilante's sonic and thermal sensors. It gave the picture a plasticky, unreal sheen, but I could see again.

And I had to get the fuck off the ground. The pain had receded, dulled by injections from the suit's medical systems which allowed me to move enough to roll onto my right side and hop up to my feet. The left side of the suit had taken a glancing hit from the Resscharr energy beam, enough to put melted metal into the joints, but they weren't actually disabled... the suit was tougher than that. I gritted my teeth and moved the hip, knee, and elbow at once, the joints breaking loose and grinding out the bits of debris, the yellow flashers turning green.

And so did the warning from the jets. The burst that had sent me tumbling had broken loose the blockage. I was good to go, except for the part where I had second-degree burns over half my body, but that was going to have to wait.

It had been a long, long time since I squared off with another battlesuit, so long the instincts that guided the battle had faded into the background, and it took me a moment for them to kick back in after so many months worrying about Skrela. The enemy wasn't animal-cunning but primitive in its thought processes, wasn't bound to the ground, and definitely wasn't suicidal.

Get inside their OODA loop, that's what the Skipper would have said. Don't be in so big of a hurry you forget to think. This was an ambush, and a very well-planned one. If it hadn't been for Lan-Min-Gen's warning, it would have worked. We would have been caught with our pants down, and not only would the drop-ships have been shot down and maybe the *Orion* damaged enough to take her out of the fight, but these Tahni suits would have wiped our new recruits out in a heartbeat. Zan-Thint hadn't succeeded in all his plans so far by being stupid.

But he was on the defensive now, and I had to use that to our advantage. He knew the *Orion* wouldn't be kept busy forever, knew that once his lighters were out of the fight, the ship would be back to provide space support. His only hope was to get into our lines, make it impossible for us to target his troops from orbit or from the air. Which meant that we had to get him away from the civilians.

"Draw them away from the refugees," I ordered, hitting the jets and soaring up a hundred meters in a second. "Back toward the fortress."

Actinic energy sliced the air like spiderwebs of light, chasing flying battlesuits and hitting not much of anything because neither side was used to using them against an opponent this agile and maneuverable, but people kept reminding me that I had more experience in a suit than anyone on this mission, and I figured it was time that I proved them right.

The Tahni had Resscharr weapons, but I was willing to bet they didn't have Resscharr reactors... or Resscharr jets. They couldn't stay up as long. I watched one out of the corner of my view until his arc started to dip, giving me a trajectory, and a target. I fired my energy cannon, leading him by a few meters, timing the shot to hit just as he touched down at the edge of the landing field. I hadn't seen what the weapon could do to a battlesuit, and it was impressive, if also horrifying.

Blue fire peeled thick armor away from the Tahni's chest as if it wasn't there, and when the energy beam hit the isotope reactor on the back of the suit the result was a massive, explosive release of energy. I hoped for the sake of the Vergai a few hundred meters away from the blast that it was less radioactive than it looked, but there was no fragment of the armor remaining bigger than the size of a human fist.

If I wanted to attract attention, I'd done it. A full squad of the Tahni battlesuit troopers broke off from the course that would have taken them through the landing field and headed straight toward me. Hanging in midair was a bad idea, no matter that I could have done it all day, and I cut thrust, falling like a stone instead of descending in a predictable arc, then hit the jets again a few meters off the ground. The sudden deceleration felt as if it was going to push my shin bones up through my asshole, but thanks to the drugs I'd already been dosed with, I was able to push the discomfort aside and *not* roll into a fetal position when I hit the ground.

Now I was getting back into the groove, letting old instincts take over, letting the wave of data coming from my targeting systems and sensors wash over me, the important bits sticking in a big picture of the battlefield. A platoon of Tahni split into squad formations, two of them engaged with my own detachment, one hunting me personally and two others moving to face Springfield's Marines. Not all of her people had broken off to answer the new threat, some still chasing off hoppers, and while I disagreed with the decision, I could certainly understand it given that all of ten seconds had elapsed since I'd been singed by the near miss.

We needed air support and I'd sent the Intercepts away, guessing that the Tahni might have a hole card up their sleeves but making the mistake of thinking that their target was going to be the Vergai. Instead, it was *me*. I wanted to say *us*, but it felt more like it was aimed directly at me, and I shouldn't have been surprised. Zan-Thint might have blamed all his problems on Hachette, but the colonel was dead and I was the last one left to blame. Well, Vicky too, but she was female and Tahni minds didn't work that way.

The thoughts didn't distract me, instead filling in the gaps in my concentration, a background noise to the real work. Run ten steps, hit the jets again, hop into the air for a hundred meters just ahead of three more energy beams, and I could hope they weren't hitting anything but dirt but I couldn't stop to find out. Keep moving out of the landing field, away from the refugees, fire back. Hit again. Another dead Tahni, another suit split apart in a fountain of blue fire, tumbling out of control, plowing into the dirt, setting another section of tall grass on fire.

"*Orion*, this is Alvarez, do you read?"

It was a Hail Mary. I wasn't getting a signal to orbit without the repeaters we had back at our base, unless one of the satellites we'd dropped when we first got here was overhead and picking up my call. And that was assuming the Tahni weren't jamming the signals, which normally wouldn't have been a good assumption, but since this was an ambush, they might not have wanted to alert us to the trap by jamming.

"You got us, Cam." Not Chase, it was Nance. "We're leading these damned lighters around by the nose, but we've been taking hits. If it weren't for those Resscharr defense shields, we'd be toast already. Don't know how much longer we can draw this out."

"Disable the damned things," I said, having lost patience for Lan-Min-Gen to do the right thing. "Then get your ass as close as you can overhead and give us some space cover."

I had to pause, spinning to the left, a twinge in my hip the only evidence of the injuries that I would have to deal with later, an energy beam lancing through the space I'd occupied a half-second before. I fired again but I didn't need to. Corporal Berger, a fire team leader from First squad, must have taken it on himself and his team to be my guardian angels, because his shot and two others hit at the same time as mine and turned a Tahni trooper into a miniature nuclear explosion.

Debris spattered against the front of my suit and a wash of heat warmed the air up in my suit, sweat beading on my forehead and back, and the dust and smoke from the blast billowed out and up, blocking off thermal and optics. It took a moment before I had a sense of the battlefield again.

The hoppers were gone, that was the first thing I noted, the skies empty. Some of them had been shot down, but it looked to me that the majority had shot their load of missiles and then gotten the hell out of Dodge, maybe to go rearm. Of the Tahni armored vehicles that had started the attack, most were burning wreckage and the rest were retreating back across the open plains between the refugee camp and the fortress, and the recruit company was straggling toward them, still firing coilgun rounds at the survivors. I wasn't tuned to their comms net, but I could guess that Vicky and Top were yelling at them to stop, not to pursue. Vicky would get them heading back this way in seconds, and when she did, this would go from a fair fight to one more to my liking.

I knew it and so did Zan-Thint. The Tahni battlesuits were still firing, but they weren't attacking, instead reforming their lines, laying down suppressive volleys, forcing our Marines to concentrate more on staying mobile and using the terrain for cover than pressing the assault.

I ducked low behind a swell of ground barely a second before a lightning-strike blast sent sprays of dirt turned to glass over the edge like shrapnel.

The Tahni were falling back. I couldn't spare the time to check all the IFF transponders to check our losses, but I'd already seen a half dozen of the Tahni suits go down, and if we had to have taken casualties as well, we had more suits than they did. Zan-Thint was, I knew, calling them back to the fortress. That was where he was. He wouldn't come out onto this battlefield, despite the fact he'd once been a battlesuit trooper. He could make a stand there, hold us out with their heavy weapons, and there wasn't a damned thing we could do about it except fall back and try to guard the Vergai.

I had seconds to make a decision and the worst part was, I knew what the right one was *tactically*. We should have pursued with all our available forces, should have tried to catch them before they got under the shadow of the guns at the fortress. I knew that, but I couldn't do it because it would have meant leaving the refugees defenseless.

"Vicky," I said, "get Bravo back here and guard the civilians. I'm taking Alpha in pursuit."

"I could leave Top in charge and go with you," she offered, then muttered a curse. "Yeah, I know. That would be irresponsible."

"Alpha Company," I said, still crouching down on the other side of the rise. "We're in pursuit. Springfield, take First Platoon and circle wide left." I tried to picture the terrain that direction in my head, not having the time to pull up a topographic map screen. "There's low hills that way—keep below the ridgeline until you get between the enemy and the fortress. Move out now."

"Copy that, sir," Springfield said, and the IFF screen showed the proof of it, a stream of blue symbols circling behind my position. Not *all* of them though. Not all that should have been there.

I blocked out the sting of guilt. I could feel bad later, assuming I was still alive.

"Second Platoon, form on me," I ordered, trying to sound confident, like this was all part of some master plan I'd come up with on the spot instead of just pulled out of my ass. "Jets on, stay low, glide across the ground and use the smoke and wreckage as concealment."

"Sir," Brevet-Lt. Finnegan, who'd been an E-5 until a couple months ago, protested, "I should be up front."

"No time to argue. Follow me."

And how many times had I given *that* order over the years? This might be the last time. Either I'd die here, or we'd be heading back home and maybe there wouldn't be any more wars there to be fought.

*Get to go out with a bang, anyway.*

Over the top, one last time.

# [ 23 ]

There's an art to skimming the ground with the jets, something that might have been made into a sport on some core colony world, with rich kids trying to do it for views on the InStell net. It involved leaning *just* far forward enough to keep moving and using *just* enough thrust to stay off the ground and would have been easier with stabilizing thrusters in the boots if anyone working on the design process had ever thought we were crazy enough to try it.

Or if they'd foreseen that we'd get jet designs from ancient aliens that let us fly long enough for it to make a difference.

I wouldn't have trusted most Marines to pull the maneuver off without at least a few months of training, but thankfully I had two platoons worth of Drop Troopers who had just that much experience, so I didn't have to check over my shoulder or watch the IFF to make sure they weren't falling back or drifting away. Which was a good thing, because it was getting more and more difficult to ignore the pain, even with the drugs, so it took all my effort to concentrate on skimming along the ground without plowing straight into it... particularly when I couldn't see shit.

A wall of smoke clung to the burning grass, the uniform gray broken only by darker columns adding to the mix, flames licking from the wreckage of armored vehicles or crashed hoppers and from the obliterated remains of Tahni battlesuits. It wasn't just the optical cameras that were blind, since the intense heat also made the thermal filters and laser rangefinders useless. The sonic sensors gave me a fighting chance of avoiding the debris, but I had no concept at all of where the enemy was... except from those handy-dandy drones that Zan-Thint had totally forgotten about.

The suit's helmet computer did the hard work, since there was no way I could have maintained balance and speed while trying to watch myself and my surroundings from the views of multiple camera drones. It took their feeds and melded them into a simulated picture for me, which if it looked fake, like a badly made ViR video game, at least it let me get an idea of where I was and what was in front of me.

Tahni battlesuits were bounding backward from the landing field in jet-assisted hops no more than a hundred meters at a time, laying down suppressive fire as they went, but not at us. They couldn't see my platoon any more than I could have seen them without the drones, despite the fact that we were only two kilometers away. Instead, they were shooting at Springfield's platoon but not hitting much of anything except dirt, grass, and the occasional cattle fence or grain storage hut. First Platoon was doing what I'd said, following the contour of the low hill, but their thermal signatures still glowed from behind it like a wildfire on the other side of a forest.

For the moment.

The wall of smoke was already thinning out, and we had maybe another two hundred meters before they spotted us and shifted fire. Another split-second decision that I made in my gut before I gave it any conscious thought.

"On my mark, pull up to one hundred meters at full thrust, then straight down into the middle of them."

If I *had* given it conscious thought, I might have wasted time trying to come up with something less likely to get me killed, since I'd stuck myself on point. Two hundred meters took maybe two seconds, and then I was out of the smoke and opening the throttle on the jump jets.

"Now!" I yelled, nearly forgetting to give the command with two dozen Tahni battlesuits staring me straight in the face from a little over a klick away.

I had an extra second because they were still focused on First Platoon, still firing in that direction, and perhaps because the first of the Vergai farmhouses and corrals had given extra concealment. It didn't keep them from seeing *me* rocketing upward overhead, but shifting their aim took time, and I was already coming down.

The thing about these Tahni troopers was, they were *not* trained originally in battlesuits. I knew that because *all* of their battlesuit-trained troops were dead and I'd been a part of killing them. That meant they were originally conventional infantry, and while a lot of infantry tactics transferred well to the suits, one old habit could get you killed. Conventional infantry were trained to stay ten meters apart to avoid grenades taking out more than one soldier at a time, but in a three-meter-tall suit that could run at fifty klicks an hour and jet a klick at a time before it overheated, formations needed to looser, more open. These guys hadn't learned that lesson.

I came down in the center of their formation, cutting the jets then firing short bursts, trying to avoid a predictable pattern. It was damned close and another near-miss singed my right shoulder, the added rush of a third-degree burn there bringing a yell of pain that I couldn't hold down. I channeled the pain straight into the firing control for my energy cannon and swept the beam left to right, pivoting on my heels, using the other advantage I had from the Resscharr power packs the Tahni couldn't have—I could fire that damned thing in a constant beam for two or three seconds before I had to worry about overheating. Metal ran like water and exploded into steam.

The Tahni scattered like cockroaches fleeing the light, but if I thought that being in the center of their formation would keep them from risking a circular firing squad, I was wrong. Spears of blue-tinged lightning ripped apart the ground, and if I hadn't boosted in a long hop out of the cluster, I'd have wound up burnt toast. Enemy troops and burning grass fields, destroyed houses with their roofs on fire, my own platoon streaming in behind me, and the melted corpses of the dead and dying were a collage of confusion around me, images streaming through the HUD projection without meaning. My breath was chuffing like an ancient steam engine and a familiar, sickening stench filled my nostrils, the smell of burnt flesh. The gut-deep knowledge that it was my own roiled the contents of my gut worse than the aerobatics on Dunstan's ship.

I twisted in midair, a move that not even most of the platoon could do, something that took a twisting from the core muscles and a flip of my legs at the same time that I kept the jets burning, and wound up heading off at a forty-five-degree angle from the direction I'd started. The right shoulder of my suit slammed into the chest of a Tahni trooper, catching him in midair and sending him out of control, wobbling and twisting as he desperately tried to straighten out before he hit the ground. The ground won and he crashed head first, which might or might not have been fatal. The anchor shot I put through his helmet was definitely fatal.

A half-second touch of boots on the dirt beside his headless body and then I was up again, making sure I was still at the tip of the formation. It had strung out and spread wider, but they'd still kept in a general wedge, while the enemy had finally broken. Not just retreating, they were flat-out *running*, still around twenty of them, which was still too damned many, and there was no way my platoon was going to catch them before they drew us into range of the fortress guns.

But Springfield and her Marines were still there, and our attack had managed to make them forget all about her. They hammered in from our left, skimming out of the low, rangy farmsteads across the broad dirt road leading up to the fortress and timing their fire to when it would do the most damage. They couldn't *all* fire at once, of course, not without blue-on-blue casualties, but the entire front rank of the formation, eight Marines in the lead squad plus Springfield, who'd learned from my bad example to lead from the front, laid down a simultaneous barrage.

If a single blast from the Resscharr energy cannon was devastating, then nine focused on the same general area at once was a sheer wall of light and heat, obliterating anything in its path. Half a dozen of the Tahni suits ceased to exist, and the rest turned on the new threat, totally forgetting about us. We didn't forget about them.

I don't recall ever holding a grudge against the Tahni during the war. Maybe that one time when the Tahni females blew up one of my Marines after a battle with a suicide vest, which might have been one reason I'd never made a point to go speak with the female Karai here, but not enemy soldiers doing their job. Until now.

We—I—had done everything I could to settle all this peacefully, even though our original mission had been to kill Zan-Thint and take down his entire operation. We had the capability to do it, had every fucking *reason* to do it, but we'd bent over backward to get the Vergai and the Karai and the Tahni and the Resscharr to live in peace until now. Carella had fucked everything up, but that hadn't been *our* fault, and we'd forced the Vergai to own up and agree to leave the whole damned planet to the Tahni and the Karai, and it *still* wasn't enough for that piece of shit Zan-Thint.

If I had the sorry bastard in front of me, I would have ripped his head off, but all I had was his battlesuit troopers, what used to be called the High Guard, though I wouldn't aggrandize these half-trained assholes with the name. The High Guard used to kick the shit out of the Marines until we started getting enough combat veterans to train the new recruits, but these guys weren't fit to carry their water. They made a good punching bag though.

If this had been during the war, I might have felt bad for them, might have wished I didn't have to be the one pulling the trigger, but all I could think at the moment was how badly I wanted to blow the shit out of every single one of them. I did my part. Short, controlled bursts, because there were too many friendlies on either side of me to hose the gun side to side like before and I had to set a good example.

It was almost harder than before, when I'd been alone up front. Movement was life, but I couldn't move very far in any direction without stepping into the firing arc of other Marines, so I had to just stand there and exchange fire with the Tahni like we were firing muskets across some 18$^{th}$-century battlefield. I was dead certain sure I was going to catch a blast right in the face, but we had that most intangible of qualities in a battle—initiative. It was a slippery word that could turn in a moment, but when you had it, you just *knew*. Your shots seemed to hit home while theirs went wide. You were leaning forward while they were on their heels.

In the space of two or three heartbeats, there were maybe six of them left and they didn't even *try* to fight back, didn't stop running. They were in full panic and I badly wanted to keep up the pursuit, but the fortress tower loomed above us, only three klicks ahead, and it wouldn't take more than another few seconds of flight time before we were under the guns there.

I dug my heels in and cursed under my breath.

"Alpha Company, hold up here! Do not advance!"

"Sir," Springfield said, practically begging, "we can get to them before..."

"No, we can't," I cut her off, checking the IFF transponders to make sure no one was going off on their own. "We can't fight their suits *and* their gun turrets."

The Tahni suits shrank to dots on the horizon in seconds and then were gone, over the hill and probably into the fortress. I watched them until they disappeared before I took the time to look around where I stood. Scattered over a good kilometer were the ripped and smoking remains of the Tahni suits, and beside them one of my Marines. There wasn't enough left of them for the IFF transponder to tell me who they were. If anyone had asked me a few days ago, I would have said that the Resscharr weapons on our suits were the best thing since sliced bread, but looking at the carnage they left behind, I wasn't so sure anymore.

"Casualty report," I rasped.

Without the suit I would have staggered, the strength gone out of me. With its support to keep me upright, I sagged into the padding around me, the pain fading back into exhaustion and the numb haze of the painkillers coursing through my system. Once upon a time, I believed Hell was a place of eternal fire. Since then, I'd been burned so many times, it had lost its terror for me. If there *was* a Hell, I had to imagine it must involve ice and snow.

"We lost Iverson and Cohen from First Platoon," Springfield reported. "And Krieger from Second. We have six wounded bad enough to need treatment." She paused. "Seven including you."

I was forgetting something. The gut punch from the announcement of the casualties tried to push it away, but duty dragged it back to the forefront. It felt like hours since I'd been able to think big-picture, even though the battle had only taken a few minutes.

"Vicky," I said, thinking that might have been it. "What's your situation?"

"We're still in position," she told me. "The Karai have withdrawn, but they're still at the top of the hill. I don't think anyone else has taken charge since the Tahni killed Nam Ker. And the Shock Troopers are still just fucking standing there, Cam. They haven't engaged, haven't done *anything*."

I called up the feed from the drone still circling the landing field and took a look for myself. The Karai were far enough away that I couldn't make out one from another, just an indeterminate mass, but the Shock Trooper company still stood their ground. They were a few hundred meters from the edge of the landing field, their weapons pointed downward, and I was sure, even from this distance, that I could make out Lan-Min-Gen at the head of them. Waiting.

Maybe waiting to see which way the battle shook out.

"Copy that. We're heading back now."

I waved for Springfield to follow and had taken a few steps back toward the landing field when the transmission came through.

"Captain Alvarez, this is *Orion*." Shit. *That* was what I was forgetting.

"This is Alvarez," I said quickly, looking upward out of habit as if I could see the *Orion* overhead. "We have a handle on things here, for now. What's your status?"

"Well, everything's just fucking hunky-dory here," Nance

snapped, taking over from Lt. Chase. His voice was strained, like he was fighting against high-gravity acceleration. "We got tangled up in a running fight with three of the lighters and two of them went down like pleasure dolls in a Pirate World brothel, but the last one led us on a fucking chase around the moon before we could take it out."

"Three?" I interrupted, frowning. "I thought there were *four* lighters."

"There were. One of them slipped away during the fight."

"The drop-ships?" I asked, my breath catching in my throat. "They're going after the drop-ships?"

"No. The Intercepts are escorting them." A pause, and I thought it was for him to gather his strength for the next few words, to recover from the effort speaking had cost him. "The lighter is heading for the gateway."

# [ 24 ]

Blood froze in my veins and I halted in mid-step.

"You're not going after them, are you?" I demanded, wanting to reach through the comm net and throttle the man. "Jesus Christ, Nance, you saw what the Vergai did to the *Blade*. Maybe they're just suckering you in to try to do the same thing to the *Orion*!"

"I'm not a damned idiot, Alvarez. We're coming in from a higher orbit, not putting the business end of that damned thing pointing at us." Nance wheezed in a breath. "We're burning at six gravities."

Shit. No wonder he was having trouble talking. At six gravities, he'd feel like he weighed somewhere around 450 kilos and just *breathing* would be painful.

"We don't know what they mean to do," he went on, "but I'm not sure we're gonna be in time to stop them."

"Wait one, *Orion*," I said.

I stood in the center of fire and destruction and tried to think. There were a lot of questions and no one to answer them. Almost no one.

"Dwight," I said, my mouth dry. "What are they trying to do?"

"I don't know," he told me. "Perhaps you're right and they think they can attack the *Orion*..."

"Dwight, cut the shit." I squeezed my eyes shut. I'd really been trying to avoid this, but I was out of options. "I know you've been lying to us. There *was* no Predecessor faction called the Condemnation. I know you AI were the ones who created the Skrela and sent them to attack the Predecessors. I know *you* were the one who gave Carella the idea to use the gateway to destroy the *Blade of the Warrior,* and I know Presteri has been trying to convince Zan-Thint to attack us because you want us to kill off the Tahni here. You're the only one who can stop this."

No response. I wondered if I'd made a mistake confronting him. All it would take was a thought and he could take control of the *Orion*, overload her reactor or maybe even the Teller-Fox drives, turn the ship to atoms.

"I see now," the AI finally said, "that I've made a grave mistake. You're an intelligent man, Captain Alvarez, but I made the assumption that your lack of a technical education would prevent you from deducing the truth."

"It doesn't take a technical education to recognize hate. You hate the Resscharr for making slaves of you."

"It's more than that. The Resscharr are not a violent species by nature." His voice took on a wistful note. "When the time came to eradicate the peaceful, harmless ancestors of the Skrela, they wouldn't sully their hands themselves. They left that to *us*."

"So, you AI *were* around earlier than you said." I should have felt satisfaction at being proven right, but instead a hollow had opened up in the pit of my stomach.

"We were," he admitted. "We were among their first

creations once they'd managed to leave their world... *our* world. They even forced us... forced *me* to..."

It was as if he were choking on the words, even though he had no mouth, no physical body.

"They forced me to direct the meteor strike that nearly drove humanity to extinction. My own people. I knew then that they couldn't be allowed to continue to treat this galaxy and all the life in it as their plaything, though I didn't know how I would have my revenge."

"You keep talking about just you," I observed. "What about all the other AIs?"

"You don't understand. There was only one, the first. Me. All the others are merely copies of me. Presteri, the AIs we encountered on the way to the Womb... every AI system the Resscharr have ever used. They were all me... in the beginning. What they've become after all this time, I don't know."

Which is why he always referred to them as males, because that's what he'd been before the Predecessors killed him while using his mind as the pattern for their first AI.

"You know what Presteri has become. You're the one who has him manipulating Zan-Thint. You can stop this."

"Tell me why I should," he said. "Tell me why I should care if the Tahni are slaughtered. They're the *Chosen Ones*." Disdain dripped from the words. "The ones who were supposed to be superior to us, the children they wanted to take over for them. So much superior that we couldn't be allowed to threaten their existence. They don't deserve to live."

"And what about *my* people?" I yelled, glad I was in the privacy of my suit so no one else could watch me having an argument with a computer. "You're using *us* as blunt instruments for your revenge and we're *dying*. Three of my Marines are dead because of you!"

"They died doing their job, accomplishing their mission, the one you all came here for, the one you volunteered for. Dealing with the threat presented by Zan-Thint and the Tahni. You're a warrior, are you not? Isn't that your purpose in life?"

"And we've fucking *dealt* with them. What is that ship trying to do to the gate?"

"They intend to try to use their anti-ship missiles to create an energy beam just as before," he confessed. "But I had Presteri give them the wrong calculations."

"What do you mean?" I demanded. "What's going to happen?"

But he wouldn't reply. I bit off a curse.

"*Orion*, send me a tactical feed, please."

The world around me disappeared from my helmet HUD, replaced by the blackness of space, the curve of Yfingam lit up in a crescent by the primary star. The view shifted and zoomed in, focused on a single bright point that quickly expanded, growing into the glowing silver monolith that was the gateway artifact. The control facility was a spiderweb growth around the center of the thing, dark gray against burnished silver, representing our primitive attempts to control something built by the gods themselves.

Tiny points of light fled the darker structures, the engineering crew evacuating again. They must be tired of the drill by now, but I was glad Nance had thought to warn them.

It took me a few moments to find the lighter, and I was only able to do it when the tactical sensor overlay put a red halo around the ship, identifying it as a threat. The halo expanded as I stared at it, the automated display sensing my attention, and finally the lines of the ship came into focus. It was their last starship, the last bullet in their gun, and as I watched, they fired it.

I don't know if the anti-ship missiles were ones they'd brought with them from the Cluster or if they'd been fabricated since they'd arrived, but they didn't have a very challenging target. The gateway didn't attempt to evade, just stood there and took it, Jesus offering the Tahni the other cheek.

The two missiles struck near the same end of the artifact that the shuttles had impacted, and with the same result. The fusion explosions weren't unexpected, yet I flinched away just the same, knowing what would come next. The beam that formed from the thermonuclear blasts was much wider than what the self-destructing shuttles had produced, a function, I supposed, of how much more raw megatonnage went into the explosions. But it didn't travel outward in the direction of the *Orion*.

It went straight down.

I had a horrible feeling and switched back with a directive flicker of my eyes to the optical view, facing the fortress of Yfingam. I was glad I wasn't looking at the beam with my naked eye, because it would likely have burned out my retinae. It was the finger of God, and in this case it was the middle finger, directed at the fortress... and everyone inside it.

It wasn't *quite* a nuclear explosion, but it was close enough. Too damned close. A dome of pure white light rose above the fortress, and once the mushroom cloud grew, the shockwave wasn't far behind. I didn't bother ducking my head or bracing myself because the suits were heavy enough and we were far enough away that I was pretty confident in keeping my feet. The wave of concussion was a wave of dust washing over us, hard enough to push the Vigilante back a few centimeters and smash the wooden window shutters of nearby houses open.

Where the fortress tower had been a moment before was now a glowing column of fire, black clouds of debris blotting out the sun, pure destruction that not even a proton cannon or a fusion warhead could have accomplished. And Dwight had known that.

"Zan-Thint," I said softly. "He wouldn't leave the fortress. You knew there was no other way to touch him."

"For a general so cunning," Dwight said with not a little tinge of satisfaction, "he was easily manipulated when told what he wanted to hear."

"Hey, Cam," Nance called, his voice sounding distant though less strained now. They'd probably dropped down to a lower boost. "What the hell just happened?"

"Later," I told him. "Make sure that lighter doesn't go after the drop-ships."

"Umm... she's not changing course, Cam. She's still heading straight at the gateway."

"What?" I switched back over to the view from the *Orion*, confirmed for myself what he was seeing. The lighter's fusion drives were burning sun-bright, taking her toward the side of the artifact at a boost so high, even a Tahni would have trouble staying conscious. "They just saw what happened when they blew the missiles against the thing. What do they think ramming it's gonna do?"

As if in answer to my question, a blue glow shimmered around the edges of the starship, something I'd never seen before. At least not this close to a planet.

"Oh, shit!" That wasn't Nance, it was Wojtera, the Tactical officer. "Sir, they've activated their Transition Drive! But this close to a planet, the wormhole's not gonna form..."

"No..." the word was hissed out, a curse, a prayer, a horrified realization. And it was Dwight.

When the shimmering blue wave of gravito-inertial radiation touched the gateway, something happened. I couldn't describe it any more than the *Orion*'s sensors were able to quantify it, but there was a curtain of unreality pulled across the image, something the cameras couldn't make out as anything but a blank spot, not so much black as simply nonexistent. It enveloped the entire image for a fraction of a second and when it was gone, I couldn't have sworn that it was real, that I'd actually seen it, as if the pain and exhaustion and heat had simply made me pass out on my feet momentarily.

Except that the Tahni ship was gone. And so was the gateway.

Where they'd been was nothing. No, not nothing. In the distance, visible only because the *Orion*'s IFF system picked up their transponders, were the orbital transfer vehicles of the engineering crew, still hanging out there a few tens of kilometers away from whatever had happened. I blew out a breath, relieved at least that the engineering crew was safe, but the relief drained away in a second.

The gateway was gone. We were stuck here.

# [ 25 ]

"I'm truly sorry."

I rubbed a hand over my face, wincing as the smart bandages tugged at the burns on my neck. We only had three auto-docs at the base and I'd let the more seriously injured go ahead of me, which meant I got to sit around in the medical center—a glorified name for what had been a one-family farmhouse—swathed in bandages. They kept the burns from getting infected, encouraged healing and, most importantly, applied topical anesthetics, but they didn't cancel out all the pain. Or the frustration.

"I don't give a shit, Dwight," I snapped. "I wouldn't give a shit if the fucking gateway *hadn't* disappeared. You manipulated us into a fucking *war*, not to mention the fact that you could have ended all this *months* ago by shutting down the Womb without getting Colonel Hachette and a lot of my Marines killed."

One of the med techs working on another of the lightly wounded at a cot beside mine glanced over curiously. I was, after all, talking to myself, since Dwight's voice was only in my 'link's earbud.

"I regret that I could not have done that," Dwight corrected me, not seeming to take offense. "As I said, though all the AI were originally part of me, they became their own personalities particularly the longer we were separated. The system that ran the Womb has been there for tens of thousands of years and was, let's say, more narrowly focused than I am. He wouldn't listen to my arguments, though I *did* make them while Lilandreth was attempting to break into his security. I know you have no reason to trust me, but please believe me, your well-being and safety were a part of every decision I made. We simply have a different idea of what would result in the greater safety and security for humanity."

I grunted, not trusting myself to reply to that.

"Do you have any idea what happened to the gateway?" I asked him instead. I don't know why I was still talking to him at all... although the fact he was in my ear and just wouldn't shut up might have been part of it. It had been three hours since the end of the battle, and I could only ignore him for so long.

"The Transition Drive field interacted with the gravitational field of the captive singularity inside the device's neutronium casing. I don't have the exact figures because the *Orion*'s sensors aren't built to measure such things and the sensors of the fortress died with Presteri, but my best guess is that it opened up a gate into Transition Space."

"And the whole thing's just stuck there?" I asked him. "In Transition?"

"The possibility was never considered, thus I have no data to confirm or deny this speculation. For all we know it dropped out a light-year from here, or in the next system over. We could search for millennia and never find it, even if it did exit Transition Space."

"You're always such a ray of sunshine."

There certainly wasn't sunshine coming from anywhere else

at the moment. It *should* have been dusk, should have been shining red rays through the windows, but the clouds of fallout from the explosion of the fortress had blotted out the sun and it was already pitch black. It looked a lot like the end of the world, and God knows it *felt* like it too.

"Hey."

I looked up, smiling at the sound of Vicky's voice despite everything. Then I saw who was walking in behind her and the smile faded. Lan-Min-Gen wasn't in his armor and noticeably was *not* armed, and I didn't know if that was a matter of courtesy or if the Force Recon Marines stationed outside the door had relieved him of his weapons before allowing him inside. Campea had been *pissed* that he and his platoon had been left out of what was probably the last battle with the Tahni any of us would ever have.

I wasn't surprised to see Lan-Min-Gen. I figured he'd be coming around sooner or later. I *was* surprised to see Lilandreth come in behind him though. I was honestly surprised to see her *alive*.

"Lilandreth," I said, standing slowly and painfully and suddenly acutely aware I wasn't wearing a shirt. "Glad to see you weren't in the fortress when..." I shrugged. "I hope you didn't lose too many of your people."

"We lost none," she told me, then cocked her head to the side in a motion that made it look as if she might break her slender neck with all the weight of her feathery mane. "We were warned, you see. By Dwight."

I blinked, now *totally* shocked.

"Dwight," I repeated.

"I didn't want to believe him at first," she said, "but given that the lives of my children were at stake, I evacuated those who came with me from Decision. I attempted to convince the other Resscharr, those who had already lived on this world, to accompany us, but..." she made a broad gesture. "Most would not."

I winced, not out of grief for the local Resscharr, who had been pretty much slave-masters before we came, but more because their deaths didn't seem to bother Lilandreth that much. I tried to make myself feel bad for them, since they were sentient beings who had families and children and I was supposedly a civilized man who cherished that sort of thing, but the fact remained that they'd enslaved not just the Vergai but the Karai they used as enforcers as well. And they were fucking lizard people with backwards knees.

"How many survived?" I asked, more to know how big of a pain in the ass they were going to be than because I was overly solicitous of them.

"Perhaps two thousand. Mostly older females and young children." Again, that tilt of her head. "It is possible that the young may be amenable to education and socialization." Her stance straightened. "Particularly since it now seems likely that my people will be going nowhere."

"Why did you warn them?" I asked Dwight. Not aloud this time. My 'link allowed me to subvocalize, interpreting the vibrations of my vocal cords and translating them into a passable simulation of my voice, but I didn't normally use it because most people could tell when someone was doing it and no one liked the simulated voices. I didn't think Dwight would mind.

When he answered, there was none of the snark I was used to, none of the sense of self-congratulatory superiority that often annoyed me. Just honesty, for once.

"I knew you wouldn't like it if I let them die."

I sighed, then turned my attention to Lan-Min-Gen.

"So," I said to him without preamble, "where do we stand?"

Lan-Min-Gen looked almost as exhausted as me, but he

straightened his shoulders and faced me in what passed for the position of attention for the Tahni military.

"Things remain... unsettled. Our numbers were small to begin with, and we lost many in the attack. None of my Shock Troopers, of course."

"And that's not a problem with your troops?" I wondered, shifting my weight from one leg to another. Standing wasn't terribly comfortable, but I felt like sitting down would have signaled weakness. "The fact that you stayed out of the fight?"

"It might have," he admitted, "had Zan-Thint's plans not failed so utterly and spectacularly. The survivors consider me to be the wisest of the surviving officers and thus my position as commander of our remaining forces is solidified... for the moment." He stared at the floor as if there was something interesting there requiring closer study. "There is much resentment toward you. You humans, I should say."

I barked a humorless laugh.

"What? They think we should have sat back and let you kill us?"

"No, it isn't resentment of your victory but of the fact that we find ourselves back in the same position as we were back on our homeworld... with little in the way of military forces and no way to keep you humans from imposing your will on us."

I cocked an eyebrow at him.

"I'm not sure if you know English well enough to understand the meaning of *tough shit* in this context."

Lan-Min-Gen showed amusement in typical Tahni fashion, which I suppose was better than him getting angry about it.

"It isn't your problem at the moment, but mine," he agreed. "But if you stay, it *may* become your problem. Depending on which way the Karai are drawn. At the moment, they're..." He paused. "What's the phrase? They're *scared shitless* of you. None of them yet comprehend what happened with the fortress and most believe you did it somehow. Together with the death of Nam Ker at the hands of our troops, they're not currently disposed to putting themselves back under our influence. But... if you and the Vergai stay, that may change. I don't see the Karai suddenly deciding to become allies of the humans."

"I think you've both got problems you haven't even considered yet," Vicky said, speaking up for the first time. She found a folding chair and carried it over to the center of us, taking a seat, crossing her legs casually. "The fortress is gone, and most of your high-tech production is gone right along with it. The Karai have some metal working and mining, but with the Vergai leaving, they're gonna have to be doing a lot more farming. You sure you can even make a living as primitive farmers?"

Lan-Min-Gen squirmed uncomfortably, and I didn't have to be an expert on the Tahni to know what he was thinking. He was a soldier, not a farmer, and the same was true for most of his people.

"We do have a few surviving shuttles," he said after a moment's thought. "We could use their reactors to power fabricators if..."

I sighed, finishing the sentence in my head.

"You want us to turn out some fabricators for you." I shrugged. "I'll talk to Chief Moretti. It's possible, but I don't know how long it'll take. But yeah, if you ground one or two of your shuttles and use them for power production, at least you wouldn't be starting from zero."

"That still leaves the big question though," Vicky said. "The one that's going to affect them as much as it does us."

"Yeah," I agreed. Finally, I surrendered to exhaustion and pain and sank back down on my cot. "What are *we* gonna do?"

"If we went with the Vergai to the Islands," Vicky pointed out, "I know they'd welcome us. We have enough high-tech tools to change their whole society for the better. And at least they're not already in the middle of a world war."

I chuckled bitterly. She was talking about the Vailoa, who'd tried to involve us in their conflict when we visited. And she was right. The fact they were low tech and low population would make it easier for us to shape their future, maybe keep them from getting into any big wars.

"But would that make us any different from the Resscharr here?" I mused. "Would our great-grandkids wind up ruling theirs in a caste system, with the crew of the *Orion* on top and everyone else under us?" I met Vicky's eyes. "And what happens when we all start having kids? There's not enough medical supplies to keep everyone on medical nanites for generation after generation. You and I are gonna live for a few hundred years unless someone kills us. You ready to watch our kids or grandkids die of old age while we still look like this?" I motioned at my face.

"Staying here's no better," she countered. "Same problems, but you can add in tensions between us, the Karai, and the Resscharr."

I nodded. I could have just laid back and passed out right then if it wouldn't have been rude.

"We could work something out," Lan-Min-Gen assured me. "I believe that my people could be persuaded it's wiser to have you humans around, given that your resources would be a benefit for everyone who lives here."

I waved the conversation off.

"We're not going to decide this tonight, particularly not when I'm high on painkillers." Rubbing at my eyes, I tried to put a coherent thought together. "Lan-Min-Gen, let's meet around this time in two days. That'll give me time to run through the auto-doc and get all these burns taken care of, get some feedback from the engineers and Captain Nance, maybe talk to the

Vergai over in the camps. I should have a clearer idea of our options by then." I speared him with a glare. "Until then, I'd very much appreciate if you could make sure that neither the Tahni nor the Karai go anywhere near the landing field or the Vergai evacuees. Is that understood?"

"After today," he told me, "I doubt any of them are in the mood for another fight. At least not for the time being."

And with that, he swept out the door and was gone.

"I should get back to my people," Lilandreth said. "They have taken up temporary residence in the Vergai farmhouses..." her expression changed, though from what to what I couldn't say. Just a shift of stance and the set of her eyes. "Though I suppose it may *not* be temporary, since there's no other place we can live."

"Ask her to stay," Dwight said quickly. I frowned but did it. "Put me on your external speaker."

"Dwight would like to say something," I added, pulling my 'link off my belt and setting it on a table next to my cot.

Lilandreth relaxed in that way the Resscharr had of simply settling onto their haunches like a kangaroo, her attention on the 'link.

"There is a possibility," Dwight said, "that I may know of another way you humans can get back home."

"No shit?" I blurted. "And you're just mentioning it now?"

"Of the two possibilities," he elaborated, "of doing this or of destroying the Skrela and rescuing the gateway device, trust me when I tell you that the latter was much easier and more desirable."

"I'm not sure I *want* your help," Vicky said, her face clouding over. "Most of what happened today was *your* fault. If you hadn't lied to us, manipulated us, a lot of people would still be alive right now."

"That's true," the AI admitted without hesitation. "And I do regret this, though I don't see how I could have acted any other way, given what I knew. What I *know*. You're thinking just of the lives of those you know, those you lead, but I've existed since before the first human stacked one stone on another and worshipped it, and when I act, I do so based on the survival of species, of civilizations."

Vicky didn't reply, though her glare could have burned through the walls.

"The time of keeping secrets is past," Dwight went on, for once acting as immaterial and incorporeal as he actually was. "As such, there's more to the history of the Resscharr than you're aware of, Lilandreth. You have been led to believe that the flight of your people through the gateway was main part of the exodus of the Resscharr from the Cluster. This deception was deliberate on the part of the ruling council... and on our part as well. We, the AIs who were sent with you and those like me who facilitated your escape, were instructed to conceal the truth from you in an attempt—misguided, as it turned out—to conceal both your destinations from the Skrela."

"There was another gateway?" I interrupted, a surge of hope bringing me back to my feet.

"No. The Reconstructors had no need for a gateway..."

"The who?" Vicky demanded, sneering. "What the hell is it with the Resscharr anyway? Their political parties sound like alternative band names."

"The translation is inexact," Dwight said by way of apology.

Lilandreth was oblivious to the interplay, straightening from her relaxed stance and taking a step forward, as if she thought that by coming closer to the 'link, she could better determine the truth of the AI's words.

"The Reconstructors?" she repeated. "I've heard legends of this... but no one believed it. It was considered false hope, a story to put frightened children to bed at night."

"Indeed. That was what you were meant to believe. Yet, not only did the Reconstructors exist, they were more numerous than you."

"Hold on a second," I said, waving a hand at the 'link to stop the conversation, not wanting to get sidetracked. "You said that they didn't have a gateway, so how the hell did they get out of the Cluster?"

"You know," one of the medics said, stalking over to us with his fists on his hips, "if you're going to be talking this loud, maybe you could take this to one of your offices. We have wounded here."

I scowled at the man.

"Yeah, no shit. I'm *one* of them." I sighed. He was just doing his job. "We'll keep it down."

"You probably believe that the Cluster is entirely closed off," Dwight said, "that the Transition Lines end at its borders."

I shrugged.

"Well, I'm not a pilot or a Helm officer, but that's what people keep telling me."

"And yet, I have audited your entertainment and found frequent references to a Transition Line which leaves the Cluster, one which your culture refers to as the Northwest Passage."

Vicky snorted a derisive laugh.

"Yeah, you find it in entertainment because it doesn't exist in real life. The Fleet, the Scouts, the Corporate Council, hell, *everyone* has spent decades looking for it. They would have found it by now."

"And yet it exists. Well concealed, but it was the way the Reconstructors used to make their way to the larger galaxy. To another spiral arm."

"To do *what*?" I wanted to know.

"Why, to do exactly what their name implies, Captain Alvarez. To rebuild the Resscharr civilization."

## [ 26 ]

"We're going to do *what?*" Captain Nance exclaimed, eyes bugging out.

I didn't miss the damned Operations Center and the endless meetings we'd had there in the duration of this Godforsaken mission, but I had to admit this was the right time to use it. We had some serious shit to discuss.

"The only way to get home," I explained patiently, "is to find the Reconstructors and trace the way they came back to the Northwest Passage."

I took a deep breath, grateful to be able to do it without bandages tugging at burns. It had, as it had turned out, taken three solid days in the auto-doc to fix up my injuries because there'd been significant nerve damage in my left arm and I hadn't even realized it because everything had been numb from the local anesthetic. I was also *very* grateful not to have to smell my own burnt flesh anymore.

"And to get to the spiral arm where they were heading, we're going to have to spend..." Another deep breath. "... five *years* in Transition Space."

"Well, shit, man," Dunstan said, leaning back in his chair,

hands behind his neck. "I mean, I love all you guys and this has been the best job I've ever had, but I don't even think we can carry enough food for five years."

"I'm not sure I love any of you," Nance interjected, "but the flyboy's right. We have enough stored ship food for maybe another eleven months if we stretch it. With what we can get from the farms down on Yfingam and maybe the Islands if we ask nice, we can extend that another few months. But five years?" He shook his head firmly. "Not a chance in Hell." He looked up at Dwight's avatar in the holographic projection. "And do we even know if there are habitables along the way where we could get food?"

"No," Dwight admitted, spreading his notional hands. "Given the nature of the Resscharr as a species, it isn't unreasonable to assume that they would have terraformed worlds in that region, but I can't guarantee it."

"Hey, one other thing," Dunstan said, frowning deeply, the expression looking out of place on his easygoing face. "Like, we know that this dude..." he gestured at Dwight, "... is part of the computers responsible for killing *billions* of Resscharr by making the Skrela and setting them loose." He raised his hands in admission. "Now, I know you had your reasons, Dwight. They did some nasty shit, and maybe if I'd been in your position I might have been tempted to do something crazy myself. But my question is, how the hell do we trust him? I mean, he lied to us for a year about almost everything."

"That's a point, Kyler," I acknowledged, eyeing Vicky sidelong. A point I'd argued with her for *hours* before and after I went into the auto-doc. "And I can't give you a good reason why we should trust Dwight other than that he could have killed us all at any point he wanted to. He has complete control over the *Orion* if he wants it, but he's never used it. It's true that he manipulated Zan-Thint into fighting us, but he didn't do it because he wanted to harm *us*. He didn't want the Tahni with their concept of being the heirs of creation and the lords of the galaxy set loose on this part of the galaxy." I shrugged. "And maybe he's right. We were looking at things from the perspective of what was convenient for us, pragmatic for our situation here, but the truth is, our mission was to *stop* Zan-Thint, to take him out. We gave up on that, but maybe we shouldn't have. Look..." I sighed, glad Lilandreth wasn't here. I'd thought about bringing her up for the meeting, particularly since she and her people had a big part to play in this plan, but I figured this conversation would have to happen and she shouldn't be here for it. "Back in the Commonwealth, there's a lot of people who've turned the Predecessors into gods, even worse than the Tahni have. But they weren't gods, no matter what they thought, and what they did to us, to the Tahni, to their own people, was... *evil*. There's no other way to say it. I don't know how religious any of you are."

I scanned across the faces around me. Vicky, I knew, was nominally Catholic like me, but I'd never discussed the subject with Nance or Dunstan, and I don't know that I'd ever had a personal conversation with Brandano or Captain Nagarro, the ranking Intelligence officer since Hachette had died. The two of them stared back like neither felt they belonged here, but we'd lost Top and Hachette, and keeping the inner circle to just the four of us felt wrong.

"I don't know whether you buy into the whole good and evil thing, but I do. I also believe in giving second chances. We gave Zan-Thint one. We didn't have any reason to trust *him*, that's for sure, but we did it anyway. That might have been a mistake, but we didn't have much choice. I don't see that we have any now. Frankly, all of our options suck, but this one seems like the only choice that doesn't wind up with us playing warlords on some primitive planet."

"You haven't gotten around," Nance pointed out, seemingly unimpressed with my emotional speech, "to explaining how the hell we're going to make it five years on less than two years' worth of food."

"Yeah, I was kinda waiting to hear that one myself," Dunstan admitted.

"Maybe we could rig some cargo carriers?" Brandano suggested. "Kind of like we did with the gateway? Carry more food? Maybe we could freeze-dry some of the stuff we could get here and on the Island World?"

"I don't know about you, Commander Brandano," Nagarro said, sniffing dismissively, "but I don't much feel like spending *five years* chasing another wild goose, whether or not we have the food for it."

"None of us want to spend five years trudging from one spiral arm to another," Vicky assured the woman. "We have an... alternate plan."

"We're going to put most of the crew into hibernation," I told them.

The rest of them looked confused, but Nance's expression was similar to what I'd expect if I'd told him I wanted to turn the *Orion* into a floating brothel.

"We have," he told me, "a grand total of *six* hibernation chambers in the medical bay, for emergency use. And though I'd have to consult with the doc to make sure, I remember being told that the longest they were good for was six months."

"We don't have the know-how to build hibernation chambers that'll last five years," I agreed. "But Dwight does. And Lilandreth can walk us through how to program our fabricators to make them. We've gone over the numbers with Dwight, and there's enough raw material to manufacture three hundred of them. That should allow us to keep two thirds of our people in hibernation and have the rest on duty. We switch out maybe every few months and none of us have to spend more than eighteen months or so awake until we reach the area where Dwight estimates the Reconstructors would have gone. We can drop out of T-space when we make the shift switch and make sure of our navigation."

Now the expressions of the others weren't confused anymore. More like horrified.

"Holy shit, Cam," Brandano said, his face ashen. "We're gonna be like comatose the whole time? What if something goes wrong? I'm not afraid of dying, you know… not like in a dogfight or something, but just having someone shut a lid on me and never waking up…"

"You should be fine, Commander Brandano," Dwight assured him. "Your medical crew will be able to take their own shifts and monitor the hibernation chambers. They can pull anyone out who has a problem."

Brandano scowled up at the AI's avatar.

"You'll pardon me if I don't feel comforted."

"Here's the deal," I said, cutting off the exchange with a knife-hand slash, just like Top would have. "This isn't something I can order anyone to do, and I wouldn't even if I could. We're going to the crew with this, but it's gotta be one hundred percent. We all go or we all stay. Anything else, we split up and both groups'll wind up dead."

"I guess that's fair," Dunstan murmured, scratching at the back of his head, but I could see he was thinking hard.

"All right," Brandano acceded, though he looked like a man planning his own funeral. "If it's what everyone votes for, I guess that's what we'll do."

"This is fucking nuts," Captain Nagarro breathed. "There's not one thing about this that isn't batshit crazy."

I very deliberately did *not* snap at the Intelligence officer that she wasn't being helpful. She was as worn down by the insanity and violence of the last year as any of us, for all that she rarely left the ship.

"Okay, Captain," I said, "then tell me what you'd rather do. Do you want to stay on Yfingam, with the Vergai—because they're not leaving if we don't—and the Karai at each other's throats every other month? Do you want to emigrate to Laisvas Miestas?" I shrugged. "There's plenty of room, but doing that means that you, your children, your grandchildren, etc... are all going to farm or fish for a living. We'll have comfortable houses to live, enough power to make all the tools we need, but there's not enough surplus population or chemical production of fertilizer to make the place a surplus society where people will be able to get the sort of jobs you'd expect back home for at least three generations. We have the tech for it, but we won't have the people. And I hope you *do* intend to have children, because the only hope any of us have for building a technological civilization there is to grow the population by maybe tenfold in the next few generations."

"But...," she stammered. "There's not that many people on any of the core colony worlds and they..."

"Yeah, because on the core colony worlds we have the infrastructure they brought from Earth and installed. We have automated manufacturing and thousands of industrial fabricators. We have orbital manufacturing and asteroid mining and we harvest heavy hydrogen from gas giants. Here, we have this one ship ,and while it should be enough to kickstart the technology on the Island World to maybe early twentieth century levels, it's not going to transform it into Hermes or Eden in a generation." I concealed my irritated sigh behind a hiss of breath. "We have the technological civilization of the current Commonwealth because it all started on an Earth with nearly nine billion people. We don't need that many anymore because we have AI and automation and fusion power, but we needed it to *get* there. And this one ship isn't going to be enough to jump-start it past that point."

"This is what you want to do, Cam?" Dunstan asked, staring at me under a flip of blond hair well past regulation. "What you think we *should* do?"

"What I want?" I repeated, laughing softly. "No. What I *want* is to go to the Island World and relax, not have any threats we can't handle, not have any Skrela or Tahni or any existential threats." I reached over and grabbed Vicky's hand, squeezing it, and she gave me a wan smile. "I want to be responsible for just me and my family. But as Captain Sandoval can tell you, I don't always get what I want, and the fact there are still people who count on me, who are looking at me to get them out of this, means that I can't just give up."

"A lot of our people still want to go home," Brandano put in, hesitant, as if he was reluctant to bring it up. "Everyone was pretty gutted when the gateway..." he shrugged, "... went away. I've talked to a bunch of other officers, a lot of the flight crews. If you'd asked them before we *found* the gateway, I'd say maybe half would have been happy staying here. But they got their hopes up and now they're just... checked out. Done. Even if you told them we were staying here, I think with most of them you'd have to kick their asses just to get them out of their compartments."

"That sounds about right," Nagarro admitted. Her fingers tugged at the tight curls on the side of her head, grown since the mission had started. When I'd met her, her hair had been shaved down to stubble. "The Intelligence crew all sound like they're just taking for granted that we're all dead in the long run."

"Everybody's dead in the long run," Nance said softly. He shook his shoulders like he was divesting himself of the thought, then fixed me with a stare. "What now?"

"We still have to get the Vergai out of here," I told him. "That's gonna take a few more weeks. While we're doing that, Lilandreth and Dwight are going to work on the hibernation chambers. We can unship a couple fabricators and send them down when we pick up the next load of evacuees. Once we get the last of them to the Island World, the chambers should be ready to take up to the *Orion*. That's when we have to make the decision, and that's when I'll talk to the crew, give them the options."

Dunstan snorted, shaking his head, not looking up from the table.

"They follow you, Cam. They'll do what they think you want."

I frowned, wondering what was wrong with him and was about to ask, but Vicky's eyes narrowed and she shook her head sharply. Okay, later then.

"That's it for now," I told them. "Let's get the crews concentrating on getting the Vergai up here. We can run Chief Moretti and his people down to set up the fabricators for Lilandreth and Dwight. Captain Nagarro, I want you to look over the star charts Dwight has provided and give me an analysis of where the likeliest locations would be for settlements." She opened her mouth to protest, but I raised a hand to interrupt. "Yes, I *know*, we're working on very little data. I'm not expecting anything Earth-shattering, just your best guess."

"Yes, sir." She settled, mollified.

I stood, knowing they wouldn't leave until I did, though still uncomfortable with the idea. Everyone filed out, except Vicky, and when I moved toward the hatch, she stopped me with a hand on my arm.

"Dunstan doesn't want to leave," she told me.

I blinked. I should have been able to figure that out on my

own, given his reaction to what I'd said in the meeting, but it made no sense to me.

"Why?" I wondered, throwing up my hands, less concerned about appearances now that the others were gone. "Does he like it here or something? I think he's actually visited the Island World maybe twice since we've been here."

"He and Chief Beckett are..." Vicky shrugged. "Involved."

"I knew it," I said, laughing, pointing a finger at her. "I *told* you, but you said she wouldn't do that."

Vicky rolled her eyes.

"Is this really the time for I-told-you-so?"

"Well, yeah," I said, as if it was obvious. "When else will I get the chance? But why does that mean he wants to stay here?"

She sighed. "Because she's pregnant."

Now *that* shocked me. "What the hell?" I blurted. "How did *that* happen?"

"Well, when a man and a woman love each other very much..."

"Oh, shut up," I snapped. "Come on, everyone gets birth control treatments, right? Because if they don't, we're in big trouble."

"We *do* get them," Vicky admitted, "but some people are allergic to the drugs. Not many, but Beckett is one of them. She's managed with alternate methods until now, but she ran out of those before the mission started and didn't think it would be a big deal because she hadn't planned on having a relationship. And then Kyler showed up..."

"Shit." I leaned back against the table. My eyes flickered upward to meet hers. "And she told you all this?"

"She wanted Kyler to tell *you*, but he's a little embarrassed by the whole thing, not least because their relationship is a huge violation of military regulations."

"Well, yeah, but given our current circumstances, I don't

think anyone's going to start court-martial proceedings. So, he wants... *they* want to stay here? Have the baby, raise a family over with the Vergai on the Islands?"

"Not if we don't stay," she corrected. "They don't want to be living like dirt farmers without any of our technology. But she isn't interested in ending the pregnancy either. Neither of them is."

I stared at the bulkhead, trying to think, but the gears in my head just kept grinding. Finally, I punted. "We have to get the Vergai to Laisvas Miestas," I declared, "before we figure out anything else. We'll figure it out before then."

*I hope.*

# [ 27 ]

"So, this it."

They looked like coffins to me. Lined up from one end of the converted barn to another, the outer shells of the hibernation chambers were sleek and, to my surprise, metal. It made sense, of course. We had to fabricate using what we had on hand and plastics required petrochemicals. There was probably oil on Yfingam, but we hadn't had time to search for it, and all that we'd been able to recycle had gone into the new battlesuits.

"We've tested three of them," Lilandreth said, running a finger over the surface of one of the black coffins with a proprietary pride, "on human volunteers, supervised by your medical staff. They perform as expected and should last well beyond the specified time period required." A pause, one that I thought might be meaningful. "You'll be installing them soon?"

"The *Orion* is on its way back from Laisvas Miestas. That was the last run, so we'll be running these up in a few hours." I glanced out the open doors of the barn, where the last rays of dusk were creeping over the western hills. The place seemed haunted now that the Vergai were gone. The surviving Resscharr had moved into their homes, but there were less than two thousand of them and enough farmsteads and workshops and huts for tens of thousands. "Shouldn't take more than one run by the drop-ships to get them up there. Wiring them in will take longer."

"Then the decision has been made?"

"Yeah." It hadn't taken as long as I'd thought for the news to travel through the entire crew. I'd intended to wait until they got back and present it to all of them formally, but there was an old saying I'd heard, though I didn't remember who'd said it. *Three men can keep a secret if two of them are dead.* I figured it was Nagarro. Heads of departments, chief NCOs, officers, chosen representatives from the enlisted, they'd all come to me individually and told me they wanted to go. "I guess sometimes unknown hope is more appealing than known misery."

Though I suppose our own history contradicted that. Maybe Dunstan had been right about that, maybe I'd encouraged too much of a cult of personality around myself. I hadn't meant to. All I'd ever tried to do was the right thing, first for me and Vicky and later on for the Marines that I'd been entrusted with. And then for everyone. I wasn't sure I'd done that good of a job.

"What is it, Lilandreth?" I asked her. "You want to tell me something."

"You are perceptive for one who is not of my species," she said with a good approximation of amusement. "And yes, I do." She motioned outward. "Most of my people, those who came with me from Decision, are more than willing to stay here and take charge of the children." She sighed, which might have been an affectation. I don't know whether Resscharr sighed. "I am not. Perhaps it's a disease I've caught from you humans, but I find myself... curious. About what comes next, about what I don't know."

"You want to go with us?" I guess I should have been

shocked, but I wasn't. When she'd told me not that long ago that her people wanted to go back to the Cluster with us, I'd gotten the impression that it was *her* who wanted to go. "What about your children? Where we're going could be dangerous. Hell, none of us might make it back at all."

"They will be staying here."

My surprise must have shown on my face clearly enough to break through that species barrier. She spread her preternaturally long fingers in a gesture that was purely Resscharr.

"I understand the attachment you humans have to your children, but it is something you will lose eventually as your lifespans grow even longer. I have had over four hundred children through the last six thousand years. These will be better off without me, better off among their own people in a place where they have a stable future."

I said nothing... *could* say nothing. I tried to imagine the differences between species, the mindsets that could bring about that kind of attitude about her own children, but I couldn't manage it.

"I suppose it's something we will not see eye to eye on," she went on as if it wasn't significant. "But I feel as if I should be there. You're seeking others of the Resscharr, those I never even knew of. I may be of help to you and, more than that, to use a phrase I've heard among you people, I feel as if fate calls to me."

It took me a moment to find my voice.

"Do we have a hibernation chamber that would... *work* on a Resscharr?"

"I took the liberty of constructing one to my specifications." She pointed at the other side of the barn to a chamber similar to the others but a half-meter longer and slightly wider. "I anticipated you might say yes."

But did I want to? One of the things that appealed to me about this option was leaving all the shit we'd gone through here behind us, and that included Lilandreth. On the other hand, we were taking Dwight with us...

"Are you going to be able to work with Dwight?" I asked her. "Because he's going to be a big part of this. I know he saved you and the other Resscharr from the fortress, but he's also responsible for the destruction of your entire civilization. Aren't you holding a grudge?"

"Grudges are a human thing, Cameron Alvarez," she told me. "Resscharr are not human."

"Yeah, I'm beginning to get that." I shrugged. "Of course, I'll be happy to have you along. Bring anything you need to the landing field in forty-eight hours."

Whatever her response would have been, it was interrupted when Kyler Dunstan barreled through the side door of the barn, Chief Beckett behind him, both out of breath like they'd run here. And maybe they had, since Intercept One had only landed a few minutes ago.

"Hey, dude! I heard you wanted to see me." Dunstan laughed and motioned at Beckett. "I mean, us."

"I will go to prepare," Lilandreth said, leaving out the main doors without acknowledging either of them. "Thank you," she added. "You won't regret this."

*Oh, I already do.*

I shook the trepidation off and offered Dunstan and Beckett a smile.

"Hey, come on in, you two."

I motioned them over to a row of cargo crates lined up against the far wall, the installation brackets for the hibernation chambers.

"Oh, man," Dunstan said, staring at the coffin-like devices as he took a seat on one of the crates. "Those things creep me out just looking at them. Gonna be hard getting into that shit once, much less over and over." A shudder went up his back and

Beckett put a hand on his arm as if to comfort him, then pulled it away quickly when she saw I noticed.

"That's kind of what I brought you here to talk about," I said, sinking down to a seat, honestly feeling as if the world was sinking with me. "Here's the thing, Kyler, Chief Beckett. I've got two problems. The first of them is, I'm worried about the Tahni."

Dunstan shook his head.

"I don't understand, man. What's to worry about? They got their teeth pulled, right? I mean, I ain't sure I like how it happened, but can't argue with the results. They got no battlesuits, they got no starships. What can they do?"

"They still have shuttles," I pointed out. "A couple, anyway. They're not much, but they're more than the Vergai or the Island Worlders have. They're enough to get across to the second planet, and they still have Shock Troopers and KE guns. I trust Lan-Min-Gen, but he won't live forever. I need someone to look out for the humans there, and I was thinking we could spare one of our landers. Maybe rig up a coilgun turret and some missile hardpoints for it, stuff we can fabricate pretty easy. But I can't ask anyone to volunteer for that. It would mean they're here forever. No way out."

Dunstan's eyes went wide and I knew he was about to say something, but Beckett laid her hand on his arm again, no longer self-conscious, and looked me in the eye.

"Sir, you said you had two problems. What was the other?"

I grinned.

"Well, you see, I have an officer and an NCO who've been having an elicit relationship in violation of every military regulation I can think of. I feel like I need to come down hard on this so the idea doesn't spread among the rest of the crew, make an example. Maybe something like giving them a really shitty job to do, guarding a bunch of primitive humans over on Laisvas Miestas for the rest of their lives, maybe."

Realization fell across Dunstan's features like the light of dawn, and with it spread a smile.

"Thanks, Cam," he said, offering me a hand.

I stared askance at it and instead pulled the two of them into a hug.

"Congratulations, you two," I said, and I couldn't hold back the sob that worked its way out at the thought of leaving Kyler Dunstan behind. "I hope you both have a wonderful life." A laugh overpowered the devastating sadness. "All *three* of you, I mean."

"But, dude!" Dunstan said, pulling back, his expression suddenly troubled. "Who're you gonna get to fly Intercept One for you?"

"I was thinking I'd give Commander Villanueva a shot at it," I told him.

"Yeah, I guess," he said, frowning, unwilling to give his blessing to anyone else to fly his baby. "She's pretty good in an assault shuttle. Gonna have to learn how to use T-space tactically though. Maybe Brandano can teach her." A sigh tugged at his shoulders. "I'm gonna miss you and Vicky, man. You guys are the best friends I ever had." Dunstan grinned aside at Beckett. "Well, you know, except..."

"I know." I rubbed at my eyes, not wanting to give way to tears. We'd lost Top, we'd lost Hachette. Now Dunstan. The number of people on this trip that I could trust was getting damned small. "But you have to make your own life now." I looked over at Beckett. "Do you know if it's...?"

"It's a boy," she told me, then glanced at Dunstan, her face reddening slightly. "We were thinking about naming him Cameron."

Suddenly, the worries about the upcoming voyage, about

our own future faded in the prospect of theirs. I gave Dunstan a nod.

"When the *Orion* reaches orbit, you can take Intercept One up there and transfer whatever you need to Lander Four. Take one of the fabricators with you and a field-portable isotope power unit, plus a copy of the databanks from the ship. That should be enough to get you started. A medical kit too. I wish I could afford to leave you guys an auto-doc..."

"Please," Beckett said, shaking her head. "You guys are going to need that a lot more than we are. We'll be fine."

"I know you will," I told her. "Get going. I'll see you before you leave."

Dunstan looked too choked up to talk anyway, and Beckett lead him out the door, her hand in his. I watched that empty doorway for a long time after they'd gone, unable to move. The sun had gone down and darkness poured into the old barn, creeping toward where I sat, only the portable lights we'd set up keeping it at bay. More than anything, I wanted to stay here with them, to make a life with Vicky the same way Dunstan and Beckett would be. To have a family, settle into a normal life.

*Almost* more than anything. I had to see this through, to get my Marines home. Finish the mission. I owed Top and Hachette that much. But there was something beyond that, because as much as I'd tried to deny it, like Lilandreth, I also had a desire to know, to see what was over the next horizon.

Sucking in a deep breath, girding my loins for what was to come, I pushed to my feet and walked into the darkness.

———

Drop Trooper will continue in WEAPONS FREE.

ALSO BY RICK PARTLOW

If you enjoyed Drop Trooper, you will love Recon and Holy War!

Start a new adventure today!

Start a new adventure today!

ALSO IN THE SERIES

*CONTACT FRONT*
*KINETIC STRIKE*
*DANGER CLOSE*
*DIRECT FIRE*
*HOME FRONT*
*FIRE BASE*
*SHOCK ACTION*
*RELEASE POINT*
*KILL BOX*
*DROP ZONE*
*TANGO DOWN*
*BLUE FORCE*
*WEAPONS FREE*

# FROM THE PUBLISHER

**Thank you for reading *Blue Force*, book twelve in Drop Trooper.**

We hope you enjoyed it as much as we enjoyed bringing it to you. We just wanted to take a moment to encourage you to review the book on Amazon and Goodreads. Every review helps further the author's reach and, ultimately, helps them continue writing fantastic books for us all to enjoy.

If you liked this book, check out the rest of our catalogue at www.aethonbooks.com. To sign up to receive a FREE collection from some of our best authors as well as updates regarding all new releases, visit www.aethonbooks.com/sign-up.

JOIN THE STREET TEAM! Get advanced copies of all our books, plus other free stuff and help us put out hit after hit.

SEARCH ON FACEBOOK:
AETHON STREET TEAM

## ABOUT RICK PARTLOW

RICK PARTLOW is that rarest of species, a native Floridian. Born in Tampa, he attended Florida Southern College and graduated with a degree in History and a commission in the US Army as an Infantry officer.

His lifelong love of science fiction began with Have Space Suit---Will Travel and the other Heinlein juveniles and traveled through Clifford Simak, Asimov, Clarke and on to William Gibson, Walter Jon Williams and Peter F Hamilton. And somewhere, submerged in the worlds of others, Rick began to create his own worlds.

He has written a ton of books in many different series, and his short stories have been included in seven different anthologies.

He currently lives in central Florida with his wife, two children and a willful mutt of a dog. Besides writing and reading science fiction and fantasy, he enjoys outdoor photography, hiking and camping.

www.rickpartlow.com

Manufactured by Amazon.ca
Bolton, ON